UNCIVIL WAR
BOOK SEVEN OF
ABNER FORTIS, ISMC

P. A. Piatt

Theogony Books
Coinjock, NC

Copyright © 2022 by P. A. Piatt.

All rights reserved. No part of this publication may be reproduced, distributed or transmitted in any form or by any means, including photocopying, recording, or other electronic or mechanical methods, without the prior written permission of the publisher, except in the case of brief quotations embodied in critical reviews and certain other noncommercial uses permitted by copyright law. For permission requests, write to the publisher, addressed "Attention: Permissions Coordinator," at the address below.

Chris Kennedy/Theogony Books
1097 Waterlily Rd.
Coinjock, NC 27923
https://chriskennedypublishing.com/

Publisher's Note: This is a work of fiction. Names, characters, places, and incidents are a product of the author's imagination. Locales and public names are sometimes used for atmospheric purposes. Any resemblance to actual people, living or dead, or to businesses, companies, events, institutions, or locales is completely coincidental.

Cover Art and Design by Elartwyne Estole.

Ordering Information:
Quantity sales. Special discounts are available on quantity purchases by corporations, associations, and others. For details, contact the "Special Sales Department" at the address above.

Uncivil War/P. A. Piatt -- 1st ed.
ISBN: 978-1648554575

"You can't kill your way to success in a counter-insurgency effort."
Admiral James G. Stavridis

"There is no clear or meaningful difference between insurgency and civil war, or between national terrorism and civil war for that matter."
Anthony H. Cordesman

"Insurgencies are easy to make and hard to stop... The recipe is simply a legitimate grievance against a state, a state that refuses to compromise, a quorum of angry people, and access to weapons."
Richard Engel

DINLI

DINLI has many meanings to a Space Marine. It is the unofficial motto of the International Space Marine Corps, and it stands for "Do It, Not Like It."

Every Space Marine recruit has DINLI drilled into their head from the moment they arrive at basic training. Whatever they're ordered to do, they don't have to like it, they just have to do it. Crawl through stinking tidal mud? DINLI. Run countless miles with heavy packs? DINLI. Endure brutal punishment for minor mistakes? DINLI.

DINLI also refers to the illicit hootch the Space Marines brew wherever they deploy. From jungle planets like Pada-Pada, to the water-covered planets of the Felder Reach, and even on the barren, boulder-strewn deserts of Balfan-48. It might be a violation of Fleet Regulations to brew it, but every Marine drinks DINLI, from the lowest private to the most senior general.

DINLI is also the name of the ISMC mascot, a scowling bulldog with a cigar clamped between its massive jaws.

Finally, DINLI is a general-purpose expression about the grunt life. From announcing the birth of a new child to expressing disgust at receiving a freeze-dried ham and lima bean ration pack again, a Space Marine can expect one response from his comrades.

DINLI.

* * * * *

Prologue

GRC EXECUTIVE ARRESTED FOR TREASON

By Liz Sherer, Terra News Network

(TNN) – Weldon Krieg, executive director of the Galactic Resource Conglomeration (GRC) Military Sales and Affairs Division, was arrested without incident in an early-morning raid on the GRC headquarters in Cologne.

Krieg, 53, is charged with Treason for his role in supplying Precision Crafted Soldiers (PCS) to Maltaani nationalist forces in contravention of UNT laws covering the transfer of military equipment to foreign governments without government approval. The alleged violations occurred during the build-up to the invasion of Maltaan.

"Mr. Krieg authorized the sale of third-generation PCS to the People's Army of Maltaan with full knowledge that those PCS would be deployed against our own forces," UNT Solicitor General Ariana Gomez told reporters. "In peacetime, the transaction would have been reviewed and possibly received retroactive approval. In a time of war, his actions amount to nothing less than the betrayal of the human race."

As the largest supplier of military hardware and contractor services to the UNT Ministry of Defense, the GRC was quick to distance themselves from Mr.

Krieg. "Krieg did not act with Conglomerate approval in this matter. It has always been and will continue to be GRC policy to support the men and women charged with defending Terra Earth."

Attorneys for Mr. Krieg did not respond to a request for comment.

Krieg is being held without bail in the UNT prison in L'viv. No other GRC employees have been arrested in connection with this case, but UNT officials, speaking on the condition of anonymity, confirmed that the UNT is actively pursuing Krieg's alleged co-conspirators.

* * * * *

Chapter One

Captain Abner Fortis adjusted the hospital bed until he was sitting upright. He'd grown bored after two hours flat on his back, and now he'd sit up in complete boredom for two more. The hemodialysis machine plugged into the port in his arm *whirred* as it drew his blood, filtered and conditioned it, and pumped it back in. The entire process took four hours, during which he was stuck on the bed.

He looked at the empty bed next to him and scowled. Gunnery Sergeant Petr Ystremski, who'd just vacated the bed after he'd completed his own course of dialysis, had winked at Fortis as an orderly led him from the room.

"Pace yourself, Captain. It's for your own good."

All six survivors of Tango Company's recon mission were quarantined aboard the hospital ship *Solicitude* for treatment. They'd each received a massive dose of radiation from the nuke they'd detonated near the spaceport during the invasion. Two of them had completed their treatment and departed after a week, and two more had finished theirs four days after that. Fortis and Ystremski were in the middle of their fourth week, and the lead physician of the Radiology Ward, Dr. Ayad, had given them no sign of when they might complete their treatment.

"Radiation affects everyone differently," she'd told Fortis when the captain had asked why he and Ystremski were still in quarantine.

"In your case, the radiation around your pancreas resisted our efforts to remove it all. Do you remember the chills and pain across your stomach and back? That was the radiation. The nanobots we used to condition your blood needed a little help, so we took additional measures. It all takes time."

"What about Gunny Ystremski?"

Dr. Ayad had smiled and shook her head. "Sorry, Captain. I can't discuss his private medical information without specific authorization."

Ystremski had later confided to Fortis that he had issues with both his colon and prostate. After watching his friend suffer through the targeted therapies, Fortis considered himself lucky that he only had his pancreas to worry about.

That was a week ago, and both Space Marines had since made remarkable progress. Fortis' body was radiation-free, his hair had begun to grow back, and Dr. Ayad had told him his current round of hemodialysis was precautionary and not therapeutic. Ystremski was also free of radiation.

As their health improved, their patience with the confines of quarantine wore thin, and they fantasized about how to make their escape. The previous night, they'd stayed up late, brainstorming how they could seize control of *Solicitude* and sail it to Eros-69 for some well-earned liberty.

The door slid open, and Fortis smiled when he recognized the two men who entered the room. Colonel Anders, his friend and mentor from the Intelligence, Surveillance, and Reconnaissance Branch; and Jerry Wagner, Science and Technology advisor to General Boudreaux, commanding general of ISMC 2nd Division.

"Abner!" Jerry said. "You're looking well."

"Thanks, Jerry. I feel great," Fortis said. "Welcome to the war, Colonel. Well, my part of it, anyway."

Anders had missed the invasion because of wounds he'd received weeks earlier, when the humans had evacuated the UNT embassy in the Maltaani capital of Daarben.

"Believe it or not, I'm happy to be here," Anders replied.

"Me, too," Fortis deadpanned as he gestured at the hemodialysis machine.

"Speaking of happy to be here, I've got some good news for you, Abner," Wagner said. "When you've completed this round of blood conditioning, you're done."

"Done? As in I can leave?"

"Yes. Return to full duty."

Fortis guffawed. "Fantastic! It'll be good to get back to Tango Company."

"Yeah, about that," Jerry said.

"What about it?" Fortis asked.

"A lot's happened since you entered quarantine," Anders said. "Major combat operations have ended, and the war has become a nationalist insurgency again. Five of the nine ISMC divisions deployed for the invasion have already returned home."

"What?"

Wagner nodded. "1st, 2nd, 3rd, and 4th Divisions are all that remain of the invasion force. General Tsin-Hu took the rest back to Terra Earth. General Boudreaux is now the commander of the new Military Assistance Command–Maltaan, or MAC-M."

"But the 2nd Division is still here, right?"

"Yes, but they don't need a recon company to accomplish their new tasking."

"What's their new tasking?"

"PCS management."

Anders chimed in. "We captured records that show the GRC sold two hundred thousand PCS to General Staaber of the PAM."

"Two hundred thousand?" The number shocked Fortis. "Fleet intel told us ninety thousand."

"They were wrong."

"Yeah, by a lot."

"A conservative estimate is that there are still one hundred and fifty thousand PCS on Maltaan," Anders said.

"What's the plan?" Fortis asked. "Please don't tell me it involves me."

Wagner held up his hands. "We'll get into all that later when you're back on the flagship. There will be a shuttle waiting for you when you're released the day after tomorrow."

"I thought you said we were finished after this round?"

"You are. Gunnery Sergeant Ystremski needs a day to recover from surgery, and then you'll be free to go."

"What surgery?"

Just then, the door opened again, and an orderly wheeled Ystremski to his bed. A thick swath of bandages covered the gunny's head, and he looked groggy.

"Here we are, Gunny," the orderly said. He helped Ystremski climb onto his bed. "Safe and sound."

"Fuck off," Ystremski slurred as the orderly raised the safety rails. He peered over at Fortis, who waved from his bed. "And fuck you, too."

Anders and Wagner chuckled.

"Gunny Ystremski just received a cochlear translator implant," the colonel told Fortis. "The technique they use here on *Solicitude* is more intrusive than the one we underwent back in Kinshasa. Don't worry, that's just the anesthesia talking."

The cochlear translator implant was a small device placed under the skin behind the wearer's left ear, connected to electrodes wired to the speech centers of the brain. With some training, it allowed the wearer to understand and speak foreign languages without the services of a translator. Fortis had received an implant before his previous mission to Maltaan, and now he was conversant in the Maltaani language.

"The day after tomorrow?" Fortis asked to confirm what Wagner had told him.

"Correct. In the morning, you'll board a shuttle to *Mammoth*," Wagner said. "I gave the staff temporary uniforms for you, so you don't have to travel in those well-ventilated gowns. The colonel and I will meet you there, and we'll proceed."

"Hey, Gunny, did you hear that?" Fortis asked, but Ystremski had already fallen fast asleep. He smiled at Wagner and Anders. "I'll tell him later."

* * *

General Staaber sat in the holding pen with a hundred other Maltaani prisoners and waited for the humans to interview him.

Interview.

Staaber frowned at the euphemism. It was typical of the humans. Their weakness and cowardice even permeated their language. The only reason they'd defeated the Maltaani was their reliance on mechs to make up for their lack of physical courage. He was certain torture awaited.

All around him, former Maltaani soldiers speculated about their fate at the hands of the humans. Would the humans keep them as slaves or release them?

Staaber knew the answer, but he didn't share his thoughts with the others. The less attention he drew to himself, the better. As the former commander of the People's Army of Maltaan, he was easily recognizable by other Maltaani, even if the humans couldn't tell them apart. Since they'd captured him masquerading as a low-ranking soldier, he knew all it would take was one careless remark or one moment of recognition to expose his ruse.

His other concern was that the humans had placed traitors in their midst; royalist dogs or nationalist turncoats eager to serve their new masters by spying on their fellow Maltaani. Just the thought that some Maltaani would betray their own race to the humans made the otherwise stoic Staaber furious, and he struggled to contain his anger.

"Number One Zero Eight Four Six," the human guard announced from the holding pen gate. His Maltaani lackey translated, and the prisoners checked the numbers sewn onto their prison smocks.

"That's you, brother," one of the Maltaani said as he pointed at Staaber's number. "They've called you."

A hundred sets of eyes watched as Staaber picked his way through the crowd. He hunched his shoulders in anticipation of the betrayal he felt certain was coming, but no one spoke.

The human pointed to the interview tent. The Maltaani guard propelled him along with a firm hand to the back, and Staaber walked on wooden legs.

My name is Baardek. I am a miner from Ulvaan. They drafted me to fight in the infantry.

Staaber had settled on the simplest cover story he could concoct. Most of it was true, which meant it was easy to remember, and might resist chemical interrogation. Staaber's older brother's name was Baardek, and Staaber's family owned many mines near Ulvaan. With any luck, by the time the chemicals compelled him to tell the truth, he would have created enough doubt that his actual story couldn't be put together easily.

Inside the tent, the human pointed to a Maltaani-sized chair in front of a table containing a data pad and computer terminal.

"Sit."

Staaber sat, and the Maltaani guard took a position next to the table as the human sat across from him.

"Do you speak Terran?" the human asked. The guard translated, and Staaber shook his head. The human continued in Maltaani.

"Name?"

"Baardek."

"Where are you from?"

"East, near Ulvaan."

The questions continued, and the human entered each of Staaber's answers into the computer. The human read through the questions twice before he seemed satisfied with the general's answers.

He's trying to trip me up.

Staaber gave the same answers as before, and the human ticked his answers off the list. When he finished, the human held up the data pad.

"I'm going to take your picture for your identification card," he said.

After the picture, he had Staaber press all ten of his fingers on the data pad. Then he nodded to the guard, who went to the back door of the tent and admitted another Maltaani. Staaber's heart leaped into his throat when he recognized the newcomer. It was Prince Aashdu, a member of the royal family, whom Staaber had known when he was a general before the war.

"His name is Baardek. Do you recognize him?" the human asked the prince. Recognition flickered in Aashdu's eyes, and Staaber braced himself for the betrayal, but it never came. Instead, Aashdu shook his head.

"No, he is not familiar to me."

Staaber struggled to contain his sense of relief as the human thanked Aashdu, and the prince left the tent. Another human entered and placed a plastic card on the table in front of him.

"Baardek, this is your permanent identification card. You must always carry it. You'll go through this process again if we find you without it. By accepting this card, you promise to be a loyal citizen of Maltaan, and never take up arms against her again. Do you promise?"

Staaber nodded slowly as he picked up the card and looked at it.

"I promise."

The human gestured toward the rear door. "Exit through there, and they'll escort you to the railhead to board the train heading east. You're going home."

* * * * *

Chapter Two

Fortis and Ystremski practiced their Maltaani as they waited for their release. The gunny made rapid progress, and by the evening before their release, they spoke only in Maltaani, which drew questioning looks from the quarantine ward staff.

"Are you sure you don't know what the Corps has planned for us?" Ystremski asked. "I didn't sign up to be a babysitter for a bunch of damn test tubes."

"Like I told you before, Gunny, all they said was that 2nd Division is tasked with controlling the test tubes. They don't need a recon company for that. Your guess is as good as mine."

"What's your guess?"

"Hmm. Since I no longer command a company, it won't surprise me if I revert to first lieutenant. They're not sending us home, so maybe I'll get an XO job. I suppose there's a company out there in need of a company gunny, too. Maybe we'll stay together, maybe not."

"I'll miss my bottom rocker. I was just getting used to wearing it."

"They won't take it. If they try, I'll go talk to Boudreaux."

"You gonna mud-suck him again?"

Both men laughed.

"I'll do whatever it takes," Fortis said. "DINLI."

Dr. Ayad entered the room. "Good evening, gentlemen. It's nice to find you both in good spirits."

"We're busting out of here tomorrow, Doc," Ystremski said. "Back to the war."

"That's what I heard. If that's what you want, then I'm happy for you."

"I like clean sheets and hot food as much as the next guy, but the sooner we get this mess sorted out, the sooner I can get home to my clean sheets and my wife's cooking."

"His wife is a wonderful cook," Fortis said.

"Back to business. Any complaints? Unusual pain, discolored urine, difficulty breathing?"

They both shook their heads, and Ayad made a note on the clipboard she carried. "Then first thing tomorrow morning, we'll give you the uniforms Colonel Anders left for you, return your gear, and release you."

"Does that mean we'll get our kukris and dog-tooth necklaces back?"

"Yes, Captain, you'll get your kukris and necklaces back, although I'm not sure why you'd want them."

"Badges of honor," Fortis said.

"We're heroes," Ystremski said with a smile.

"Heroes or not, it's bedtime. Tomorrow, you can go back to wearing bones if you want. Chopping up the enemy, too." Dr. Ayad turned out the lights. "Tonight, you still belong to me. Good night, gents."

"Good night, Doc."

* * *

Saito Mitsui led Dalia Hahn and Dexter Beck up the rocky path that led to the cave complex where they'd been hiding for the past two weeks. The former mercenary leaned on the crutch he had carved out of a thick tree branch, and their progress was slow.

The trio climbed in silence as they listened for the sound of hovercopter engines or the low buzz of surveillance drones. They were further east than they'd seen any Space Marine infantry venture, but human aircraft were ever-present in the skies over the mountains.

They reached the plateau outside the complex, and Mitsui sat heavily on a large boulder. He winced as Hahn knelt next to him and checked his bandages.

"We need to get under cover," Beck said.

"We'll go as soon as he can walk," Hahn shot back. "Can't you see how badly he's hurt?"

Mitsui pushed Hahn's hands away and heaved himself to his feet. "Beck's right," he said through gritted teeth. "We can't let them spot us this close to the cave."

Beck took the lead as they wound their way along the narrow trail. They were twenty meters from the cave entrance when Mitsui heard the unmistakable sound of a surveillance drone.

"Drone!"

Mitsui and Hahn dove for cover, while Beck took off at a run for the cave complex. The sheer mountains channeled and reflected noise in unpredictable ways, and it was best to take cover and wait for the sound to fade. The craft could have come from any direction, or been flying three valleys away. They had no way of knowing until they saw it.

"Beck, get down!" Hahn shouted, but the frightened man ignored her and disappeared among the boulders piled up around the cave entrance.

Mitsui bit the inside of his cheek to stifle a scream when Hahn kneed his injured leg as she scrambled into the underbrush next to him. Nausea swept over him, and he forced himself to ignore the pain and focus on the drone.

After several long minutes, they couldn't hear the drone anymore. Hahn helped Mitsui crawl out of the bushes and climb to his feet. The nausea returned in waves as he straightened up, and he would have fallen if she hadn't grabbed him around the waist and held him erect.

"Thanks, little darlin'," he drawled with a weak smile.

"You need a doctor," Hahn said as they staggered toward the cave.

"Last time I checked, we were all out of doctors," Mitsui said. "Unless you rustled one up somewhere, I'm out of luck."

"The Space Marines have doctors," she said. "We can contact them—"

"No!" Mitsui stopped and stared into her eyes. "No Space Marines. I'd rather die from this than have them save me so they can hang me for treason. I mean it. No Space Marines."

Hahn blinked away worried tears as he leaned on her for the last few meters. Once inside the cave, he slumped to the ground.

"Let me rest here awhile."

"I'll get some water," Hahn said before she disappeared deeper into the cave. When she was gone, Mitsui allowed himself several dry sobs. His chest heaved from the pain, but also because of the futility of their circumstances.

Pointless.

Mitsui had been the lead trainer for the two hundred thousand PCS sold to the Maltaani. When war became inevitable, he'd accepted a colonelcy in the People's Army of Maltaan and control over all the PCS. He planned to leave the actual command of the clones to the Maltaani, but their limitations forced him to move troops in response to the changing strategic situation. When the Maltaani nationalists couldn't prevent the Space Marines from landing, he'd fled his headquarters with Hahn, Beck, and Mitsui's PCS assistant, Gabby.

On the second day of their eastward journey, a patrolling hovercopter found them and strafed their vehicle. The humans got clear, but Gabby was too slow. A round punched a hole in his back. Without thinking, Mitsui broke cover to drag him to safety, and a ricochet gouged a deep furrow through the meaty part of his right thigh. He'd been in agony ever since.

Under normal circumstances, a medic would have treated a wound like Mitsui's with antibiotics, sewn it up, and limited his movement while it healed. Because they kept moving, the wound didn't have the chance to heal. All their medical supplies had burned up with the truck, so they had to use makeshift bandages. The wound festered, but circumstances forced Mitsui to use his leg as they continued east. To make matters worse, the Maltaan rainy season had begun, and periodic showers kept everything damp.

When they happened upon the other former mercenaries hiding deep in the mountain cave, it was a mixed blessing. The cave system was a perfect place to hide from aerial surveillance, but it was cold and dank, and they had to venture down into the valley to find wild game and edible plants.

Hahn was the only female in a group of mercenaries who hadn't seen a woman in months and had no compunction about obeying norms of human decency. Mitsui had warded off their suggestive approaches twice since they'd arrived at the cave, but as his health deteriorated, her safety became less certain.

Hahn returned with a crude wooden cup and put it to his lips.

"Drink this," she said, and Mitsui gasped as the cold water shocked his parched throat. He hadn't been thirsty, but suddenly he couldn't get enough. When the cup was empty, he sank back to the cold cave floor.

"We have to get you to a doctor, sweetie," Hahn said in a low voice. "I can't bear to lose you."

Her voice was thick with emotion, and Mitsui knew she was on the verge of tears. He closed his eyes and willed the pain in his leg to subside, but his leg throbbed with every beat of his heart. After a long pause, he nodded.

"When I wake up, we'll go."

* * *

The 36-hour journey down the mountain to the railway had been a nightmare for Hahn and Mitsui. He was much larger than Hahn, and she couldn't stop him from half falling, half crawling all the way down the mountain. It was all she could do to get him moving again when they reached the bottom. Delirious from the pain, Mitsui experienced a weird sort of second wind. He marched through the thick Maltaani forest singing martial songs in a weird English accent, punctuating his singing with the occasional shout of, "Tally ho!" or, "Bully!"

When his manic energy was exhausted, Mitsui collapsed, unconscious, in a puddle on the forest floor. It was all Hahn could do to roll him out of it and sit him upright. Fearful that he was in his death throes, Hahn wrapped herself in his arms and cried herself to sleep.

When she came to, he was stroking her hair as his breath wheezed in and out of phlegmy lungs.

"Where are we?" Mitsui asked.

"We're in the valley, near the railway," Hahn said. "We're going for medical help."

"Let's just stay here like this, forever," he mumbled as he fell back into unconsciousness.

Hahn propped him up as best as she could. She covered him with a layer of wide, flat leaves to keep the rain off and preserve as much of his body heat as possible. Satisfied that she'd done everything possible, the diminutive GRC executive turned west and walked along the railway. Somewhere ahead, she'd encounter Space Marines and their medics, who'd save Mitsui's life.

After three hours of walking, Hahn's uncertainty about her mission had become raging doubt. She stopped and looked up and down the tracks. It seemed crazy to walk any farther, because there were no Space Marines within walking distance and there would be no aircraft flying in this foul weather.

Saito is going to die.

Determined to die with her lover, Hahn turned back. A hovercopter zoomed overhead from behind, but she was so deep in her dejection that she didn't hear it until it was past her. After a moment of confusion, Hahn waved her arms and shouted at the craft.

The hovercopter turned around and settled onto an open section of ground long enough for a squad of Space Marines to disembark with weapons at the ready. The hovercopter climbed back into the air and maintained an overwatch position as the Space Marines approached her.

"Who are you?" one of them demanded. "Where are you from?"

Hahn sank to her knees at the sound of another human voice. "My name is Dalia Hahn. My partner, Saito Mitsui, has a terrible injury and needs immediate medical attention." She pointed east. "Please. He's not far."

The squad set a defensive perimeter as their leader had a brief conversation with the hovercopter.

"Okay, lady. Let's go get your friend, but let me warn you. If this is a trap, I'll kill you first."

Hahn scrambled to her feet. "No trap, no tricks. Please, hurry."

The Space Marines followed Hahn back to where she'd hidden Mitsui. When she uncovered her wounded lover, she saw his face had taken on an unnatural gray pallor, and she feared he was dead. Panic gripped her, and one of the Space Marines pulled her away.

"Let the medic do his job," said the sergeant, a female named Ezuedu. "He can't help your friend if you're in the way."

The medic gave Mitsui a quick once-over before he cut away the filthy bandages on his leg. Hahn almost passed out when she saw the wound. It had become a gooey mass of suppurating flesh, and the edges had drawn back to expose the femur. The medic dug out two large packets of antiseptic powder and dumped them into the wound. He emptied a tube of cream on top, wrapped Mitsui's leg in fresh gauze, and looked up at Hahn.

"Does he have any other injuries?"

Hahn shook her head. "I don't think so. Just his leg."

The medic unfolded a crinkly silver space blanket, wrapped it around the injured man, and fastened it in place with straps. When he finished, he stood and turned to the sergeant.

"You saw the fungus on his leg. He's got hypothermia, and his lungs sound like he's developing pneumonia. We need to get him on the bird, stat."

"Roger that. I called Bare Knuckle while you were working, and they're standing by to pick us up where they inserted us."

"Give me a minute to cut a couple poles to rig up a litter, and we'll be ready to move."

While the medic cut the poles he needed to fashion the litter, the sergeant stood next to Hahn as she stared down at Mitsui. She put a reassuring arm around Hahn's shoulders.

"We'll be on our way in just a minute, and he'll get the best care available on the planet."

As the hovercopter touched down and the Space Marines filed aboard, Hahn had a momentary urge to stay behind. She wasn't sure how the UNT would view her role in the PCS transfers to the Maltaani, but she knew her father would be furious when he found out she'd turned herself in.

Screw it. I'm going with Saito.

* * * * *

Chapter Three

Fortis and Ystremski giggled like schoolgirls as they traded their hospital gowns for ISMC sweatsuits. They both wore their Maltaani dog-tooth necklaces outside their tops and strapped on their kukris, and the orderly assigned to escort them to the waiting shuttle could only shake her head. Neither Space Marine looked back as they climbed aboard and buckled their restraints.

After a brief ride, the shuttle recovered aboard *Mammoth*, the 2nd Division flagship. When they disembarked, a female sergeant named Ramon greeted them in the hangar.

"Welcome aboard, Captain." She nodded to Ystremski. "And to you, Gunny. Mr. Wagner tasked me to meet you and requests your presence in the division intelligence center after you've changed into proper uniforms."

Ystremski agreed to meet them at Fortis' stateroom and headed for his berthing area. The sergeant waited outside while Fortis changed into clean utilities he'd left behind when they deployed to Maltaan. He tried but failed to ignore the empty lockers and bare mattress once used by First Lieutenant Quentin Moore, his deceased XO. It occurred to him that he needed to send condolence holos to the next of kin for Moore and all the other Tango Company Space Marines who'd died during the invasion.

I don't even know all their names.

He made a mental note to get a company roster from the 2nd Division personnel who'd remained behind when the division dropped. When he finished dressing, he met Ystremski and Ramon in the passageway.

"This way, gentlemen." Ramon led them through a maze of passageways, and when they turned the last corner, Fortis had to stifle a smile. The passageway dead-ended at a blue door guarded by a Space Marine sergeant. "Flag Suite," a sign above the door announced. "Authorized Personnel Only." It was the same blue door a sentry had turned Fortis away from when he'd searched for Wagner before the invasion.

Ramon showed the sentry her ID. "This is Captain Fortis and Gunnery Sergeant Ystremski. I'm escorting them to see Mr. Wagner."

The sergeant scrutinized Ramon's ID and eyed Fortis and Ystremski with practiced suspicion. Satisfied, he stood aside. "Proceed."

Ramon waved her ID in front of a sensor by the door, and it clicked open. Fortis didn't see anyone in the passageway beyond or in any of the offices he looked into on their way to the flag suite.

"Almost everyone is on the surface," Ramon said as she led them through a set of double doors into a large planning space. Anders and Wagner were there, along with another civilian and a Fleet major who hovered over a large map table.

"Welcome!" Wagner said when he saw them. He approached and shook their hands. "That's it for now, Sergeant," he said to Ramon. "Thanks for your help."

Ramon left the space, and Fortis and Ystremski followed Wagner to the table. "Captain Fortis, Gunny Ystremski, this is Mr. Bell from the Grand Council Select Committee for Intelligence. This is Major Parisi of the Joint Intelligence Center, and of course, you know Colonel Anders."

The men exchanged handshakes all around before Wagner waved them into seats around the table.

"I'd like to open this by telling you how pleased I am that you accepted General Boudreaux's invitation to work with us," Wagner told the Space Marines. "You could have opted to return to Terra Earth, and we're grateful that you didn't. I plan to run this as a group effort, so get involved, ask questions, and provide insights. Everyone here has unique knowledge and experiences, and we want to leverage every bit."

Ystremski raised a hand. "In that case, I'll start. Who are you? Or we, I guess."

"This—we are the MAC-M Special Support Group, or SSG for short," Wagner said. "We operate to support the commanding general's mission to defeat the nationalist insurgency and stabilize the legitimate Maltaani government."

"And how do we do this?"

Wagner smiled. "Gunny, give me a few minutes to bring you up to speed on the situation on the ground, and then we can get into the way forward, okay? Trust me, it'll all make sense when we're done."

"Yes, sir."

Wagner tapped a keyboard, and a holo of Maltaan appeared over the desk. "As you know, major combat operations on Maltaan are over. ISMC has control over the areas in blue. We're contesting the red areas, and the green areas are unknown."

The western half of the continent was blue all the way to the western edge of the mountains. The eastern half was green, with blotches of red and blue scattered throughout. Ulvaan, the only large city in the east, was also blue, but there were many spots of red around it.

"As you can see, we control the west and several strategic areas in the east. Most of the east remains unknown, and there's a burgeoning insurgency, as evidenced by the red."

"We're back where we started," Fortis said.

Wagner shrugged. "Fair point, but we're in a much stronger position than before. When the remnants of the People's Army of Maltaan fled to the mountains, they left behind most of their weapons and equipment. The insurgents have limited their operations to minor sabotage, theft of supplies, and an occasional sniper attack. None of that is a major concern."

"Unless you're the one being sniped," Ystremski said.

"Another good point, but compared to the PCS, the insurgency is a minor problem. Our estimates are that we killed fifty thousand PCS during the invasion. When the PAM collapsed, they abandoned their PCS charges and headed east. That means there are somewhere around a hundred and fifty thousand PCS spread throughout the central forests and mountains. They're armed, hungry, and leaderless.

"Four days ago, a group of approximately a thousand PCS overran a Maltaani farm three hundred klicks east of Daarben. A 3rd Division patrol investigated, and they discovered the PCS had murdered all the Maltaani and destroyed the farm. The PCS detected the patrol, and before air assets could respond, wiped them out. Thirty-two Space Marines died in the attack."

"Fuck." Ystremski shook his head. "What happened to the PCS?"

"We destroyed them with air strikes," Wagner replied.

"Sounds like a good way to deal with them to me."

"From your perspective, it does," Bell said. "The Grand Council disagrees. Destroying two billion credits of GRC property isn't a workable solution."

"I thought they sold the test tubes to the nationalists," Fortis said.

"They transferred them for future considerations, including the rights to the helenium mines in the eastern mountains," Bell explained. "Since the nationalists lost, the GRC didn't get paid."

Ystremski scoffed. "Tough shit. You take your chances when you side with the enemy."

Wagner held up his hands. "Gentlemen, we gain nothing by debating legal technicalities in this forum. There are considerations outside our sphere of control that guide our actions. The GRC is making amends for the actions of some of their executives, and they've requested our help in rounding up as many loose PCS as possible."

"For what?"

"For the original purpose the GRC sent them here. To work the helenium mines. The GRC has leased the mineral rights to several helenium mines, but they're hesitant to hire Maltaani miners who fought for the nationalists, which means there are almost no Maltaani miners available to employ. Many refuse to work for humans or the royalists."

"Are you shitting me?" Gunny Ystremski stood up. "The GRC sent two hundred thousand troops to the nationalists for some helenium. Now that their plan has fallen through, we're supposed to help them make amends by bleeding and dying to round up their property so they can still profit from the same helenium?" By then, Ystremski was shouting. "They're traitors. They deserve to be treated like traitors!"

"Calm down, Gunny," Major Parisi said. "Mr. Wagner already explained that there are larger forces at work here."

Fortis cringed. Ystremski didn't get angry very often, but when he did, it was a mistake to tell him to calm down. Even if one was a major. He braced himself for the gunny's response.

"My guys didn't die for fucking helenium," Ystremski barked. "They died because a bunch of staff pukes couldn't figure out how to suppress the Maltaani air defenses long enough to land a division, much less the rest of the invasion force. Where were you while we were down there fighting and dying, Major?"

Parisi didn't respond.

"That's what I thought." Ystremski pointed at the major. "With all due respect, Major, fuck you, and fuck your larger forces at work, too. You can bust me down to private and send me to the brig, but I'll be damned if I'll round up a single test tube for the fucking GRC." He turned and started for the door. "I'll be in my quarters if you want to send the MPs."

"Gunnery Sergeant Ystremski, at ease!" Colonel Anders shouted.

Ystremski hesitated.

"Petr, stop," Fortis said. "Don't do this."

Ystremski stopped and turned at Fortis' use of his first name.

"Please."

The anger drained from Ystremski's face as he stared at Fortis.

"Seriously." Fortis gestured to the gunny's chair. "I won't round up a bunch of test tubes either, but I don't think we're here for that." He looked at Anders. "Am I right?"

The colonel nodded. "This isn't about collecting PCS for the GRC. Assigning that task to you two would be like spreading butter with a scalpel. It can be done, but it would be a hell of a waste of a sharp knife."

Ystremski's eyes flicked from face to face until they settled on Fortis, who nodded.

"Have a seat, you old napalm pisser, and let's find out what our mission is."

Wagner took a deep breath. "The PCS issue is a problem for 2nd Division. Our tasking is counterinsurgency."

"You just said the insurgency was a minor problem," Fortis said.

"Compared to the PCS issue, it *is* a minor problem. In fact, there's little interest in it outside this room. The primary focus is on the PCS."

"Focus on making money from the mines, you mean," Ystremski said.

"Profit is a powerful motivator," Bell said. "It's also shortsighted, in this case. The long game here is a stable Maltaan. The UNT can't afford to maintain a significant troop presence here, but we can't leave without dealing with the insurgency and restoring order. If we pull out now and leave the Maltaani to their own devices, we could be fighting them again in ten or twenty years. We want to avoid that, so we're taking action to preempt the possibility."

"Let's move on." Wagner said. "Colonel Anders, why don't you go ahead with mission specifics?"

Anders zoomed the holo in on an outlined area southwest of Ulvaan. There were three blue circles and several red ones surrounded by green.

"This is Baat-Doh Province. There are two helenium mines here, marked in blue. The third blue mark is a forward operating base named Camp Zulu-Five. As you can see by the red, there has been recent insurgent activity in the area, and it is increasing.

"Your team will deploy to Zulu-Five. You will report to Major Sokolov, who commands the counterinsurgency teams operating out of Zulu-Five, for tasking."

"What team, sir?"

"You and Sergeant Ystremski, plus two Space Marines from the four divisions still present in theater. Any preference in who you'd like?"

Fortis and Ystremski exchanged glances, and the gunny shrugged.

"All the good guys I know are dead."

"Sergeant Bender," Fortis said.

Anders nodded. "He's in 3rd Division. Who else?"

"I don't know, sir. Tell Bender to pick somebody, I guess. He'll know who to bring."

"Okay. I'll have Bender plus one brought up to *Solicitude* for cochlear implants this afternoon. They should be here tomorrow morning at the latest."

"What kind of tasking are we talking about?" Ystremski asked.

"I'll take this one, Colonel," Bell said. "We believe the best way to stop the insurgency from growing is to decapitate the insurgency organization. Without leaders, most insurgents are just hungry malcontents, and we can feed them. Your job will be to find those leaders and neutralize them."

"Neutralize?"

"Execute. Assassinate. Call it what you want," Bell said. "Speaking frankly, the royalists don't have facilities or manpower to hold prisoners, nor do they have a legal process to prosecute them."

"Maybe not, but the ISMC has a process to prosecute Space Marines who murder prisoners," Fortis said.

"Turn over any prisoners you take to your Maltaani counterparts. What happens after that is not your responsibility."

Fortis glanced at Anders, who gave him a look that said, *We'll discuss this later.*

Wagner held up a data stick. "Everything you need is on here: frequencies, callsigns, etc. Read it tonight and return it when you're through. Sergeant Ramon will take you to the quartermaster and armorer to arrange for new skins, armor, and weapons. We'll meet back here tomorrow evening for a final briefing to make sure you're good to go. The following morning, you'll take a shuttle to the spaceport in Daarben and catch a hovercopter to Zulu-Five. Questions?"

"No, sir," Fortis and Ystremski said in unison.

"That's it, then. See you tomorrow."

* * * * *

Chapter Four

It was midday before they finished at the armory, so Fortis and Ystremski agreed to link up after lunch. There were no Space Marines in the dirty-shirt wardroom since almost all the 2nd Division officers were down on Maltaan, so Fortis sat alone. When he finished, he went back to his stateroom to wait for Ystremski.

"That fucking major is a piece of work," the gunny blurted as soon as he entered and shut the door. "That Bell character isn't much better. 'Execute. Assassinate.' Who the fuck is he kidding with that bullshit?"

Fortis nodded. "I don't think he understands what he's talking about. I'm going to talk to Anders and get some clarification on that. I also want to get more information on these 'Maltaani counterparts' Bell talked about."

"Who's Bender?" Ystremski asked.

Fortis told him about the mission he'd been on with Bender and the massive Aussie's one-man war on slavers afterwards.

"He went AWOL to hunt slavers?"

"Hell, yeah, he did. They trafficked his goddaughter. He hit them so hard that—well, let's just say that it's good to have him back in uniform." Fortis affected a thick Aussie accent. "He's a top bloke and a right wanker, and you can tell him that when you meet him later."

"If you say he's squared away, that's good enough for me."

"You'll like him. He's a good guy, and he has experience climbing back up the rank ladder too, so you'll have a lot in common."

"Thanks, dickhead."

The two men laughed.

"You know Anders and Wagner a lot better than I do. What's up with this mission?"

"The strategy makes sense. Stop the insurgency before it gets too big. I don't know about the prisoner situation; we might get useful intel from the prisoners instead of just killing them. Who knows? The Maltaani have very different ideas than we do about life and death."

"I don't have a problem killing those pricks, but I'm not killing prisoners."

"Me, either."

"Since we have nothing to do until tomorrow night, maybe we should hit the gym this afternoon?" Ystremski asked with a smile.

Fortis shook his head. "I can't this afternoon. I have something to do."

"What's that?"

"I have to write holos to the families of Tango Company's KIAs."

"Oh, shit, I forgot about that. You want some help?"

"I appreciate the offer, but it's a commanding officer's duty. It's already been three weeks, so I need to get it done before we head back down to the surface."

"Okay, sir. If you need some help, look me up." Ystremski held out his hand. "Why don't you let me have the data stick Wagner gave you, and I'll read through it this afternoon?"

"Yeah, sure." Fortis dug out the data stick. "You can read, right?"

"I'm sure there are pictures, maybe a map or two."

* * *

Dalia Hahn sat on a bench in front of a medical tent on the Space Marine base at the Daarben spaceport. Everywhere she looked, the Space Marines moved with purpose. Hovercopters came and went from the tarmac, and she'd seen two shuttles land in the last hour. The activity didn't bother her; she'd been living on a base with thousands of PCS for a month. What disturbed her were the many conversations she caught snippets of. The PCS were passive and didn't talk much, which made the stoic Space Marines seem like chatterboxes by comparison. It was a little overwhelming, and she hugged herself and leaned forward to shut out the noise.

"Are you okay, ma'am?"

A female Space Marine corporal named Vincent had become Hahn's escort as soon as the authorities had realized who Hahn was. They'd said she needed an escort for her own safety, but Hahn knew a guard when she saw one.

As if I'm going to escape after surrendering.

"I'm fine, thank you. I'm not used to so many humans at once."

Inside the medical tent, doctors worked to save Mitsui's leg. It had been over an hour, but no one had come out with an update. At last, a doctor in blood-stained surgical scrubs came outside, stripped off his gloves and mask, and approached.

"Miss Hahn?"

Hahn shot to her feet. "I'm Dalia Hahn. How is he?"

"His prognosis is good," the doctor said. "There is some tissue damage, of course, but the femur is intact." He frowned and shook his head. "Our chief concern now is controlling the infection. The fungus here is unlike anything we've seen before, but I think we've got it figured out. I put him on a regimen of the most powerful antibiotics available, but only time will tell if it's effective. Why did you wait so long to bring him in?"

"Things got confused after the invasion. We've been hiding in a cave system up in the mountains."

A serious-looking civilian approached, accompanied by a Fleet major. "Miss Hahn, I'm Supervisory Agent Thomas Leighton with the UNT Ministry of Justice. Come with me, please," the civilian said.

"Justice? What is this?" Hahn asked. "I'm waiting to see a friend."

"You *were* waiting. Now, you're coming with me," Leighton replied in a clipped voice. He motioned to Hahn's Space Marine escort. "Corporal, bring her along."

The doctor gave Hahn an apologetic look as Leighton and Vincent escorted her away from the medical tent. She felt the first twinges of misgiving when they reached a large tent guarded by a pair of civilians straight from central casting: squarish heads on thick necks, wide shoulders, and permanent scowls etched on their faces.

"Inside, please." Leighton motioned to the tent, and Hahn ducked through the door. Leighton and the major followed.

The interior of the windowless tent was stuffy and smelled like mold. Under the funk, Hahn caught a whiff of something more visceral.

Fear?

In the middle of the tent was a table and three chairs. Leighton pointed to one of them. "Sit, please."

"What's going on here?" Hahn asked as she sat down. Instead of answering, the agent placed a small electronic device in the center of the table, and when he pressed a button, two lights came on. Hahn recognized it as a miniature holo generator.

"This is Supervisory Agent Thomas Leighton with the UNT Ministry of Justice," Leighton said. "Present is Major Jean-Paul Bisset of the Fleet Legal Counsel Office." He noted the time and date. "This is the initial interview of Miss Dalia Hahn. Miss Hahn, before we begin, I am required to apprise you of your rights under the UNT Human Rights Declaration. You have the right to remain silent. If you exercise that right, the interview will end, and we will take you into custody until we adjudicate your case."

Hahn's mouth became dry. "Custody?" she squeaked.

Leighton held up a finger. "If you choose to answer my questions, your answers will become part of the legal record of your case, and we can hold you liable for any false statements. You have the right to legal counsel during all legal proceedings, including this interview. Because routine access by civilian attorneys is forbidden in an active war zone, Major Bisset is your court-appointed attorney. Although he is a Fleet officer, Major Bisset must provide you with the best defense possible, and you enjoy full attorney-client privileges, just like any Terran attorney. Do you understand your rights, Miss Hahn?"

"Yes, I understand."

"Do you have questions before we begin?"

Hahn decided that her best option was to reveal nothing until she found out what this was all about. "Just a request. May I have something to drink?"

"Of course." Leighton retrieved two hydration packs from a box in the corner. "Anything else?"

Hahn reveled in the taste of water that hadn't come from the muddy puddles and dirty wooden cups she'd been using over the last several days.

"Nothing else, thank you."

"Your father is Weldon Krieg, Executive Director of the Galactic Resource Conglomerate's Military Sales and Affairs Division?"

"Yes."

"You are the executive assistant to Dexter Beck, Galactic Resource Conglomerate trade representative to the Maltaani government?"

"Yes."

"Are you aware that the Ministry of Justice arrested your father and charged him with many alleged felonies, including treason, for the illegal transfer of military equipment?"

Hahn gasped, and her hands went to her throat. "Treason?"

Leighton nodded. "Providing military technology to the enemy is an act of treason."

"But he didn't! He—"

Leighton cut her off with a wave of his hand. "We're not here to adjudicate your father's case. We're discussing yours. Let me repeat my question. Are you aware that we arrested your father and charged him with many alleged felonies, including illegal transfer of military technology and treason?"

"I am now." Hahn fumbled for the other hydration pack and opened it with trembling hands.

"Did you transfer or abet the transfer of military technology to the Maltaani government?"

"No."

"Did you transfer or abet the transfer of military technology to any individuals inside or outside the Maltaani government?"

Hahn thought for a second. "No."

"Are you sure?"

Hahn was sure her name didn't appear on any of the agreements that facilitated the PCS deal with Staaber.

"Yes."

"Were you involved in the deal to transfer two hundred thousand PCS from the GRC to the Maltaani government? In particular, General Staaber?"

"I was aware of the deal, but I had no personal involvement."

"Who facilitated the deal on Maltaan?"

Here goes nothing.

"My boss, Dexter Beck. He made the deal to provide the Maltaani with sufficient manpower to revitalize their helenium mining industry."

"By sending them military technology?"

"Agent Leighton, I don't think you understand how the PCS program works. The word 'Soldier' is a legacy term from when the original intent of the program was to develop artificial soldiers for the UNT. They could change it to 'H' for 'Humanoid' or 'W' for 'Worker,' but it means the same thing.

"When the GRC creates a PCS, it's a blank slate. It has no innate military training or capabilities. We develop those traits through basic military training. It was my understanding that Staaber and his family have significant interests in helenium mining, and he wanted the PCS to develop those interests."

"Did you know Staaber was a general in the Maltaani military when the GRC struck the deal with him?"

"Yes."

"And they made the deal anyway."

"The Maltaani have no compunction about using their positions within the government or military for personal benefit. What we on Terra Earth consider blatant corruption is business as usual to the Maltaani."

"So, it's your contention that the PCS transferred to General Staaber were not military technology?"

"To the best of my knowledge, no, they were not." She paused for a second. "I recall Mr. Beck met with Ambassador Brooks-Green about the transfer. Mr. Beck informed the ambassador of the deal, and she had no objections."

The meeting had occurred, during which Beck and Hahn had given the ambassador the same story about the PCS not being military technology. Hahn doubted any record of the meeting existed outside their memories. The ambassador had ordered the embassy evacuated a few days afterwards, and she was sure the staff had destroyed most of the records.

"Did the GRC provide personnel to assist the Maltaani with the PCS?" Leighton continued.

"I recall they brought in some contractors, but what their exact roles were, I don't know," Hahn replied. That was her first outright lie, but it would be almost impossible to *prove* it was a lie, despite her relationship with Mitsui. She'd spent even less time with the mercenaries than Beck had, and her only knowledge of their activities had come to her through Mitsui.

"Was Mr. Beck in frequent contact with Mr. Krieg?"

The question took her aback, and her mind raced as she tried to remember the many messages she had exchanged with her father. She responded in slow, measured words.

"I wouldn't characterize it as frequent. They communicated as often as necessary."

"That's an odd way for Mr. Beck to show his appreciation to Mr. Krieg, wasn't it?"

"It was unfortunate, but the relationship between my father and Mr. Beck was strained. I sometimes took on the role of intermediary," she said. "They had history from before I came to work for Mr. Beck, and I felt it was an unwritten part of my job to facilitate communications between them. I acted as a conduit, but whether they were also in direct contact, I can't say."

It was a non-committal word salad, but Leighton seemed satisfied with her answer. The agent looked at Major Bisset and back to Hahn.

"That's enough for now, Miss Hahn. I urge you to keep what we spoke about confidential, and I appreciate you taking the time to meet with me today. I'd like to speak with you again soon."

"Agent Leighton, I'm at your disposal."

As if I have a choice.

"This is Supervisory Agent Leighton, concluding the interview with Miss Dalia Hahn." He noted the time and date again, and then turned off the holo recorder. "Miss Hahn, thank you for your candor. I believe Major Bisset wants to speak with you for a moment before you're taken to see Mitsui."

After Leighton was gone, Bisset slid into the seat opposite Hahn. He fixed her in an unflinching gaze.

"Miss Hahn, as your legal counsel, I want you to understand something. You're alone in this. There is no honor among thieves in this situation; it's every person for themselves. Even between you and your father.

"The Ministry of Justice is serious about this prosecution, and public sentiment is very strong since our victory here on Maltaan. What I'm trying to say is, if you have information about the roles played by your father, Mr. Beck, or any other GRC employee or contractor involved in this affair, now is the time to talk. I encourage you to be forthright during these interviews."

"Thank you, Major. I'm grateful for your advice." Hahn stood. "May I return to the medical tent to check on Mitsui?"

As Corporal Vincent escorted her back to the medical tent, Hahn had to suppress a smile.

Public sentiment doesn't grease the wheels of government like GRC money does.

* * * * *

Chapter Five

Fortis accessed the Tango Company personnel files, located the final company muster submitted by Lieutenant Moore the day before the invasion, and checked off the six survivors from the mission. He pulled up the first name on the muster and compared it to the official casualty list published by the ISMC.

Lance Corporal Sergio Adamski.

Fortis tried to conjure up an image of Adamski, but he couldn't put a face to the name. He opened Adamski's personnel file and immediately recognized the picture. Adamski had been a member of 1st Platoon. Adamski had listed his mother listed as primary next of kin, and the father's name was blank. He turned on the holo recorder, and after two false starts, ended up with a satisfactory final product.

Dear Mrs. Adamski, I am Captain Abner Fortis. I was your son's commanding officer during the invasion of Maltaan. There is nothing I can say to assuage the grief you must feel at the death of your son, but I hope I can offer you some small bit of solace.

Sergio was an exemplary Space Marine who carried out his orders to the best of his abilities. I can't share specific details about our mission on the night he died, but you should know that Tango Company was engaged in tasking critical to the success of the invasion. Our success was a testament to the valor of men like Sergio, and his sacrifice was not in vain.

Please accept my most sincere condolences and know his fellow Space Marines will always remember their brother, Sergio.

Sincerely, Abner Fortis.

Fortis watched the holo twice and decided it would do. He made a few notes for the next one and checked the list.

Sergeant Moussa Cisse.

* * *

Three hours later, he'd finished all the holos but one.

First Lieutenant Quentin Moore.

He'd skipped over Moore's file because he knew he wanted to send more than what equated to a holographic form letter. In the brief time he'd spent with Moore, Fortis had grown fond of him, and he wanted to capture some of those feelings and share them with his wife. He regretted not meeting her before they deployed, but at the time, he hadn't wanted to intrude on the few hours she and Quentin had left before 2nd Division deployed.

Dear Mrs. Moore, I am Captain Fortis. Quentin was my executive officer during the invasion of Maltaan. He was my friend, and I hope this will help ease your grief.

Quentin was an outstanding officer in every way. He was an efficient administrator, and his performance as executive officer enabled the entire company to operate at the highest levels. He was a brave and resourceful tactician, and his courage and technical prowess were critical to the success of our mission. Although

I only knew him for a few days, I am proud to count him among my friends, and we Space Marines will always remember him.

If there is anything I can ever do to help you and your family, please contact me.

Sincerely, Abner Fortis.

* * *

Beck fought to control the urge to run out of the cave as he surveyed the angry mercenaries in the dim firelight. Fight or flight, it was called, and he knew if he took flight from the deep, dank cave, they would catch him before he could make it outside. He had no idea what would happen after that.

"Where are they?" the largest mercenary, an ugly bastard named Walker, demanded as he brandished a club fashioned from an enormous bone he'd discovered deep in the cave.

"I told you, I don't know. The last time I saw them, they were on the ground by the entrance. I woke up a few hours later, and they were gone."

Mitsui and Hahn had disappeared within hours of their return to the cave. Beck was certain they'd gone back down the mountain in search of Space Marines to treat Mitsui; that was all Hahn had talked about in the twelve hours before they'd vanished.

"You should have been watching them," Walker said. "You knew they wanted to leave."

"Watching them? We're not prisoners here, and I'm not a guard."

The group grumbled at his answer, and Beck couldn't tell whether they agreed with him or not.

"We'll be prisoners soon enough if Mitsui and that bitch tell the Space Marines where to find us."

The grumbles became loud growls. Beck knew he was losing the argument and maybe his life. He had to think fast and talk faster.

"Why would they do that?" he retorted. "Hahn is the daughter of a high-ranking GRC executive. Do you think anyone will ever sign on with the GRC again if they betray us?" He looked around the semi-circle at the faces of the desperate men. "Mitsui's dead by now, anyway. I could smell his leg from five meters away, for God's sake. It wouldn't surprise me if we find his body at the bottom of the mountain."

Several of the mercenaries traded looks, and even Walker lowered his club. Beck was just getting warmed up, and he knew it was time for some misdirection. He pointed to the small pile of wood next to the fire.

"The rainy season is here, and that's all the dry firewood we have left. The rain soaked everything else. It's going to get mighty cold in here when that's gone. We're going to get hungry, too. We went all the way down the mountain, and I saw nothing. Not even one of those giant tree rats we saw everywhere when we got here. The rain has driven the animals into hibernation, or they've migrated down into the valleys. Either way, they're not here anymore. Maybe Mitsui and Hahn leaving is a sign that we need to leave, too."

"You want us to surrender?" an angry voice demanded.

"No, of course not. I want us to move to a place where food and shelter are easier to come by. This cave is an excellent place to hide out, and maybe we can come back to it when the seasons change. Right now, if we stay here, we die here."

"Where do we go?" Walker asked.

"I don't know; I'm not a geographer. The railway runs east and west, and it's the easiest way to travel, so let's follow it. At some point, we're going to run into someone."

"Yeah, like Space Marines," one man growled.

Beck knew he had to talk fast, so he appealed to their mercenary natures.

"There are eleven of us, and eight rifles. That's plenty of firepower to take over one of the little farms we saw along the way here. We grab it, hunker down for a couple days to eat and sleep in a warm, dry hut, and move on. I doubt the farmers would even report it, and if they do, we'll be long gone. Besides, who would they report it to? The Space Marines won't dedicate assets to locate a phantom group of humans, and a provisional royalist government in Daarben won't care what's happening to a bunch of poor farmers this far from the capital." There were more grumbles, but this time Beck recognized the agreement in some of their voices. "The key is not to give the farmers a reason to report us. If we don't kill everybody or burn everything, and leave them with enough to get by, they'll just go on with their lives."

Beck was spinning straight-up bullshit by that point, but he had the momentum, and he knew if he gave the mercenaries time to think, somebody would find a reason to argue with him. He forced himself to smile at the dirty faces around him.

"I don't know about you guys, but I'm tired of shivering on the floor of this fucking cave all night while the rumbling in my stomach keeps me awake. I want to be warm, I want to be dry, and I want to eat." For dramatic effect, he pointed up toward the cave mouth. "All that is out there somewhere. We just have to find it and take it."

The band of mercenaries didn't even take time for a vote. They collected what few belongings they had and trooped out of the cave, with Walker in the lead. The rain was still falling as they slipped and slid down the mountain trail. Beck kept one eye on the surrounding forest, half-expecting to see Mitsui and Hahn huddled together in death.

When they emerged onto the railway, everyone stopped and looked up and down the tracks. Without a word, Walker gestured with his bone club, and the mercenaries turned to follow him.

East.

* * *

There was a tap on Fortis' door, and Colonel Anders stuck his head in.

"Abner, do you have a minute?"

"Yes, sir. Please, come in."

"I have some news you'll be interested in. You've heard about the arrest of Weldon Krieg, right?"

"I have. Long overdue, if you ask me."

"Perhaps. Anyway, Division Intel just reported that we captured Saito Mitsui and Dalia Hahn."

Fortis searched his memory for the names. "I'm sorry, Colonel, but—wait a second. Saito Mitsui? Isn't he the Asian cowboy we met at the spaceport when we first got here? The guy with the farm equipment?"

Anders nodded. "The same guy. It turns out Mitsui was the lead overseer of the PCS training program for the Maltaani. There's even been some reporting that he was an officer in the People's Army of

Maltaan in command of all the PCS during the invasion, but that's unconfirmed as of now."

"Good. Good catch. Who's the other person? Hahn?"

"Do you recall the meeting we attended at the embassy when General Staaber burst in and started shouting about the fliers with your picture on them?"

"How could I forget?"

"You saw Beck there, and a female companion. The female was his executive assistant, Dalia Hahn. Dalia Hahn is the daughter of Weldon Krieg."

The news stunned Fortis, and then he felt a sudden surge of hope. "That's fantastic. Please tell me we captured Beck, too."

Anders frowned. "I wish I could, but I can't. Beck remains at large, along with many of the GRC mercenaries who fought with the PCS. Still, we've cut off several snakes' heads, and the rest can't be far behind."

"Do we have a line on where Beck might be? Have Mitsui or Hahn given us anything?"

"Not that I've heard."

"Well, when we do, let me know. Nothing would make me happier than to pop in on my old buddy Beck."

"You're forgetting yourself, Abner. Unless Beck is part of the insurgency, he's a law enforcement problem for 2nd Division, not us. We're counterinsurgency, remember?"

Fortis scoffed. "Shit. I don't care whose problem Beck is, sir. I'll shoot the bastard in the face if I get the chance."

Anders didn't respond, and the ensuing silence lasted well beyond comfortable.

"Is there something else on your mind, sir?"

The colonel nodded. "That was quite an outburst from Gunny Ystremski this morning."

"I can't blame him. Every time we get involved with the GRC and their test tubes, things go to shit, and Space Marines pay the price. After all the killing and dying because of those fucking things on Pada-Pada, only one person faced discipline. Me. Nobody from the GRC was ever called to account.

"Now we come here to liberate Maltaan and restore the royalist government, and who do we find working with the enemy? The GRC and their test tubes. After the fighting ended, the same GRC now asks for our help with rounding up their creations so they can put them to work and turn a profit for the Conglomerate. We're dying, and they're getting rich."

Anders took a deep breath. "I know how it looks, and from one perspective, you and Gunny are right. It's the height of hypocrisy for us to pretend they're guiltless, but there are steps being taken to hold them accountable. Krieg, Mitsui, and Hahn are proof of that, and if there's any justice in the universe, we'll get Beck, too.

"That doesn't solve the immediate tactical problem of a hundred and fifty thousand armed troops with no conscience or moral compass wandering the landscape. We can't just wash our hands of the problem; the attack on the farm and the patrol is proof of that." Anders stood up and paced.

"Like it or not, there *are* bigger forces at work here. Major Parisi isn't an operator. He doesn't understand war from the pointy end of a kukri, but he understands the economic politics of the situation. I have a friend with insider knowledge who tells me the Grand Council has begun informal discussions about breaking up the GRC into independent component companies. That includes their Military

Sales and Affairs Division, most recently headed up by Weldon Krieg. As they're a major military contractor, what happens to them impacts our military readiness. Still, the PCS are a problem for 2nd Division, not the counterinsurgency."

"Speaking of the counterinsurgency, what about captured Maltaani insurgents?" Fortis asked. "I don't take orders from a civilian spook like Bell, even one from the Grand Council. I'll kill every Maltaani soldier I encounter on the battlefield, but I'm sure as hell not going to murder prisoners."

"If you capture insurgents, turn them over to the Maltaani. That's our guidance."

"Sounds like the same situation as Eros-28. Catch the resistance, turn them over to the Kuiper Knights, and find them dead later on."

Anders shrugged. "I don't have all the answers you want, Abner. It's not too late for you to request reassignment. That's not a threat, it's just the way it is."

Fortis thought for a second before he responded. "I'll do it. DINLI, but I don't think this is going to turn out the way some council committee members think it will."

* * * * *

Chapter Six

Mitsui was conscious when Hahn arrived in the medical tent, and she knelt by his side and took his hand. "My love, it's good to see you awake," she said. She looked over her shoulder at Corporal Vincent, who stood right behind her. "Corporal, could we have some privacy?"

"Ma'am, my orders are to maintain a close escort until I'm relieved."

"What are you afraid of? I'm not going to make a dash for freedom. I surrendered, remember? Besides, we're in a tent full of Space Marines, on a base full of Space Marines. I can't run fast enough to dodge all of you. I'm only asking for a little room so we can talk in private. Please?"

Vincent looked around the tent before she nodded and took several steps back, far enough that she was out of earshot for a whispered conversation.

"Hey, little darlin'," Mitsui slurred. "I missed you."

Tears welled in Hahn's eyes. "I missed you, too."

"Where are we?"

"A Space Marine field hospital at the spaceport in Daarben."

Mitsui tried to sit up. "Wha-what? Space Marines? Why?"

"Dearest, you were dying. Your leg…" She shuddered at the memory. "You had a terrible infection in your leg. It was going to kill you if you didn't get proper treatment. They saved your life."

"Saved it so they could hang me," Mitsui said as he slumped back. "You think your daddy can help?"

"Oh, my sweet, I don't think so. They arrested Daddy for treason."

Mitsui groaned. "I'm dead."

"No! You mustn't talk like that. I'll think of something."

"I hope so."

She leaned in close. "There's an agent named Leighton from the Ministry of Justice here. He just interviewed me, and he's going to interview you, too. What's important is that we stick to our plan. You remember our plan, don't you?"

The mercenary grunted.

"Remember our plan?"

Mitsui's breath grew deep and steady, and Hahn realized he was asleep. She held his hand for a long time and watched him sleep while a million thoughts tumbled around in her mind.

Despite Leighton's show of informing her of her rights and recording her interview, Hahn suspected the agent would use every dirty trick in the book to get the information he wanted, including interviewing Mitsui under sedation, or lying to him about what she'd revealed. Hahn could only hope Mitsui would remember the story they'd concocted during the nightmarish journey down the mountain: Beck alone had worked out the deal for the PCS, and if the GRC had militarized them before the transfer, it was someone else's responsibility.

She didn't share Mitsui's pessimism about his position, or hers. She wasn't a lawyer, and the Ministry of Justice was preventing them from obtaining top-notch counsel by holding them in a war zone, but she didn't think the treason charge would stick. Mitsui had been there to supervise the contracted human trainers. He hadn't commanded troops in the field; his role had been advisory only. Besides, he was a mercenary, and there was no law against him accepting a position in a foreign military. Once the invasion began, he'd abandoned his post almost immediately, further evidence that he wasn't involved in the actual fighting.

The more she thought about it, the more she convinced herself that Mitsui was in a better position than she was. There were communications between her and her father about the PCS deal. As far as she knew, there was no hard evidence implicating Mitsui. It all came down to the statements of one person.

Beck.

* * *

Ystremski found Fortis in his stateroom, deep in thought.

"Hey, Captain. Sorry to interrupt, but what do you say we hit the gym? It's been a long time since I pumped some iron and even longer for you."

Fortis nodded. "Yeah, Gunny. That's sounds exactly what I need right now. Exercise is good for the soul, you know. Hey, before we go, there are a couple of things I want to tell you. First off, I got the holos done."

"Huh. Tough job. DINLI."

"Indeed." Fortis then related what Anders had said about Mitsui and Hahn.

"No Beck?" Ystremski said.

"No, no Beck. Not yet."

"It's probably too much to hope that we'll get close enough to take a shot at that prick."

"I brought it up, but Anders told me to concentrate on counter-insurgency. Still, if we get the chance…"

"Boom."

"The other thing I want to talk about is Major Parisi."

"Ah, fuck. Did he file a formal grievance?"

"No, not that I'm aware of. That doesn't matter. What matters is that you apologize to him for your outburst this morning."

Anger welled up in Ystremski's chest. "Apologize? Fuck that. That smarmy bastard hasn't set foot on anything more hostile than a rub-and-tug doorstep in the red-light district outside the base back home, and he's lecturing me about 'larger forces at work' here?"

"He's a major, Gunny. You can't say 'fuck you' to a major, no matter how much of a prick he is. Like it or not, there *are* some higher stakes here than killing nationalist insurgents." Fortis explained the implications of the PCS crisis. "If we don't unfuck this mess right now, we might end up fighting this war all over again."

Ystremski glowered at Fortis. "I told you not to get mixed up with these fucking spooks. This is the bizarre shit they thrive on. They talk about 'larger forces,' but the only forces I care about are my kukri and my pulse rifle."

"I can't argue with you about that," Fortis said. "I brought up the same stuff with Anders, and he made it clear. DINLI or turn down the mission and get reassigned. We've chewed enough of the same dirt for you to know that I don't care who rules Maltaan, as long as it doesn't involve us any longer than it has to. Maybe we should've nuked the whole fucking planet."

Ystremski had to smile. "Yeah, you're right." His mood shifted from angry to happy. "Fuck all that stuff, sir. Change your clothes, and let's hit the gym."

* * *

Beck and Walker crouched in some thick undergrowth and examined the miserable collection of huts huddled together on the banks of a swollen stream.

"I don't know. This doesn't look promising," Beck whispered. "Maybe we should look for another one."

"Fuck that. We've been walking for hours, and we haven't seen anybody. The boys are wet, tired, and hungry, and it's getting dark. These aren't the guys you want to be stuck with all night in the rain."

"Okay, fine. How do you want to do it?"

Walker thought for a second. "Send five guys around the far side in case there are runners. The rain will cover their movement. We give them ten minutes to get into position, and then move in from here. There are only five huts, so maybe twenty Maltaani. We'll put all of them in a hut and take turns guarding them until we're ready to move on. Like you said, if we don't give them a reason to report us, they won't."

Beck nodded. "Sounds good. Let's go brief the others."

When they got back to the group, Beck stood back and let Walker do the talking. He liked the quasi-advisory position he'd developed behind Walker. He didn't take orders like the lowest ranking mercenaries, but he wasn't responsible for any of Walker's decisions, so they couldn't blame him if things went wrong.

Walker scratched a rough diagram of the village in the mud, and the mercenaries gathered around it. He pointed to the first five to his left.

"You five, move around this way to watch the back door. Go quick, because in ten minutes, the rest of us will move in from this side. There are five huts, so I don't expect over fifteen adults. After we round them up, we'll clear one hut and put them inside with a guard. Everybody…" Walker turned and looked at Beck. "Everybody will take a turn as the guard while the rest of us get out of this fucking rain and get something to eat."

Heads nodded as the group agreed to the plan.

"Flankers, move out," Walker ordered. "The rest of you, follow me."

The mercenaries spread out to watch for signs of alarm as the other group circled to the other side, but there was no reaction. After several minutes, Walker stood and brandished his club.

"Let's take this place."

The mercenaries formed a skirmish line and moved in on the village. At first, their presence went unnoticed, but a voice shouted in alarm from one hut, and then another. Frightened Maltaani poured from the huts, and Beck realized there were well over fifteen adults. A *lot* more.

There must be a hundred of them.

Screaming women dashed around with babies clutched to their chests, while toddlers clung to their skirts. Other Maltaani shrank back in fear as the mercenaries used their boots and rifle butts to herd them together. Two Maltaani males dashed up to Walker and protested in rapid-fire Maltaani, but the mercenary leader didn't have a translator, so he pushed them aside.

Several villagers tried to escape into the forest, but the flankers turned them back toward the village. Somewhere in the back of the village, Beck heard a ballistic rifle shot ring out, followed by a pulse rifle, and then a third. Maltaani shrieked and ran in all directions, and the mercenaries opened up on them.

Beck stared, open-mouthed, as blue-white bolts of energy tore through the villagers. Men, women, and children fell under the guns of the mercenaries, and it took him a long minute to remember he had a pulse rifle. He slid it off his shoulder and ran to the nearest mercenary.

"Stop it!" Beck shoved the man, who took his finger off the trigger long enough to throw a fist at Beck. Beck dodged the strike, but the mercenary returned to shooting down the villagers.

Beck looked around and spotted Walker, who swung his club at a passing Maltaani.

"Walker, stop this!" Beck screamed. He leveled his rifle at the mercenary leader. "Stop it, now!"

A bomb exploded behind his ear, and Beck's legs went out from under him. He fell face-first into the bloodstained mud as pain thundered through his head. He couldn't move his arms or legs, and all he could do was watch in horror as the mercenaries completed their grisly assault. Finally, it was done.

Boots appeared in front of Beck's face, and Walker hauled him to his feet and held him face-to-face.

"What the fuck are you doing, Beck?" Walker demanded.

Beck struggled to put a sentence together through the loud ringing in his ears. "Shooting innocents," he said before he collapsed to his knees.

"Fuck innocents," Walker said. One mercenary threw an ancient-looking ballistic rifle down in front of him. "They fired first."

The mercenaries gathered around Walker, laughing and chatting. Two of them supported one of their comrades, who had a bloody hole in his leg. They lowered him to the ground next to Beck.

"One of them had that rifle stashed away," a mercenary reported. "He shot Baniewicz and made a break for it."

Beck had recovered enough to stand on his own. "I'm not surprised, the way you were beating on them."

"What's your problem, Beck? They were running around and wouldn't follow orders."

Beck gestured to the dead Maltaani scattered around the village. "What do we do now?" he asked Walker.

"Stash the bodies in one of the huts, find some food, and get some sleep out of this rain," Walker said. "Where did all those fuckers come from, anyway?"

When the mercenaries investigated the huts, they discovered a tunnel system dug under the village. The tunnels connected the huts, and two side tunnels disappeared somewhere under the forest. The mercenaries stacked crude Maltaani furniture and other debris over the holes to block anyone else from coming out, while others gathered everything that looked edible.

"Some of this meat smells funky," a mercenary complained.

"It's probably skunk," another quipped, and the group laughed.

"Get a fire started in that hut," Walker ordered. "Throw it all in that cauldron there and boil the hell out of it. Beck, you're the cook."

"I'm not a cook," Beck said.

"You've done nothing on this trip so far but complain. It's time you pull your weight, unless you want to head out on your own."

"Whatever you say, Walker," Beck said as he headed for the huts to find some firewood and get supper started.

I hope that skunk meat gives you the shits.

* * * * *

Chapter Seven

First thing the following morning, Anders summoned Fortis and Ystremski to the 2nd Division flag suite. "Bender's shuttle just docked," the colonel told them. "They'll be here in a few minutes."

When Bender arrived, Fortis greeted him at the door.

"G'day, Lucky," Bender said when he saw Fortis. "What happened to your hair, mate?"

Fortis smiled. Bandages swathed Bender's enormous head, the result of his cochlear translator surgery. The two men embraced.

"Same thing as your head. *Solicitude.* How are you?"

"Bit of a headache, but nothing to fuss about." He gestured to another bandaged Space Marine behind him. "This is Woody. Top bloke, knows a thing or two about explosives and bullet wounds."

Fortis and Woody shook hands. Woody was shorter than Fortis, but his build was like a fireplug: barrel-chested with thick shoulders and no neck. "Sergeant Woods," Woody said in a clipped English accent. He tipped his head toward Bender. "This bastard has a nickname for everyone."

"He does."

Ystremski stepped up and stuck out his hand. "I'm Gunny Ystremski," he said as he shook hands with Bender. "My nickname is Gunny."

Bender chuckled and slapped him on the shoulder. "No worries, Gunny."

Colonel Anders stood back and gave the men a few minutes to become familiar with each other. A few sea stories about mutual acquaintances and deployments they had in common would build unit cohesion, critical to their success on an accelerated deployment timeline.

With introductions out of the way, Colonel Anders stepped forward. "Gentlemen, let's get down to the business at hand."

The four Space Marines took seats at the large table, and seconds later, Wagner, Bell, and Parisi entered the room. After a brief round of introductions, Anders started by putting up a holo of Baat-Doh Province, with Camp Zulu-Five and the two helenium mines marked in blue.

"A quick recap of the big picture brief. Baat-Doh Province is part of 4th Division's area of responsibility. You'll be one of three teams operating out of Camp Zulu-Five under the command of Major Andrej Sokolov. Your mission is to run operations against the insurgents in the province. The goal is to kill or capture them."

Fortis and Ystremski exchanged glances but said nothing.

"Now that Sergeants Bender and Woods are here, and appear to be no worse for wear, I'm speeding up your deployment timeline. When we break from this briefing, Sergeant Ramon will take Bender and Woods to the armory to get recon armor. While that's happening, Captain Fortis and Gunny Ystremski will determine what your expected logistics requirements are and submit it to me. After everything is complete, you'll proceed by shuttle to the spaceport and meet a hovercopter from Zulu-Five. Questions?"

Woody raised his hand. "What's our intel support like at Zulu-Five, sir? How will we know where to find the insurgents?"

"Major Sokolov has been building up a network of spies and informers over the past couple of weeks. You'll combine the organic reporting with the technical intelligence provided by Major Parisi and his people at the Joint Intelligence Center to develop specific operations. Anyone else?"

"Colonel, how far from logistics support will we be operating?" Fortis asked. "Will we get routine supply hits from the hub at the spaceport? That's going to be important when we calculate how many cases of pig squares to bring."

"Before the rainy season, we sent flights at least weekly. Since the rain started, the flight schedule has been less reliable. The hovercopters can fly through some pretty nasty stuff, but they're weight-limited when they do. Take a week's worth of everything. You might have to tighten your belts."

"Roger that, sir." Fortis looked at Bender and Woody. "Do you have any requirements?"

"Fifty meters of det cord and a hundred caps, to start," Bender said. When Fortis raised his eyebrows in surprise, the Australian giant laughed. "It comes in handy."

"I'll need a standard trauma kit, plus another kit's worth of antibiotics," Woody said. "Every minor scratch gets infected in this weather, and the infections spread quick."

Sergeant Ramon collected the newcomers, and Wagner and Parisi headed for the door.

"Major Parisi," Ystremski called. He approached the major and hung his head.

"Sir, I was out of line and disrespectful yesterday. I failed to live up to the standards expected of an ISMC gunnery sergeant, and I hope you will accept my apology."

Ystremski's apology shocked Fortis. He'd never heard the gunny speak like that, and he knew it took everything Ystremski had.

Parisi extended his hand, and the two men shook. "Apology accepted, Gunny. Sometimes our passion for the fight overtakes common courtesy, and I took no offense. I owe you an apology, too. I sometimes forget that real people who bleed and die fight our battles."

"It's unnecessary, but thank you all the same, sir."

After Wagner and Parisi were gone, Fortis caught Anders' eye and nodded to the door.

"You two work on your logistics request," the colonel said. "I need to run out for a second."

When they were alone, Ystremski let out a long breath.

"Damn, Gunny, that was the nicest thing I've ever heard you say. It almost brought a tear to my eye," Fortis said with a smile.

"Shut up, dickhead. You wanted me to apologize, so I apologized."

"It was a good apology, too. So good that you made *him* apologize. For a second, I thought you two were going to kiss and make up for real."

"I should have suffocated you with a pillow on *Solicitude* when I had the chance," Ystremski retorted, and both men broke into laughter.

They were still laughing five minutes later when Anders returned.

* * *

"Mr. Mitsui, I'm Supervisory Agent Leighton with the UNT Ministry of Justice. This is Major Bisset of the Fleet Legal Counsel Office."

"What?" Mitsui blinked at the strange man standing over his bed.

"I'm Supervisory Agent Leighton with the UNT Ministry of Justice, and this is Major Bisset of the Fleet Legal Counsel Office," the man repeated, louder. "I'd like to ask you a few questions."

Mitsui feigned confusion, but he was awake and alert. Since the doctors had eased up on the heavy pain medication, he'd been expecting a visit from Leighton. Hahn's words echoed in his mind.

Stick to the plan.

"Questions?" Mitsui mumbled.

"I'm collecting routine information about the GRC here on Maltaan, and I'm hoping you can fill in some gaps. Would you mind?"

"Mmm-kay." Mitsui looked around and saw the hospital staff had set up privacy screens to shield him from view.

"Great." Leighton set a small device on a bedside table and sat in a chair next to him. "I'm going to record this," Leighton told him. "It's so much easier than making notes. That's okay, isn't it?"

"Sure."

The other man, Bisset, stood at the foot of his bed with his hands folded in front of him.

"This is Supervisory Agent Thomas Leighton with the UNT Ministry of Justice," Leighton began. "Present is Major Jean-Paul Bisset of the Fleet Legal Counsel Office." He noted the time and date. "This is the initial interview of Mr. Saito Mitsui. Before we begin, I am required to apprise you of your rights under the UNT Human Rights Declaration. You may remain silent. If you exercise that right, the interview will end, and we will take you into custody until we adjudicate your case.

"If you choose to answer my questions, your answers will become part of the legal record of your case, and we can hold you liable for any false statements. You have the right to legal counsel during all legal proceedings, including this interview. Because we are in an active war zone where routine access by civilian attorneys is forbidden, Major Bisset is your court-appointed attorney. Although he is a Fleet officer, Major Bisset must provide you with the best defense possible, and he enjoys full attorney-client privileges, just like any Terran attorney. Do you understand your rights, Mr. Mitsui?"

"Uh-huh."

"Do you have questions before we begin?"

Mitsui waved a hand at Bisset. "What's his name again?" Mitsui took care to speak in a slow monotone to mimic a drugged stupor.

"Major Bisset, from the Fleet Legal Counsel Office. He's your attorney."

"Okay."

"Are you aware that we arrested your employer, Weldon Krieg, the executive director of the Galactic Resource Conglomerate's Military Sales and Affairs Division, for treason in connection with transferring military technology in time of war?"

"Yeah."

"Did you transfer or abet the transfer of military technology to the Maltaani government?"

"Military? No."

"Did you transfer or abet the transfer of military technology to any individuals inside or outside the Maltaani government?"

"No."

"Are you sure, Mr. Mitsui?"

Mitsui waited a long second before he responded. "Uh-huh."

"Were you involved in the transfer of two hundred thousand Precision Crafted Soldiers from the GRC to the Maltaani government? In particular, General Staaber?"

"Uh."

"Mr. Mitsui, were you involved in the transfer of two hundred thousand PCS from the GRC to the Maltaani government? In particular, General Staaber?"

"Staaber. I know him."

Leighton turned off the recorder and leaned over until his face was almost touching Mitsui's. "Mr. Mitsui, I'm not buying your sedated act. I'm an expert at chemical interrogation techniques, and I know what pain meds the doctors gave you, and how long they last.

"You can continue your charade, but if you do, you need to understand something. Your pain medication is optional, and I'm the guy who exercises that option. You might avoid answering my questions for now, but in a couple hours, your meds will wear off. I'll have you gagged so your screaming won't disturb the other patients, but you'll have a clear mind to answer my questions. The choice is yours. Do you understand?"

Mitsui's heart raced, and he gave a slight nod. He'd encountered many dangerous individuals in his years as a mercenary, but he'd never felt as threatened as he felt right then. Leighton wasn't a large man, but he exuded complete confidence in the power of the government that he wielded. As if to emphasize the danger, a spasm of pain made his foot twitch.

Leighton sat back. "Okay. Let's try this again." He switched on the holo recorder. "Mr. Mitsui, were you involved in the transfer of two hundred thousand PCS from the GRC to the Maltaani government? In particular, General Staaber?"

"Yes."

"Good. Can you elaborate on your role in the deal?"

"The GRC contracted me to train the Maltaani in how to develop the PCS into a useable workforce. I'd been what we called a PCS 'wrangler' when I worked for the GRC in the past, so they brought me back as the head contractor for the project. It was my job to oversee the other contracted trainers and facilitate the transfer of the PCS to training camps in the east."

"Were you aware the PCS had received basic military training before the GRC shipped them here?"

"Not at first. They seemed easy to organize, but I assumed that was a feature of the new generation. I'd only worked with first- and second-generation PCS before."

"The GRC sent them here to General Staaber. Why would a general want demilitarized PCS?"

"I asked Mr. Beck about that. You know Beck, the GRC head honcho here? Anyway, I asked him, and he told me the general's family owned some dormant mines and needed a lot of manpower to get them producing again."

"Did you know General Staaber was a leader in the nationalist movement?"

Mitsui shook his head. "I don't follow politics. I came here to make a lot of money training the Maltaani."

"Why didn't you leave when the ambassador ordered the embassy evacuation?"

"Headquarters told Beck we were to stay put. As far as I knew, the war had nothing to do with our deal. Staaber offered us a safe place to stay, so we took it."

"Did you become an officer in Staaber's army?"

Fuck.

"Yeah, but it wasn't like I was an actual officer. He gave me rank so I could get things done without the rest of the Maltaani getting in my way, but I didn't lead troops. It wasn't a good time to be a human here, you know? We weren't real popular."

"Were you aware that the invasion by the ISMC was imminent?"

"Again, I don't follow politics. Beck talked about all kinds of moves and countermoves between us and the Maltaani, but I tried to ignore him. As soon as I got word that the Space Marines had dropped on the spaceport and there was fighting in Daarben, I grabbed Dalia Hahn, and we took off. Beck attached himself to us kind of as an afterthought."

"What was your plan?"

Mitsui shrugged. "Didn't have one, to be honest. Head east and stay clear of the fighting until we could figure out how to get home." He motioned to his leg. "That's when I got this."

"How did it happen?"

"A hovercopter strafed our truck, so we bailed out. My assistant Gabby got hit. When I went back for him, I got hit myself."

"Where's Gabby now?"

"Dead. Gabby was a PCS, and company protocol says that we kill wounded PCS rather than spend medical resources treating them."

"That's harsh. If Gabby was a PCS, why'd you go back for him?"

"Instinct. It was my mistake for getting attached to the little fella." Mitsui cleared his throat. "Do you think I can get something to drink?"

Leighton motioned to Bisset, who disappeared and returned seconds later with a hydration pack.

"What else do you want to know?" Mitsui asked after he finished quenching his thirst.

Leighton turned off the holo recorder. "I think that's enough for now, Mr. Mitsui. If my guess is correct, the pain meds are wearing off, and your leg is throbbing. We can pick this up later. Wouldn't want to cause you any unnecessary suffering, would we?"

* * * * *

Chapter Eight

Beck leaned against the wall of the cooking hut and listened to the snores and farts of the sleeping mercenaries scattered around him. None of them had gotten the shits from the skunky meat, but something in the stew he'd created with it had left them all bloated and flatulent. It was funny at first, but as the night wore on, and their gas pains became painful cramps, everybody stopped laughing. Most of the mercenaries escaped their intestinal discomfort by falling asleep, but not Beck.

He stirred the embers of the fire with a stick and then dropped it onto the glowing coals. Despite the foul smell in the hut, and the cramps that twisted his stomach, Beck was warm and dry for the first time in several days. With his immediate physical needs met, he had time to contemplate his situation and options.

The massacre had come as a terrible shock, and when it was over, he'd discovered the mercenaries had planned it.

"We're not leaving any of those bug-eyed bastards alive to report us," Walker told him when Beck complained.

"What about our discussion back on the mountain? We were supposed to just hold them."

"I guess we changed our minds. If you don't like it, the railway is that direction. Just be careful that you don't get hurt going over there."

Beck recognized a threat when he heard one, so he backed off.

Beck was at an extreme disadvantage among the band of mercenaries here in the forest. None of them had connected Beck to their current circumstances. Yet. They were fugitives in the forest because the GRC had abandoned them, and the closest GRC executive was within arm's reach. The group had seen his reaction to the village massacre, and some had been giving Beck sideways looks ever since.

He wanted to leave, but he wasn't certain where they were, only that they were somewhere north of the railway. Walker had taken his pulse rifle away, and Beck knew it would be futile to ask for it back. He didn't have any supplies, so walking away wasn't an option. Alone, unarmed, and lost in the forest were the makings of a disaster.

Staying with them presented a whole different set of problems. He didn't want any part of what he'd witnessed earlier, because he knew that eventually there'd be an accounting. They might attack a village that was better prepared to defend themselves, or they could raise enough anger and alarm that other area villages might band together and pursue them. That was the nightmare scenario; Beck had heard stories of what happened to human captives at the hands of the Maltaani.

I gotta get out of here.

He stretched out next to the fire and tried to forget his worries and get some sleep. The fire warmed him, the hut kept him dry, and at that moment, nothing else seemed to matter.

* * *

It was early evening by the time Fortis' team was equipped and their logistics request filled. They gathered in the shuttle hangar to check their gear and make final preparations.

"This recon armor is a good bit of kit," Bender said. "The regular stuff is too bloody small for us full-figured girls. Chafes my boys." He nodded at Fortis' kukri. "What's with the crimson handle, mate? You been telling porky pies?"

Fortis stared back. "Porky pies?"

"Porky pies. Lies," Woody translated. "A bit of the English language hijacked by our penal colonists a long time ago."

Before Fortis could respond, Ystremski spoke up. "No lie. Damn near chopped a man in half with one swing. I saw it myself."

Bender blinked in surprise. "Fair dinkum?"

It was Ystremski's turn to be puzzled by Bender. "What?"

"Is that the truth?" Woody said. "Another bit of the mother tongue, shredded by convicts."

"It's the truth. Split him open from crotch to chin. I tied that crimson cord myself," Ystremski said.

"Fuck me, but you've led an interesting life," Bender told Fortis.

"I'm just trying to pay off my student loans," Fortis replied. Fortis, Ystremski, and Bender laughed, and it was Woody's turn to be puzzled.

"The ISMC said they'd pay my student loans if I signed up," Fortis explained. "I figured I'd spend a few years nuking bug holes and be debt-free at the end."

Woody chuckled. "I can see how that's working out for you."

Colonel Anders and Jerry Wagner entered the hangar. "What's your status, Captain?" Anders asked.

Fortis looked around the group, and everyone gave him a thumbs-up. "We're ready, Colonel. We loaded the supplies, and we've got all our gear. We're standing by for your order to mount up."

"Mount up!"

Fortis led the team aboard the shuttle, and they buckled in as the crew chief secured the cabin. The craft gave a slight jerk as the launch rail engaged.

"Cleared for launch," the pilot announced over the PA system. After another bump, the artificial gravity of *Mammoth* vanished, and they were free.

"It's going to get a little bumpy after we get into the atmosphere," the pilot said. "It's storming at the spaceport."

"Why are we in a rush to land in a storm?" Ystremski asked. Fortis could only shake his head in response.

The shuttle bucked as it punched into the atmosphere and descended to the spaceport. Fortis' stomach lurched after one especially nasty drop, and when the shuttle slammed down on the tarmac, he smiled with relief.

"I've made smoother landings on a drop ship," Woody said as they unbuckled their restraints.

The pilot came back into the passenger cabin. "Hey, Captain, as soon as I get clearance to taxi, I'll take you over to Hanger Nine. That's where you're supposed to meet your ride, and you can offload the cargo without getting soaked. The air boss grounded everything because the weather socked in the spaceport, so we're stuck here tonight. Thanks for that."

Fortis grinned. "You can always come with us."

The pilot, a kind-faced warrant officer named Appleton, shook his head. "No thank you, sir. I didn't join the Fleet to run around in the rain and mud. I'll take a lumpy mattress on the flagship over a wet hole every time."

"Thanks, Warrant," Fortis called after the pilot, and the Space Marines shared a laugh.

They made quick work of transferring their cargo to the hangar before the shuttle taxied away. The hangar was empty, and there was nobody there to greet them, so Fortis went in search of someone who knew what was going on.

"You three stay here. I'm going to check things out at the air boss' tent," he told them.

"Don't get wet," Bender called after him.

The light rain that was falling when they'd landed and offloaded had become horizontal sheets of wind-driven water as Fortis trudged along the flight line until he found the air boss' tent. He paused for a moment to let the water run off his armor before he took off his helmet and looked around. A surprised sergeant looked up from a holo player on her desk.

"Can I help you?"

"I'm Captain Fortis. I just came down from *Mammoth*, and I'm supposed to meet a hovercopter here."

"Nobody's going anywhere tonight, sir. Flight operations have been suspended due to weather. Try back tomorrow morning." She turned back to her holo.

"Sergeant, I'm not looking to fly out tonight. I'm trying to find out where my ride is. I was told it was in Hangar Nine, but Hangar Nine is empty."

The sergeant got an annoyed look on her face. "Sir, nothing is flying tonight." She sounded like someone admonishing a small child.

Fortis ran out of patience. "Sergeant, where the fuck is the hovercopter from Camp Zulu-Five? Either you tell me, or I'll find the fucking duty officer, and *they* can tell me."

Her annoyed look became petulant. "Fine, Captain, I'll look it up, but you're not going anywhere."

Fortis bit back his response as she tapped her keyboard.

"Here we go. Fender 454. Scheduled departure to return to Camp Zulu-Five shown as TBD. Hangar Eight. Like I said, Captain. Nothing is flying tonight."

Fortis resisted the urge to unload a verbal barrage on her. Instead, he nodded, put his helmet on, and went back outside. The rain was still falling as he walked to Hangar Eight.

An aging hovercopter squatted inside. Someone in a flight suit stood atop a ladder next to it with the top half of their body buried under open engine cowlings. Music played over speakers inside the craft, and Fortis recognized the sounds of classic rock-n-roll.

"Excuse me," he shouted up the ladder. "I'm looking for Fender 454."

The Space Marine on the ladder extricated himself from inside the engine and looked at Fortis. "Hold on, buddy." With practiced ease, he slid down the ladder side rails, ducked inside the hovercopter, and the music ceased. The nametape on his flight suit read "Brumley," and when he doffed his protective cranial, Fortis saw bright red hair and a youngish face. "Now, what can I do for you, pal, er, sir?"

"I'm Captain Fortis. I'm looking for Fender 454. She's supposed to take me to Camp Zulu-Five when the weather breaks."

"You're Fortis? Great." The redhead stuck out his hand, and the pair shook. "This is Fender 454, and I'm the lead pilot, Warrant Brumley. Everybody calls me Red, for obvious reasons."

"Pleased to meet you, Red." Fortis nodded to the hovercopter. "What's the story with the bird?"

"Nothing a multi-million-credit overhaul can't fix," Red replied. He chuckled. "I'm kidding, Captain. I've been flying with a faulty gearbox temp sensor, and I found one here. Routine repair." He must have seen something in Fortis' face, because he continued. "She looks a little rough, but she's a warhorse, sir. I keep her looking that way to avoid ferrying VIPs around for photo-ops."

Fortis nodded. "Understandable."

"Captain, 454 is a beast. They built her before Fleet decided to save money by reducing weight instead of building bigger engines, so she's armored from nose to tail. She was built as a cargo bird, but now she's got rocket pods and chain guns. The only gun we're missing is the nose-mounted pulse cannon, and I couldn't convince them to buy it for me." Red patted 454 on the nose. "She's heavy, but when the shooting starts, she can fly straight and level a lot longer than the new birds."

While Red spoke, Fortis walked around the hovercopter. She was old, but she was well-maintained. The ground crew had even touched up all the minor dings from stones or other debris thrown up by the engines.

"Where's the rest of the crew?" Fortis asked.

"When the air boss suspended flight ops, I sent them to the chow hall to get something to eat and find some spare bunks to get a little shut eye."

"What about you?"

"I get plenty of sleep when I'm flying," Red deadpanned. When Fortis didn't react, he grinned. "A little pilot humor, sir. I'm going to finish with that sensor and call it a night myself. Someone has to stay with the bird, so I'll rack out inside."

"The rest of my team is next door, in Hangar Nine," Fortis said. "I'll go get them and our gear so we can get it loaded before you turn in."

"Sounds good, sir."

The rain had slacked off to a chilly drizzle when Fortis walked between hangars.

"Fender 454 is in the next hangar over," Fortis told his team. "The rain's let up, so let's get this stuff over there while we can."

They moved everything in two trips, and when they were done, Red had just bolted down the cowlings. He slid down and greeted the newcomers.

"You look young to be a pilot," Ystremski said. "Does your mom know you're playing Space Marine, son?"

Red smiled at the barb. "You sure got me good that time, Gunny. That's the first time anyone has *ever* told me I look too young to be a Space Marine."

Fortis, Bender, and Woody laughed at Red's deft table-turning, and even Ystremski chuckled.

"But since you ask, my mom was a Space Marine pilot, too. She dropped with 9th Division on Balfan-48. Shot down on the first day."

Fortis and Ystremski traded surprised looks. They, too, had been with 9th Division and dropped on Balfan-48 for the first battle between the Space Marines and the Maltaani. Five thousand Space Marines had faced off against twenty-five thousand Maltaani, and only five hundred had survived.

"I was on Balfan-48 with Gunny Ystremski," Fortis said.

"I know who you are, Captain," Red replied. "Why do you think I requested to be your pilot?"

* * * * *

Chapter Nine

Dalia Hahn sat in silence and tried to clear her head while Supervisory Agent Leighton went through his spiel about her rights again for the benefit of the holo recorder. Corporal Vincent had awakened Hahn in her spartan quarters and hustled her to the interview tent before she could even wipe the sleep from her eyes.

At least it stopped raining.

"I'm sorry about waking you for an interview at such an early hour." Leighton tried to sound apologetic, but Hahn suspected it was a deliberate tactic to hit her with questions while she was sleepy and not thinking straight. "I'm afraid I can't offer you any tea or coffee because the UNT Human Rights Declaration prohibits me from giving you any stimulants before questioning. Would you like some water?"

"No, I'm fine."

"Then let's begin. Where is Dexter Beck?"

The abruptness of the question unsettled Hahn. She'd expected warm-up questions meant to establish rapport and get her talking.

"I don't know."

"Come on, Miss Hahn. I know you evacuated with him when the invasion began, and you spent a couple of weeks together evading capture. So tell me, where is Dexter Beck?"

How much did Saito tell him?

Hahn shook her head. "I don't know. When I last saw him, he was at the cave we'd been hiding in. Mitsui and I went down the mountain to find medical help. I don't know what happened to Beck after that."

"Where's the cave?"

"I don't know. In the mountains close to the railway. That's all I can remember."

Leighton unfolded a map and handed it to Hahn. "That mark is the spot where the Space Marines found you. The other mark is where they found Mr. Mitsui. Where is the cave in relation to them?"

"It's... I don't know. It must be close to where they found him, because he's too big for me to carry. When we got down the mountain, we walked a little way, then he passed out."

"Did you ever discuss or hear Mr. Beck discuss his plans for how to get off Maltaan?"

"No. We didn't worry about long-range plans. We were too worried about finding food to think about much else."

Leighton considered her for a long moment. "Do you have any reason to protect Mr. Beck?"

The question surprised Hahn. "Protect Beck? No, I have no reason to protect Mr. Beck."

"Were you alone with Mr. Mitsui and Mr. Beck in the cave, or was there someone else there?"

Hahn thought about lying, but changed her mind. "There were others, maybe ten. GRC contractors."

"Mercenaries?"

Hahn thought for a second. "They're trainers, like Mitsui. As far as I know, they weren't here in a military role."

"And they're all in this cave?"

Hahn's irritation bubbled over. "Agent Leighton, I don't know where anyone is anymore. I haven't been there for a few days now. They might still be there, or they might have moved on. Send some Space Marines and find out."

Leighton scoffed. "I plan to, but I don't want to send them on a fool's errand. You're sure you don't know where Mr. Beck is?"

"Positive."

"That's all I have for now, then. Thank you for your cooperation, Miss Hahn."

It surprised Hahn to see it was light outside when she exited the interview tent. It was drizzling, and the sky was still heavy with rain clouds. For the moment, it felt like a spring day back on Terra Earth.

"I don't suppose we could go for a walk?" she asked Vincent.

The corporal just stared.

* * *

After the team finished loading their stuff, Ystremski asked Fortis about getting some chow.

"You go ahead," Fortis said. "I'll stay here with the bird. I'm not hungry, anyway."

"We can take it in turns, sir."

"Nah, I'm good. Go get something to eat. Just don't go too far. Red told me if the weather breaks, he wants to launch as soon as possible."

"We'll go eat and come back then," Ystremski said.

"I'm going to go check the weather," Red told Fortis.

Fortis paced the hangar to relieve his boredom, but after his third lap around Fender 454, he went outside to check the weather.

The sky was lightening, and the driving rain had given way to a light drizzle, almost a heavy fog. Fortis felt a surge of hope that they might be airborne some time that morning.

Two figures in rain slickers approached, and Fortis watched them as they grew closer. When they were two meters away, the taller one saluted, and he realized it was a female Space Marine. He returned the courtesy and looked at the second person. It was another female, bedraggled from the rain, but there was something familiar about her face. Then it hit him.

Dalia Hahn!

At the same moment, recognition dawned on Hahn's face, and Fortis gave her an exaggerated wink. The pair continued to walk, but Hahn turned and looked at Fortis. He smiled and shook his head as he reentered the hangar.

A few seconds later, Fortis forgot all about Hahn when Red banged through the door, followed by two other Space Marines in flight suits, and the three members of Fortis' team.

"We have to mount up," Red told him. "Daarben Control cleared us to launch, but we have to go now before they change their minds." He motioned to the other pilot, who was already climbing into the cockpit. "That's Johnson, my copilot."

The Space Marines scrambled to fold their seats down and fasten their belts while Red and his copilot ran through their pre-launch checklist. The crew chief rolled the hangar door open and waved to some ground crewmen who arrived with a boxy yellow cart.

"I'm Varney," the crew chief told Fortis as he leaned in the door and handed the captain a headset. "Channel One is the cockpit. Do us a favor and don't say anything unless I'm bleeding or burning, and then only if it's out of control."

Meanwhile, the ground crewmen hooked up to Fender 454 and towed the hovercopter out of the hangar to the correct launch pad. After they were clear, Varney made a visual inspection, and then gave the "cleared to launch" signal to the cockpit before he climbed in next to Fortis.

"I'm Staff Sergeant Varney, your flight attendant today!" he shouted over the whine of the engines. "We'll be flying at some unknown altitude while we dodge storm cells on our way to Zulu-Five, with a brief stop for fuel at Romeo-Nine. It's gonna be rough, so buckle up. If you feel ill, please inform me so I know who's going to clean the inside of the aircraft when we get to Zulu-Five. There's no beverage service on this flight, and the only place to take a piss is out the door. Stand by for takeoff."

"*Here we go*," Red said over the intercom. Fender 454 jerked into the sky and then climbed nose-up at high speed. Ystremski and the other Space Marines cursed and grabbed for handholds as the g-force pressed them into their seats. After several seconds, they leveled out above the low-hanging clouds that blanketed Maltaan.

"Combat takeoff!" Fortis yelled to his team over the engine noise. "It's good practice."

Varney secured the hovercopter doors, and the engine noise dropped to a low whine. Fortis got as comfortable as he could in the folding canvas seat and let his chin droop to his chest. Sleep was a rare commodity in a war zone, and he tried to take every opportunity to get some. There was nothing to see out the window, just heavy gray clouds all around them. He let the engines lull him to sleep.

"Captain!"

A sharp elbow from Varney jolted Fortis out of his slumber.

"Red's trying to reach you on the intercom."

Fortis scrambled to get his headset on and hit the talk button. "This is Fortis."

Red's voice boomed in his ear. "*Hey, Captain, we've got trouble ahead. A logistics bird flying to Daarben from our fuel stop at Romeo-Nine went down yesterday, and nobody knew it. She wasn't supposed to launch, but they went anyway. After she was hours overdue, somebody asked Flight Control in Daarben about her, and that's when they realized she was missing.*"

"Where is she?"

"*Supposed to be about thirty klicks out. She's been up and down on the emergency freq, but not for long. Flight Control told me they reported fighting all night.*"

"Fighting who?"

"*I don't know, sir. We'll know more when we get close enough to contact them ourselves.*"

"Any other assets in the area? Troops or aircraft?"

"*Negative. We're all there is. There's no infantry for a couple hundred klicks, and nothing else is flying.*"

"Let's go find out what's up, then. What do you need us to do?"

"*Give Varney a hand with the door guns, and then stand by, I guess.*"

Fortis briefed his team on the situation, then they assisted Varney with the door guns. They pinned the hovercopter doors open and unfolded the mounts for the guns, which were large-caliber automatic pulse rifles.

"You guys know how to work these guns?" Varney shouted over the engines.

The Space Marines responded with a thumbs up.

"Good. As we're making our approach, I'll man the starboard gun, and one of you man the port gun. Don't forget to fasten your safety lanyard if you're going to move around the cabin. If you don't, and we have to do some juking to get away from ground fire, you'll end up grabbing air on your way down."

"*We'll be overhead in one minute, Captain,*" Red told Fortis over the intercom.

Fortis heard the copilot transmit on the emergency frequency.

"*Any station, this is Fender 454. How do you read?*"

There was a burst of static, so Johnson repeated his call. They heard a garbled and broken transmission, but someone responded.

"*...copter... down... help...*"

Fortis and the team strained to search the ground below for any signs of a downed hovercopter or its passengers. Red slowed the hovercopter down as they began a low orbit around the last reported position of the downed craft.

"*This is Fender 454. How do you copy?*"

"*Help us!*" a female voice shouted over the circuit. "*We're surrounded!*"

"There!" Woody pointed, and they saw the shattered remains of a hovercopter strewn down the side of a mountain.

"Four o'clock low," Varney announced, and Red banked to starboard.

"*I can hear you,*" the woman said over the circuit. "*Please, save us!*" In the background, Fortis heard the unmistakable sound of rifle fire.

"*Troops in contact,*" Red announced over the intercom. Varney and Bender stood by the door guns as the hovercopter spiraled down over the crash site.

"*Are you at the crash site?*" Johnson asked over the circuit. There was only silence. "*Ma'am, where are you? Are you at the crash site?*"

"*She's hit,*" a man's voice reported. "*We're all in the wreck at the bottom of the mountain. Fucking Maltaani everywhere.*" There was more rifle fire. "*You gotta hurry.*"

"*Keep your heads down,*" Red told him. "*Varney, hose down the tree line.*"

Even though Fortis knew it was coming, the burst of automatic pulse fire made him smile in surprise. The stream of blue-white energy bolts tore into the undergrowth.

"*Do that again!*" the man shouted over the emergency freq.

Varney unleashed a longer burst, and Fortis saw several small trees topple as the fire shredded their trunks.

"*They're running!*"

"*Okay, sir, what's your status? How many of you are there? Any wounded?*"

"*Uh, there are five of us left. Two wounded,*" came the reply.

"*Can you move?*"

Red brought Fender 454 around, and Varney hammered the undergrowth.

"*No, I don't think so. Please, you've got to get us out of here.*"

"*Stand by.*"

"*Captain, this is Red. There are five survivors at the crash site.*"

"Yeah, I heard. Can you get in there?"

"*I don't think so, sir. Too many trees.*"

"Let's find a clearing somewhere around here, and we'll go in on foot with you in overwatch."

"*Roger that.*"

"We can't get in at the crash site," Fortis told his team over the recon circuit. "Red's gonna insert us close by, and we'll proceed on foot. Bender, bring some det cord and caps. We might need to knock down a couple trees."

"*Hey, Captain, there's a clearing two klicks west of the crash that I can get into. As soon as you're in, we'll get back overhead of the crash site to guide you in.*"

"Sounds good. If we can, we'll make some room for you over there instead of carrying out the wounded."

"*Yes, sir.*"

Red brought Fender 454 down in a low hover over the clearing. When the hovercopter was two meters off the ground, Fortis and the team jumped down and set a perimeter. The hovercopter climbed up above the trees and headed back toward the crash site.

"Count off," Fortis said as he scanned the trees with his pulse rifle at the ready.

"One," said Ystremski.

"Two," said Bender.

"Three," said Woody.

"Four. Okay, Woody, take point, then Gunny, me, and Bender. There are hostile Maltaani forces somewhere around here, so stay alert. Move out."

* * * * *

Chapter Ten

Staaber walked up the gravel drive that led to his family home. The once-manicured landscaping was now ragged and overgrown, and the overcast sky cast a heavy blanket of gloom over the scene.

He stopped and stared at the house. Broken windows gaped back at him like the eyes of an empty skull. Someone had ripped the front door from its hinges and dropped it on the ground in front of the portico. Bullet holes pockmarked the columns, and pulse rifle bolts scorched the walls up to the second floor. Humans and Maltaani together had desecrated his family home.

Animals.

Anger welled up inside him as Staaber took in the scene, and it took all his self-control to force himself to mount the steps and enter the house.

Glass shards crunched under his feet as he walked into the entryway. Broken balusters gave the grand staircase railing a gap-toothed grin, while stained wallpaper and broken furniture hinted at the former grandeur of the space. All that remained of the portraits of his ancestors that once overlooked the room were a pile of broken frames and ashes where someone had thrown them together in the center of the floor and set them alight.

Staaber's customary stoicism cracked at the sight of his proud ancestry treated with such disrespect, and he turned and made for the main dining room. The destruction was the same in every room; they'd defiled the splendor with ruthless efficiency. He forced himself to see without seeing until he reached the mantle above the fireplace in the dining room.

With a single deft motion, he unlocked the secret compartment behind the mantle. Relief washed over him when his fingers brushed the crushed velvet bundle hidden inside.

It was his family sword, carried by his father, his father's father, and countless generations before. The royalists insisted Maltaani officers carry ceremonial daggers instead of swords, one of many tiny irritants that had angered the nationalists and led to the full-scale rebellion.

He removed the velvet and examined the weapon. It wasn't a ceremonial weapon like the detested daggers; it had no fancy scrollwork or intricate carving. The sword was a plain, heavy weapon of war designed to do one thing. Kill.

Staaber drew the sword and inspected the blade. Even in the dim interior of the house, the edges gleamed. Nicks and other blemishes served as testament to the hard service the sword had seen, but the heft gave him a surge of pride. When he twisted the sword a certain way, he could make out the only adornment on the blade or scabbard; a phrase engraved on the blade.

Here we stand.

Brave words of defiance, first uttered by a distant forefather and adopted as the Staaber family motto.

Staaber reached into the hidden compartment and found the leather sword belt he'd also stashed there. He buckled the sword around his waist, and without a backward glance, strode from the house. He had a vague idea where to find other aggrieved nationalists who'd join him in continuing the resistance to the humans and their royalist lap dogs.

* * *

Woody led the way through the forest to the area where Fender 454 orbited. The urgency of the situation at the crash site demanded speed, but the natural caution they'd developed as veteran infantrymen held them back. Fortis could hear occasional gunfire and the burst of automatic fire somewhere in the forest ahead.

Woody raised his hand to signal a halt.

"Captain, I can see some of the wreckage through the trees," the point man reported.

Gunny Ystremski crawled forward and joined Woody. "Affirmative, sir," he said. "We're here."

"Can you see anybody?"

"Negative."

"Bender, are you good?"

"Rearguard all clear."

"Stand by." Fortis keyed the circuit to Fender 454. "This is Fortis. We're at the crash site. Can you confirm where the survivors are?"

"*They're under cover by the biggest piece of the fuselage. That's all I can get from them. I don't think they're military.*"

"Damn. Okay, let them know we're approaching from the west and not to shoot anything not identified as Maltaani."

"*Roger that.*"

He switched to the team circuit. "They're under cover by the biggest piece of the fuselage. It's not a lot of help, but we'll make do. Woody, take us in nice and slow."

Fortis stood to follow the point man when a figure rose from the bushes two meters away and shot him at point blank range. The bullet slammed into Fortis' pulse rifle, and the force of the impact threw him backwards. The bushes exploded in blue-white energy as Bender hosed down the attacker.

"Lucky! Are you all right, mate?" Bender asked as he kneeled next to Fortis.

His hands stung from the impact of the heavy round on his pulse rifle, but the captain was otherwise unhurt. "Yeah, I'm good." He looked at his weapon. "My rifle's fucked."

"What's going on back there?" Ystremski demanded.

"The captain got shot, but he's not hurt," Bender reported. "He's the luckiest bastard in the world."

"Captain?"

"I'm good, Gunny. The round hit my rifle, not me. We're on our way."

Bender and Fortis picked their way through the underbrush to where Ystremski and Woody waited.

"Fucker popped up out of nowhere," the captain explained. "I don't know how long he was hiding there, but I didn't see him until his rifle was coming up."

"You need to sit this one out, sir?"

"No." Fortis drew his kukri. "I'm good."

Just then, a female voice screamed somewhere ahead of them.

"Let's go!"

The team sprinted to the sound of the scream. They found a human woman wrestling with a Maltaani armed with a huge knife.

"Get your hands off me, you bug-eyed freak!"

Without hesitation, Fortis charged forward. Although his recon armor camouflaged his movements, the Maltaani must have sensed his presence, because he let go of the woman. Fortis swung his kukri in a tight arc and severed the Maltaani's knife hand in one blow. The Maltaani bellowed and fell to his knees, and Fortis finished him with another quick stroke across the neck. The woman scrambled to her feet and attacked the dead Maltaani, screaming and kicking at the corpse.

"Take it easy," Ystremski said as he dragged her away. "You're okay now. It's dead. Take it easy. Liz?"

The woman jerked and brushed the hair away from her face. "Petr?"

It was Liz Sherer, chief military affairs correspondent and field reporter for the Terran News Network. Fortis and Ystremski had met her when the ISMC had embedded her with their platoon during the Battle of Balfan-48.

"What the fuck are you doing here?" Ystremski asked as she grabbed him in a crushing bear hug.

"I'm reporting on the war, when I'm not crashing hovercopters and being raped by those bastards." She let him go and delivered another kick to the dead Maltaani's head.

"You're okay now. Where are the rest of you?" Fortis asked.

"Abner!" Liz hugged Fortis, too. "I'm not sure. We were huddled up over there, when two of these fuckers appeared out of nowhere. This one dragged me away, and we ended up here."

"Take us there," Gunny said.

"It's me, Liz," Sherer called out as they approached the hiding place. "I brought some friends. Space Marines!"

"Oh, thank God," a muffled voice exclaimed.

Three more humans gathered together under the hovercopter wreckage. Two of them, a man and a woman, wore bloody bandages on their heads, and the third had bandages on both legs. Despite his injuries, he clutched a pulse rifle to his chest.

"Woody, see what you can do," Fortis said, while Bender and Ystremski set a security perimeter around the position. "We were told there were five of you. Where's the other one?"

The survivor with the pulse rifle shook his head. "I don't know, man. Two of those fuckers snuck up and jumped in here. I got shot in the other leg, and Liz got yanked out by her hair. I didn't see what happened to Dave. Maybe he took off running."

"That's his name? Dave?"

"Yeah. Dave Fallon."

"Okay." Fortis keyed up the hovercopter circuit. "Fender 454, this is Fortis. We've located four survivors. Three wounded, none of them can travel. We're missing a fifth, so we're going to take a quick look around, and then prepare an LZ for you. Did you see any activity from up there?"

"*Negative, Captain. Foliage is too thick.*"

"Damn it. All right, we're going to be moving around down here for a few, so hold off on any more fire support until I call you, okay?"

"*Roger that. Hey, Captain, whatever you're going to do, make it quick, okay? The weather's going to crap again.*"

"Got it." Fortis switched back to the team circuit. "Listen up. One survivor just went missing. Gunny, I want you to go out with me, and let's look around. Bender, fall back to their hiding spot for security. We're gonna need some charges to take down a few trees to make room for Fender 454. We need to get moving; Red just told me the weather is turning to shit, and I don't want to get stuck here."

Fortis led Ystremski into the tree line and stopped to look around.

"Hey, Captain, maybe I should go first, since you don't have a pulse rifle," Ystremski said.

"Good idea."

They searched for any signs of someone passing through the undergrowth, but the hovercopter and the fighting had chewed it up and obscured all signs. The pair made a sweeping arc twenty meters from the crash site, but saw nothing.

"Let's get out of here," Ystremski said.

As soon as they started back toward the others, they heard a strange noise deeper in the forest.

"What was that?" the gunny asked.

"I don't know. You think it's a trap?"

They heard it again, and Fortis recognized a human voice.

"That was a human. Let's check it out."

They approached the sound, and when they discovered the source, it horrified them.

Someone had bound a human man cross-legged against a tree. A rope knotted around his neck and tied off on the tree was tight enough to hold him upright, but not tight enough to strangle him. Blood from a scalp wound spilled over his face and gave him a ghoulish appearance, but the real barbarity was the deep gash across his abdomen. He gurgled as he clutched his hands to the wound, but his pinkish-gray intestines had spilled out and coiled into a pile in his lap.

Fortis' stomach lurched at the sight, and Ystremski had to tear off his helmet to vomit.

"What the fuck?" the gunny demanded as he spat to clear his mouth.

"Animals," Fortis said. "I guess they don't have their dogs with them."

"What do we do with him?" Ystremski asked.

"Leave him," Fortis said. The man's body had gone limp, and his head lolled onto his chest. It was obvious the gurgling had been his death rattle, and there was nothing more they could do for him. "Let's get back to the others."

When they returned to the crash site, Woody had finished treating the injured civilians and was fashioning cutting charges with Bender.

"Did you find him?" Liz asked.

"Yeah, but there's nothing we can do for him," Fortis said.

"But—"

Fortis cut her off with a quick shake of his head. Liz had seen how the Maltaani troops on Balfan-48 treated captured Space Marines, and she knew not to press him for details.

"We're ready with the cutters," Bender reported. "There's a flat spot about fifteen meters up the mountain that was already cleared by the hovercopter crash, so it won't take much to make room for Fender 454."

Fortis nodded to the wounded. "Can we get them up there?" he asked.

"Yeah, I reckon so. I'll go clear it, and then me and Woody can handle the head wounds if you can help him," Bender said as he gestured to the man with the wounded legs.

"I'll crawl out of here if I have to," the man insisted.

"Gunny, head up there with Bender and cover him. I'll stay here with Woody and get everyone ready to move."

The two Space Marines disappeared up the hill, and Fortis keyed his mic.

"Red, this is Fortis. We're clearing a spot just above our current position. When it's ready, we'll pop smoke and bring you in."

"Roger that, Captain. We're seeing some movement in the trees west of the crash site. Are all friendlies accounted for?"

"Affirmative."

"Stand by for reconnaissance by fire."

Almost instantly, a stream of plasma bolts ripped into the trees. To Fortis' surprise, two Maltaani jumped up from their hiding spots and charged the crash site.

"I got 'em," Woody said. One of the Maltaani did a spectacular backflip when an energy pulse hit him in the forehead, and the other went down hard with a smoking hole in his chest. The injured civilian had rolled over and tried to engage with his pulse rifle, but the weapon wouldn't fire.

"Nice shooting," Fortis said. "Watch for others." He turned to the civilian, who pounded his hand on the defective rifle. "Let me look at that."

Fortis examined the weapon and worked the charging handle, but the action was clear. He flipped it over and discovered someone had jammed the battery into the receiver backwards. He pried it out, checked it for damage, and inserted it the right way.

"I'm gonna test fire this," he told Woody. He fired two short bursts, and the weapon operated without a problem.

"You ever shot one of these before?" Fortis asked the civilian.

The man shook his head. "I shoot cameras, not guns. I'd never even held one before last night. After the battery died, I couldn't get the fucker to work."

"Okay, how about if I hang onto to this one then?"

"Yeah."

"*Captain, this is Gunny Ystremski. We're ready to blast.*"

"Go when you're ready."

Five sharp *cracks* echoed through the forest, and Fortis watched several large trees fall on the mountain above them.

"*Good shot,*" Ystremski said. "*If Red can hold a two-meter hover, we're ready.*"

"Pop a smoke and come back down for the wounded," Fortis ordered.

"*Roger that.*"

* * * * *

Chapter Eleven

"**M**r. Mitsui?"

Mitsui opened his eyes and saw Leighton and Bisset standing at the foot of his bed.

"You weren't sleeping, were you?"

"No. Resting my eyes and thinking."

"Good." Leighton pulled up a chair on the right side of the bed and sat down. He gave Mitsui an apologetic look. "It's okay if I sit down so we can talk, isn't it? Your next pain medication isn't due for another hour. I'm not permitted to interview you for several hours after you receive it, so it's now or never."

Mitsui nodded, so Leighton pulled out his holo generator and went through his human rights speech.

"With that out of the way, let's begin. Where's Dexter Beck?"

"How should I know?"

"You spent a long time hiding with him after the invasion. Where were you hiding?"

"In a cave, in the mountains."

"Were you alone?"

"No. Beck was there, and Hahn."

Leighton's eye twitched as if Mitsui's answer annoyed him.

"Besides Mr. Beck and Ms. Hahn, were there other humans hiding in the cave?"

"Yes."

"How many, and who were they?"

"Six, maybe eight. I'm not sure. I was hurtin' pretty bad by the time we found them. They were all trainers, like me."

"What about PCS or Maltaani? Any of them present?"

"I don't remember."

"Do you recall any conversations with Mr. Beck or the other mercenaries about plans to return to Terra Earth or otherwise escape from Maltaan?"

"Trainers, not mercenaries. And no, I don't. Like I said, I was in terrible shape. Delirious, I guess."

"Do you recall any of their names?"

Mitsui searched his memory. "No."

"How could you not recognize your own men?"

"I might have been the head honcho of the trainers for the GRC, but that doesn't mean I knew them all by name. There were two hundred thousand PCS, so you gotta figure there were what, five hundred trainers spread out across the country? No way I knew them all. The guys in the cave were just faces to me."

"Are they still there?"

Mitsui scoffed. "Are you listening to me? I was so far out of my mind with pain and fever that I'm not even sure they were there at all. The cave is a hazy memory, and I don't know how I got down the mountain."

Leighton rolled his head on his neck and frowned. "Your lack of cooperation is becoming tiresome, Mr. Mitsui." He laid his hand on the blankets covering Mitsui's injured right leg. "I thought I explained how important it is for you to cooperate."

"I can't tell you what I don't know," Mitsui said. He fought to keep the panic out of his voice. "I was out of it. I mean *out of it*. You talked to the doctors. I should have died out there." He shook his head and threw up his hands. "Do what you want, but I don't remember a thing."

Leighton stood and turned off the holo generator. "That's all I have for now, Mr. Mitsui. Your doctor told me he's going to try you on crutches later today. For someone who was almost dead when he got here, you've made remarkable progress. Heal up, and I'll see you again soon."

* * *

Red guided Fender 454 into a low hover to recover the team. When the first Maltaani rounds pinged off the craft, the team formed a perimeter and returned fire. Varney blasted the trees with the automatic pulse rifle while Ystremski scrambled up into the hovercopter.

"Send up the wounded!" the gunny commanded the team. "Don't let them suck you into a gunfight."

As soon as Bender, Woody, and Fortis loaded the wounded and Liz Sherer, they clambered aboard. Fortis didn't have time to get in his seat before Red put full power to the engines and Fender 454 shot skyward.

"Buckle up!" Varney shouted. "It's about to get rough." He slammed the doors shut and cinched himself in tight.

Fender 454 slammed through the turbulent skies as they raced to get the wounded to Camp Romeo-Nine for proper medical attention. The woman with the head wound cried out every time the hovercopter bounced, and Woody did his best to comfort her. The other head-wound patient was unconscious on the deck next to her, and the man with the leg wounds sat next to Fortis.

Ground fire had starred the window on Fortis' side of the hovercopter in three places while the Space Marines loaded the casualties. Bender held up his left foot, and Fortis saw the sole of his boot holding on by a few threads.

"Wankers shot my favorite pair of boots."

Everyone laughed a little harder than the remark deserved, but their laughter eased the strain they'd been under while they were on the ground. Bender smiled as he shook hands with Fortis and Ystremski.

"Bloody good team we've got here, mates," he said. "Fucking Maltaani don't stand a chance."

"That was some damn fine shooting," Fortis said as he patted Woody on the back. "Two shots, two kills. Damn fine."

"Don't start trading warm spit just yet. We still have to get home," Ystremski growled.

"I can't thank you enough for saving us," Liz told them. "When we went down last night, I thought we were dead. Sometimes I wished I was."

"What are you doing out here, Liz?" Fortis asked.

"I heard an ugly rumor that the UNT gave the GRC control of the eastern helenium mines, provided they collect all the test tubes roaming around the country to work them," she replied. "I came out here to confirm it and to investigate an even uglier rumor that they plan to use the same mercenaries who sided with the nationalists to manage them."

"What did you find out?" Fortis asked.

"Half true. They control the mines, but the job of rounding up the test tubes was given to 2nd Division. The mercenary story is unconfirmed, but I heard about a program to rehabilitate them so the GRC could hire them."

"That's crazy!" Ystremski blurted. "They're fucking traitors. Line 'em up and shoot them."

"I don't disagree," Sherer replied, "but so far, I can't prove it's happening. I was on my way to Daarben to interview General Boudreaux and a couple other government types when we crashed."

"*Two minutes*," Red said over the intercom. "*Medical personnel are standing by.*"

Varney held up two fingers. "Two minutes."

"Where are you headed?" Sherer asked Fortis.

"Camp Zulu-Five. We're going to train some local security force personnel." He'd expected her question, but he couldn't tell her the truth. He didn't like to lie to Sherer, but he wasn't sure how much he could say about their counterinsurgency operations.

If she discovers the truth, she'll understand.

"*On final.*"

High winds buffeted Fender 454 as they made their approach to the hovercopter pad. There was nothing fancy about the landing; Red brought them in level, and when they were over the pad, reduced power until the craft touched down. Varney threw open the door, and personnel with white helmets climbed aboard and removed the wounded. The rain had started again, and they struggled to protect their patients as they carried them from the pad.

"Watch your feet, boys, or they'll take you, too," the crew chief warned. After the wounded, Varney looked at Sherer.

"You're next, ma'am."

Sherer gave the Space Marines a quick hug before climbing down. "Thank you again," she said to Fortis as she looked him in the eye. "I hope I see you soon."

"Be safe, Liz," the captain called after her.

A ground crewman hooked up a heavy black fuel hose to Fender 454's belly, and after a few minutes, he disconnected it and coiled it onto a rolling stand. The crewman dragged the hose clear of the landing pad, and after a quick visual inspection, Varney climbed back aboard.

"We're all here and ready to go, sir," he reported to Red.

"*Captain Fortis, are your men ready?*" Red asked.

"We're ready," Fortis said.

"*Then let's take her home.*"

The engines whined, and Fender 454 was soon airborne en route to Camp Zulu-Five.

* * *

Beck slipped and almost fell for the hundredth time as the column of mercenaries followed the narrow footpath through the forest. The clouds had opened up right after they'd left the village, and everything was slick with rain.

There were ten of them now. When Walker had roused the group from their huts in the morning, they'd discovered someone was missing. After a quick search, they found him with his pants around his ankles, wrapped in the thick coils of an enormous snake. To their horror, they saw the beast had its victim's head and shoulders half-swallowed. Walker dispatched the monster with a point-blank shot to the head. Nobody wanted the job of cutting the snake open so the mercenaries could give their comrade a proper burial, so they left him there in the forest.

It wasn't long before the absurdity of the man's death sank in, and the wisecracks and laughter began.

"Nobody shits alone," Walker ordered, and the group laughed even louder. Beck knew they laughed to mask the fear they felt at the gruesome death. Even he laughed, and as they moved through the forest, they found it a much more threatening place than it had been before.

The point man smelled smoke and called a halt, and Beck slumped down on the side of the trail. Walker and two other mercenaries moved up to investigate. When they returned, they gathered the group together.

"Same setup as before," Walker said. "Five huts, no sentries. Two of you go around the back, and then we'll move in. Watch out for tunnels this time."

Beck hung back behind the largest group as the mercenaries took their positions. He'd claimed one of the Maltaani rifles they'd recovered from the first village, but he only carried it for show. Being singled out in this group could be dangerous, so he did what he had to do for the sake of appearances. He didn't know how to check the load, or whether it could fire.

After a few minutes, Walker waved them to their feet, and the mercenaries advanced on the village. The reaction was the same as the previous village: screams of terror and villagers running in all directions, but there was no gunfire. The mercenaries shoved the villagers into a group in the center of the huts, and Beck counted seventeen of them.

"This hut's clear," a mercenary reported to Walker.

"Let's get them inside."

One of the Maltaani, the village leader from the way he carried himself, approached Walker and raised his hands in supplication. He spoke in rapid-fire Maltaani, and Walker pushed him away. The Maltaani persisted, and the mercenary punched him in the face. Blood spurted from his face as the Maltaani went down, and Walker booted him in the ass.

"Get moving!"

The injured Maltaani stayed down and clutched his face, which enraged Walker. He slammed his bone club across the Maltaani's back, and some villagers cried out from their temporary prison hut. Walker raised his bludgeon again, and a scuffle broke out between the villagers and their captors.

"No, no, no!" Beck shouted when the first pulse rifle pointed at the unarmed Maltaani, but he was powerless to stop the inevitable slaughter. Walker continued to beat his victim with the bone club until his head was a pulpy mess while the others murdered the rest of the captives.

Beck turned and ran back down the path to get away from the carnage. He expected a plasma bold in the back with every step, but none came, and he was soon out of earshot of the massacre. The slippery trail slowed him down, but he ran as fast as he dared, until his sides hurt and he couldn't breathe. He stepped off the trail and flopped down onto the ground, exhausted. That was until he remembered the snake. He jumped to his feet as the hairs on the back of his neck stuck up.

Paranoia overwhelmed Beck as he spun around and tried to point his rifle in every direction at once. After several panicked seconds, he got his breathing under control. The forest had closed in behind him, and he wasn't sure which direction led to the path. He made several attempts to find it, but he only got himself turned around even more. He was alone and lost in a hostile forest.

I'm a dead man.

* * * * *

Chapter Twelve

Thompson Leighton waited for the communicator encryption light to turn green to begin his call with Associate Minister of Justice Wanda Judon, his boss, stationed on *Mammoth*.

"Good afternoon, ma'am. I've completed initial interviews with Mitsui and Hahn and forwarded the holos for your review."

"And?"

"Per your instructions, I haven't applied electronic or chemical truth detection techniques to either subject, nor do I believe they're required. After some initial noncooperation, both subjects responded to verbal encouragement and answered all my questions. Their stories corroborate each other, and I didn't detect any mendacity. In short, they don't know where Dexter Beck is."

"Hmm. That's unfortunate."

"With your permission, my next step is to coordinate with the MAC-M to search the area where the Space Marines captured Hahn and Mitsui. Both claimed to have sheltered in a nearby cave. If there's a cave in the area, the Space Marines will find it. If Beck and the other mercenaries are still there, the Space Marines will capture or kill them."

"Capture."

"Yes, ma'am. Capture is the primary goal, but if they resist—"

"Capture. Make sure the Space Marines understand we need them alive. Especially Beck."

"Yes, ma'am."

"There's been an important development in the case against Krieg back on Terra Earth. His attorneys claim that, prior to transferring the PCS, the GRC representative Dexter Beck met with Ambassador Brooks-Green and received her approval for the deal."

"That corroborates what Hahn said in her first interview."

"It does, but I want you to conduct one more interview with Hahn to confirm the meeting took place. If it did, what did they discuss? The details are critical so we can compare Krieg's claim to Hahn's statement and look for inconsistencies. When you've completed the interview, find Beck. That's your number one priority. We *must* have his statements to corroborate or refute Krieg's claim. His daughter isn't enough.

"I'm leaving you in charge of capturing Beck because you've performed well as my point man since the beginning. Please don't disappoint me. Find him. Soon. We need him to move forward with our case against Krieg."

Leighton smiled. Beck's capture would make a nice highlight to Leighton's time on Maltaan.

"Thank you for your confidence, ma'am. What of Mitsui and Hahn after her interview?"

"They're not to be offered the rehabilitation program. They'll remain in custody while their cases progress through the system. Pending the results of Krieg's case, of course."

"Yes, ma'am."

"Hahn and Mitsui are lovers, correct?"

"They are, or were. As you know, they continue to ask about each other."

"Arrange for them to be confined together. Call it conjugal housing, or something like that. Before they move in together, have our best people wire the place so we can hear and see everything they say and do. Perhaps they'll reveal something about Beck that we didn't get from your interviews."

Leighton nodded. "I'll get right on it, ma'am."

"Is there anything else?"

"That's all I have for now."

"Keep me informed."

Before Leighton could respond, Judon ended the call, and the encryption light went out. He laughed aloud and pumped his fist in the air. He'd feared that a more senior agent would seize the opportunity to take charge of the hunt for the GRC personnel involved in transferring the PCS, but that seemed unlikely now. The surrender of Hahn and Mitsui had been an incredible stroke of good fortune, and they'd given Leighton a starting point to begin the hunt for Beck.

* * *

Fender 454 landed at Camp Zulu-Five without incident. Varney jumped out, opened the doors to one of five hangars next to the pad, and returned with a boxy yellow cart. He hooked it up and guided the hovercopter into the open hangar with practiced ease.

"You can leave your stuff on the hovercopter for now," Red told Fortis and the team. "Johnson will confirm which bunkroom you're in while we go talk to Major Sokolov."

When they got to the main building, Red asked the duty watch about the major.

"Major Sokolov is in the team room," a staff sergeant named Diggs told Red.

The pilot led the team down the hall to a set of double doors that opened into a large room with two rows of tables and a pair of computers on a desk against the far wall. A Space Marine hunched over a keyboard, and when he looked up, Fortis saw two things. He was a major, and he had a thick scar that started under his scalp, disappeared under a patch over his left eye, and ended in a distinct curl on his left cheek.

"Major, we're back," Red said.

The major stood, and Fortis read the name tape on his utilities.

Sokolov.

"These are the new guys?"

"Yes, sir. Captain Fortis, Gunny Ystremski, and Sergeants Bender and Woodson."

Sokolov caught Fortis staring at the scar as he shook hands with the team.

"Pretty, isn't it?" he said as he lifted the patch. An oversized prosthetic eye bulged out of the socket. "Fishing accident."

"What the fuck were you fishing for?" Ystremski blurted.

"I was the bait." Sokolov pointed to Fortis. "I heard you've got a fake leg."

Fortis nodded. "Yes, sir, I do."

"Welcome to the land of broken toys." The major waved to an empty table. "Take a seat, gents. You're now designated Team Three. How was your trip?" he asked Fortis.

"Eventful."

Fortis and Red related the details of their journey from Daarben to Camp Zulu-Five. When they finished, the major nodded.

"Good work. I hope you like Red, because he's the Team Three pilot, and Fender 454 is your team bird. My advice is to keep him flying, because if you don't, Flight Control will notice and try to grab him to fly politicians and other idiots around to get their picture taken in a war zone." Sokolov tapped a key, and a holo of Baat-Doh Province appeared.

"This is our playground, Baat-Doh Province. We're in 4th Division's AOR, but we don't answer to them. Those two blue dots are the helenium mines Baat-Doh One and Baat-Doh Two, or BD1 and BD2 for short. This blue dot is Camp Zulu-Five. Those green dots are Maltaani hamlets. The red dots mark known hostile hamlets and the locations of insurgent activity.

"Camp Zulu-Five is part of a larger Maltaani base complex, which means there is no privacy here. They hear everything you say.

"The Maltaani claim to have a military counterpart to every team. Every time you head out into the field, they're supposed to go with you, but that never happens. The Maltaani military are westerners, and they don't like to go on patrol unless there's a chance of confiscating something of value. They don't know the area any better than we do, and with cochlear implants, we don't need them to translate. Plan on operating alone. We can talk more about that offline," Sokolov said as he stared at Fortis and pointed to the ceiling.

"Your tasking is simple. Patrol the province, develop local information sources, fuse it with intel we get from the Fleet, and track down the bad guys. We're in reaction mode right now because we've had little success making friends with the locals. Our royalist allies are pretty rough on their eastern cousins, so the hearts and minds routine isn't working. The Fleet intel is imagery of groups of suspected insurgents that have so far turned out to be farmers or loggers headed off to work. Not actionable by any definition."

"What's 4th Division up to these days?" Fortis asked.

"Protecting BD1, BD2, the railway into Ulvaan, and rounding up test tubes."

"Sheesh." Ystremski shook his head. "Waste of good Marines."

"Welcome to low-intensity conflict, Gunny," Sokolov said. "We kill any bad guys dumb enough to stick their heads up and wait around, hoping the rest get bored and decide to cooperate with the government. They say it's just a matter of time. Say, ten or fifteen years." He laughed.

"All right, the useful stuff. I don't know how much experience any of you have in the Maltaani bush, but there are some things to watch out for. They have wild dogs here, big bastards, that won't hesitate to attack." Fortis touched his chest where his dog fang necklace hung under his recon armor. "I heard there are snakes out there that can take a man down, but I haven't seen that. I've also seen video of a herd of large, six-legged land animals we call elephants, too, but I don't think they're up here in the mountains. Finally, you're all rugged and manly Space Marines who don't let booboos slow you down, but the fungus here will fuck you up, especially during the rainy season. Doc needs to treat every scratch like your life depends on it, because it might. Questions?"

The team exchanged glances and shook their heads.

"Good. You have today and tomorrow to acclimate yourselves to the camp. The day after that, I expect you to make your first patrol, so work with Red to figure out where you're going, and then come brief me. That's all."

* * *

Dalia Hahn sighed as Corporal Vincent led her to the interview tent. Leighton and Bisset waited inside, and Leighton sped through his human rights speech.

"Miss Hahn, I have a few last questions for you."

Hahn perked up. Last questions? From the sound of it, her time in the dismal camp might soon end.

"Ask away."

"To the best of your recollection, did Mr. Beck or any other GRC representative receive official approval for transferring the PCS to the Maltaani?"

"Hmm, I'm not sure. I think so."

"No meetings, messages, or communicator discussions?"

Ha!

Hahn sat up and feigned excitement. "You know, I remember now. There was a meeting between Mr. Beck and Ambassador Brooks-Green, and she approved the transfer. I was there."

"You're saying you were present when the ambassador approved the transfer of the PCS from the GRC to the Maltaani?"

"Yes. Yes, I was. In fact, she was eager to release news of the deal because there'd been little else to report on," Hahn said.

"Do you have a record of this meeting? Notes, or a holo, perhaps?"

Hahn paused for a moment and then shook her head. "No, I'm sorry, I don't."

"Does Mr. Beck?"

"I don't know. He might have kept a ledger, or he might have reported it back to GRC headquarters via message or holo, but he never gave me anything like that to file."

Leighton stroked his chin as he reviewed his notes, but Hahn was certain he was only trying to increase her anxiety level. After a long pause, he looked up.

"Miss Hahn, it should come as no surprise that I've been corroborating your interview results with other testimony and evidence. This is a complex case, and we have to be careful how we proceed. I've found your answers to be truthful and consistent with the other evidence, and I'm grateful for your cooperation."

Hahn smiled and tried to project gratitude.

"The Ministry of Justice and the GRC cooperated to set up a rehabilitation program for former GRC employees who were involved in the Maltaani PCS deal. Instead of prosecution, volunteers for the program agree to assist the GRC with training and supervising the remaining PCS as they transition from soldiers to miners."

"Am I eligible for that program?"

Leighton shook his head. "Not right now. Your relationship with our prime suspect, Weldon Krieg, along with your senior position within the GRC hierarchy here on Maltaan, precludes such a program for you, at least until legal proceedings against Weldon Krieg are complete."

Hahn's face fell, and she stifled a sob, which made her angry.

"I'm sorry, Miss Hahn. I didn't intend to upset you with that news."

Yeah, right.

"You've been upfront with me, and I feel it's only right to be upfront with you. You will no doubt hear about the program, and I wanted to make sure you knew about it ahead of time, so you didn't get your hopes up."

"I appreciate your forthrightness," Hahn replied with a heavy dose of sarcasm. "What about Mitsui? Can I see him?"

"I can't discuss Mr. Mitsui's case with you, nor can I promise a reunion. The legalities of how to treat coconspirators and all that."

She frowned. "That makes no sense to me. I've answered your questions. Why punish me?"

"Miss Hahn, I think you need to accept your position, *vis-à-vis* the case against your father and other GRC officials," Major Bisset said. "This is a serious matter to the Ministry of Justice, and it should be for you, too. The penalties for treason are as severe as the penalties for murder. You could face life imprisonment if you're convicted of the current charges against you. *That's* punishment. Not seeing Mr. Mitsui is merely a condition of your pre-trial confinement."

Hahn waited a beat before she answered. "Okay, fine. Are we finished here?"

"We are."

Leighton turned off the holo generator and left the tent without another word. Bisset shrugged and followed, and Corporal Vincent stuck her head in the door.

"Let's go."

* * * * *

Chapter Thirteen

While Fortis and the team met with Sokolov, Johnson had organized a bunkroom for them.

"Sorry, Captain, no officer's quarters. You'll have to bunk with the dirty heathens."

They returned to the hangar to unload their gear from Fender 454.

"The hangar closest to the main building is the armory and gear storage area," Johnson told them. "There's a lockable cage in there for your team's gear. Make sure you store explosives and incendiaries in the blast-proof boxes. The armorer and her guys work a regular dayshift, but someone's available around the clock if you need something after hours."

Red, Johnson, and Varney pitched in, and it only took two trips to unload the hovercopter. The team made quick work of organizing their gear and storing their explosives. Fortis called the duty armorer; they agreed to meet after lunch to draw a new pulse rifle. Meanwhile, Varney took Bender to the logistics office to see about a new pair of boots.

"They don't have any big boy sizes," Bender said when they rejoined the group. "Varney fixed me up with some thousand-kilometer-an-hour tape, so I'm good until my new boots get here." Aircrews used the tape to make emergency repairs to their aircraft, and the manufacturer rated it to one thousand kilometers an hour.

"I think that's about it for now, Captain," Red said. "Let's go get some chow."

The team room doubled as the mess hall, and Space Marines in utilities and flight suits lined the tables, eating and talking. Conversations paused when they entered the room, and everyone turned to look at the newcomers before they went back to their meals. Team Three greeted the curious looks with nods of acknowledgement, and Ystremski exchanged a quick hello with two sergeants he recognized.

Red led them through the serving line and found a table with room for everyone.

"We do everything as a team around here," Red said. "The major moves around from group to group, but the teams stick together."

The smell of the food made Fortis' mouth water, and he remembered that his last meal had been aboard *Mammoth* many hours ago. "Is the food always this good?" he asked Red between forkfuls of a delicious, braised meat dish.

"We have a couple Maltaani mama sans who cook for us, so it's all local." Red speared a piece of meat and held it up. "I can't remember what they call this, but it's some kind of tree rat."

Fortis stopped chewing for a second.

"You've already eaten half of it, sir," Ystremski told him. "You might as well finish it."

Fortis shrugged and resumed eating.

"Most of it's damn good. A lot better than pig squares," Red said. "The locals love the canned crap we get from Daarben, so we trade it for home-cooked mystery meat. The only thing you have to watch out for is a yellow vegetable we call 'bum-burn.' It's mushy when it's raw, and it gets worse after it's cooked. The Maltaani love it, but it burns through us and leaves nothing behind but pain."

"Best chow I've had in the Corps," Woody said.

"You ought to slow down a little," Varney warned his fellow sergeant. "Let your body get used to it."

Woody nodded, but kept eating.

After they ate, the team lined up to return their trays. Sokolov waved to Fortis from across the room.

"I'm gonna take the lads to the bunkroom and get it squared away while you officers pow-wow," Ystremski told Fortis.

"Okay, Gunny. I'll catch up with you there."

"What do you think of the chow?" Sokolov asked as Fortis slid into the seat next to him.

"It's fantastic, for rat."

Sokolov laughed. "Before you leave here, you'll consider rat a delicacy. Is your team getting settled in?"

"Yes, sir. We got our gear and weapons stowed in the hangar, and Gunny Ystremski is taking them over to our bunkroom to get it squared away. Red and his crew are taking good care of us."

"*Your* crew, Captain. Remember that."

"Will do."

Sokolov leaned in and lowered his voice. "There are a few things I want to talk to you and your team about, but I need a more… intimate setting," he said as he rolled his eyes to the ceiling. "When I have to talk about things I don't want the Maltaani to know about, I get the aircrew to start the engines and talk inside the bird. Is Team Three available this afternoon?"

"Whenever you want, sir. I have to go to the armory to get another pulse rifle issued, but other than that, our schedule is clear. What time?"

"I've got some administrative bullshit to take care of on a holo call in a little while, but when I'm done with that, I'll send someone to find you."

"We'll be standing by."

"Good. I'll be in touch."

* * *

Fortis returned to the bunkroom and found a full-on field day in progress. The team had pushed all the furniture to one side, swabbed the deck, and was waiting for it to dry to do the other side.

"You're going all out," he said to Ystremski.

"This place was filthy," the gunny told him. "I kind of miss teaching new recruits how to clean, too."

"We'll be eating our supper rats off the deck in here," Bender said.

"Major Sokolov said he wants to meet with us in the hangar," Fortis told them.

"Any idea what it's about, sir?"

"I don't know. Red, do you know?"

"Hmm, maybe, but it's nothing I can talk about here."

"Okay, ladies. The deck looks dry. Let's get everything moved over there, and we'll give this side the same treatment."

Fortis joined in, and they had the other half of the room swept and swabbed in short order.

"Most of our operations are at night," Red told him while they were waiting for the deck to dry. "The other teams sleep during the day, between missions. That's why you got so many looks at lunch. They don't see operators very often."

The team had just finished moving the furniture when Diggs tapped on the door. "Captain Fortis? Major Sokolov is ready for you in the hangar."

The team found Sokolov in the hangar and followed him aboard Fender 454. Varney opened the hangar door, and Johnson climbed into the cockpit.

"Wind it up, Lance," Red told him before joining the team in the cabin.

After the engines were running and the cabin doors closed, Sokolov began.

"I apologize for all this, but the Maltaani bastards are experts at eavesdropping. Our first source vanished right after I talked with the team leader about him. His entire family disappeared, too. I think they heard us talking and took action."

"Why would the royalists do that, sir?" Woody asked.

"I don't know that it was the royalists," Sokolov said. "The nationalists could have bugged the place when they built it. I requested our counterintelligence guys come and sweep, but they haven't made it here yet. Until I'm certain we're clean, this is where we discuss confidential information like sources and operations.

"We've cultivated more sources through the chow mama sans. Husbands and sons, and a couple brothers, too. They've been giving us intel about insurgents operating in this area."

"Do you trust them?" Fortis asked.

"We flailed around and got nowhere the first couple of weeks we were out here. Then we got a tip about insurgents preparing to destroy a footbridge that leads to one of the mineral survey camps, and two days ago we got our first kills. Two dead insurgents, and we recovered their explosives and weapons, too.

"I still don't trust them, but if they sacrificed two of their own to lull us into complacency, that's one hell of a price to pay just to fool us. We'll continue to use their information and develop other sources, too."

"Do you know why they're helping us, Colonel?" Ystremski asked. "I thought the nationalists hated us."

"The nationalists do, but most of the Maltaani out here aren't nationalists. They're not royalists, either. The royalists treat them like shit because they're easterners, and the nationalists treat them like shit because they're not nationalists. They just want to be left alone.

"The mama sans deliver our food before every meal. Captain, this evening, I want a couple of your guys to help the cooks so they can meet the mama sans. It can't be you or the gunny; even the Maltaani aren't dumb enough to believe a captain works in the chow hall. You're not there to pass intel, just smile and trade the rations for the food."

"Speaking of operations, sir, I'd like to take the team outside the wire tonight for a short patrol," Fortis said. "We only met two days ago, and I'd like to do some work together before we head out for real tomorrow night. Nothing fancy, just movement and communications."

Sokolov nodded. "Yeah, that's a good idea. Stop in and see Diggs; he can give you the latest topographic downloads. Whatever you do, don't fall into the fucking river, or we'll never see you again."

* * *

Ulvaan wasn't a city by Terra Earth standards, but it was the second largest city on Maltaan, and the only major city in the east. It was the last stop on the railway that ran from Daarben and had a deep draft port facility that could handle the large freighters that transported helenium ore and lumber by sea to Daarben.

Ulvaan had also been the unofficial capital of the nationalist movement before the war, and Staaber thought he had a good chance of locating some of his comrades there. Still, prudence demanded he avoid exposure, so he remained under cover on the outskirts until dusk.

Few of the lights on the streets of Ulvaan worked, and Staaber stayed to the shadows as he looked for the city park where Maltaani men congregated at night to smoke their pipes and talk. His sword drew curious looks from the few who noticed it in the darkness, but nobody questioned him.

When he reached the park, he moved among the shadowy figures and glowing embers, and listened for any talk of the war or resistance, but the chief topic of discussion was the reopening of the region's helenium mines under human control. Most favored the move, but there was uncertainty whether the GRC would hire Maltaani to work there. Staaber tried, but failed to strike up conversations with several strangers, so he left and headed for another park.

He wound his way through a twisted maze of side streets to the other park, uncertain of the precise location. When Staaber was passing a dark alley entrance, several Maltaani dragged him into the darkness and pinned him to the ground.

"Who are you?" one of them demanded, while another rifled through his pockets. They found his identification card, and a small light flicked on.

"My name is Baardek. I'm a miner," Staaber said.

The light stabbed his eyes as they compared his face to the picture, and then it went out.

"I've never heard of you, Baardek," one of his assailants said. "I know all the miners in this area, but I don't know you." He felt Staaber's hands. "These aren't the hands of a miner."

More hands unsnapped his sword scabbard, and he struggled to get free.

"What's this?"

The light snapped back on, and one of them examined the weapon.

"Please. That's my family's sword. It's all I have left to remember them," Staaber said, his voice heavy with emotion.

"It's not much to look at." There was a metallic *ssshhing* as the speaker drew the sword. "Very plain."

"It's a weapon of war," Staaber said.

"Hmm. There's something engraved on it. 'Here we stand.' What does that mean?"

"It's my family motto."

"I've heard those words before," said a deeper voice that sounded older than the others.

"What's a miner doing with a family sword?" The first voice mocked Staaber, and he'd had enough.

"My father carried that sword, and his father before him. They were generals, and so am I."

"Royalist!"

"No. My name is Staaber. I was the commanding general of the People's Army of Maltaan."

"Get him inside."

They dragged Staaber into a nearby building and shoved him to the floor. He sat up and looked at his captors.

"You're General Staaber?"

"I was General Staaber. The People's Army is no more. Now, I'm just Staaber."

"No, General. The People's Army lives on in our hearts and in our minds," the oldest Maltaani said as he helped Staaber to his feet. "Give the general his sword."

Staaber buckled his sword back on. The weight on his hip reassured him.

"What's your plan, General?"

"I hope to rejoin my eastern comrades and resist the humans and their royalist dogs. They don't belong here in the east and should return to Daarben."

Growls of agreement met this statement.

"We're ready to fight, General. What do you want us to do?"

"There are others? Leaders?"

"Yes."

"Take me to them."

* * * * *

Chapter Fourteen

Saito Mitsui had just started to eat when Leighton and Bisset appeared at his bedside.

"I'm sorry to interrupt your meal, Mr. Mitsui, but I have something very important to discuss with you. Would you mind?"

Mitsui set his fork down and shook his head. He didn't mind; Space Marine rations were almost inedible, and his leg throbbed from practicing with the crutches earlier. Maybe some verbal sparring with Leighton would help him forget his physical woes.

Leighton smiled at Mitsui. "Unless there's a significant development in your case, this is the last time we'll meet."

"Oh, yeah? Why's that?"

"Well, I've verified your statements against other evidence we've collected, and everything you've told us checks out. Your answers have been truthful and consistent, and your cooperation is commendable."

Like I had a choice.

Mitsui nodded and said nothing.

"I just got off a holo call with my boss. Since I've concluded your interviews, she's given me an urgent assignment that'll require extensive travel throughout Maltaan. In fact, both you and Miss Hahn made this opportunity possible. Had either of you been more recalcitrant, she would've assigned another agent. So, thank you."

Mitsui remained silent.

"There's one last matter I want to discuss with you before I leave. The Ministry of Justice and the GRC have come to an understanding regarding the fate of the mercenaries involved in the illegal transfer of military technology to the Maltaani. As you're now no doubt aware, the PCS were to be used as labor in the helenium mines, until circumstances changed." Mitsui opened his mouth to respond, but Leighton cut him off with a raised hand. "That's not an accusation or indictment, Mr. Mitsui. That's the facts of the case as we know them.

"We—the Ministry of Justice—with GRC cooperation, will rehabilitate GRC employees who were involved in the Maltaani PCS deal. Think of it as a pre-trial diversion. Instead of prosecution, volunteers for the program agree to assist with training and supervising the PCS, and transitioning them from soldiers to miners. Participants incur a two-year obligation to remain here on Maltaan and work for the GRC unless discharged sooner.

"Given your role as the leading mercenary during the transactions, and your subsequent acceptance of a colonelcy in the People's Army of Maltaan, you're not eligible for this program. I tell you this not to taunt you, but because you'll hear about the program, and I think it's only fair that you have the full story instead of jailhouse rumors."

"What about Miss Hahn?"

"We're not permitted to discuss her case with you," Bisset said. "We consider her a codefendant."

"That's it, then? You came to say goodbye?"

Leighton chuckled. "When you put it that way, I guess I did."

"Well. Bye."

Leighton turned off the holo generator and gathered his things. "You made the right choice to cooperate, Mr. Mitsui. I believe it'll throw a positive light on you when we adjudicate your case." He stuck out his hand, but Mitsui didn't shake. After a second, Leighton lowered his hand, cleared his throat, and turned for the door.

Mitsui stared as Leighton and Bisset left the medical tent. Everything had happened so fast that he wasn't sure it had happened at all. He knew it was real when he looked at the bedside table and saw his dinner had congealed.

Where's Dalia?

* * *

"Sorry to spring tonight's patrol idea on you without warning," Fortis said to Ystremski. "It popped into my head, and I said it."

"Don't worry about it, sir. Most officers learn to stifle their good ideas by the time they make major, so you still have some wiggle room. Besides, what else were we going to do tonight? I don't know about you, but those couple hours on the ground at the crash site were the happiest I've been in a month."

Fortis chuckled. "Yeah, me too. They should rename *Solicitude* to *Solitary Confinement*. It felt like a prison."

They gathered everyone in the team room, and Fortis projected a holo of the area around Camp Zulu-Five. The Maltaani had built the camp on a level piece of ground in a north-south valley between two steep mountains. A sizable river ran south toward the sea, and several creeks fed it from east and west. The forest was thick, until about halfway up the mountains where the tree line gave way to scrub, and then bare rock to the peaks.

"Our piece of the camp is this corner," Red said as he pointed at the holo. "We have our own outside gate and another gate that leads to the Maltaani side of the camp. They keep both gates locked. When you head north out of our gate, you pass through a Maltaani hamlet and end up on the road that leads out of the valley. If you go south, you'll walk for about a week before you get to the sea if you survive the marsh."

"We're pretty boxed in here," Ystremski said. "High ground all around."

"That's true, but we're not in any real danger of attack. It would be almost impossible to get anything more than a sniper up on those mountains. It's too steep for vehicles, and even the locals know better than to climb them."

"Huh."

"That's also why our patrols like to insert via hovercopter. The valley opens up further north, and that's where the mines are and most of the locals live."

"Since the weather is shit, and this is a training patrol, I think it's prudent to keep things simple. Let's leave Fender 454 in the hangar," Fortis said.

"Okay, Captain, that makes sense. There's some maintenance we can do tonight while you're out," Red replied.

"As for the rest of us, our little adventure on the way here proved to me we can handle whatever comes our way, but it won't hurt to spend a few more hours in the bush together before we go down range for real tomorrow night."

The Space Marines nodded. They knew their combat skills required constant honing to stay sharp, so they took advantage of training opportunities whenever they could.

Ystremski proposed a simple patrol order that took them north through the nearby hamlet and followed the road until they reached the outskirts of the next village. There, they'd turn around and patrol back. Each team member would take a turn as point man, rear guard, and patrol commander, and they'd practice ambush response and withdrawing under fire as they went. The estimated duration of the patrol was six hours.

"I'll initiate all exercise contacts," Ystremski said. "If anybody else does it, or if you see me firing, it's real. Otherwise, hold your fire."

"Do the Maltaani run patrols in this area?" Fortis asked Red.

"I don't know, sir, but I can find out."

"No, that's unnecessary. I'll ask Major Sokolov when I brief him on the patrol order."

After the team members downloaded the waypoints of their intended track into their nav computers, Ystremski assigned Bender and Woody to help the cooks bring in evening chow while he went to the armory to retrieve Fortis' new pulse rifle, and the captain went to brief Sokolov.

Major Sokolov was receptive to their plan to keep the first patrol simple, and he liked the idea of swapping positions.

"Few young officers would do that," he told Fortis.

Fortis chuckled. "Gunny Ystremski is fond of reminding me that the holes in his underwear have been in the Corps longer than I have, sir. It would be a mistake to think I can't learn from watching him. And Bender, too."

Sokolov told Fortis that the Maltaani didn't run routine patrols near the camp, especially at night. "The Maltaani have never been big on night operations. Throw in some rain, and they're staying home."

"It's tough to deal with an insurgency if you only go out during daylight," Fortis said.

"That's why we're here."

After chow, the team assembled in the hangar at their gear cage. They'd travel light; pulse rifles and spare battery magazines for everyone, plus a medical kit for Woody and a small satchel of det cord and blasting caps for Bender.

"I've got the team circuit dialed up on my communicator," Red told Fortis. "If you run into any trouble, call me. I have to lock the gate behind you, so when you return, call me, and I'll open it."

By the time the team completed their preparations, the gloomy evening sky had turned dark as night settled over the camp. The team filed down to the gate, Red unlocked it, and they melted into the darkness.

A constant drizzle followed the team as they slipped into the forest. They started out in the formation they'd patrol in on actual missions: Woody on point, then Ystremski, Fortis as patrol commander, and Bender as rear guard.

Fortis adjusted his helmet optics to maximize the low-light capability and reduced the infrared input because the rain attenuated heat signatures into undefined smears. He checked the laser sight on his pulse rifle, and it made him happy to see it was sharp.

"Contact left!" Ystremski shouted. "Large force!"

The team leaped into action. They all went to ground and simulated return fire. After a few seconds, Bender simulated throwing a grenade.

"Frag out!"

"Smoke out!" Woody shouted from the point.

"Break contact!" Fortis ordered.

After another round of grenades and simulated fire, Bender and Woody moved into positions five meters behind Fortis and Ystremski.

"Go!" Bender shouted.

Fortis and Ystremski simulated smoke grenades, jumped to their feet, and moved into position ten meters behind Bender and Woody. The team repeated the leapfrog maneuver twice more.

"Contact ceased," Ystremski said. "Muster on the captain."

"That wasn't bad," the gunny debriefed after they'd gathered. "Quick response, no confusion or bullshit on the net. Let's reset with Bender at point, Woody, then me, and the captain as rearguard."

Almost as soon as they set off in the new patrol order, Ystremski announced, "Contact right! Small force!"

After their initial response, instead of ordering the team to break contact, Ystremski ordered them to assault their imaginary attackers. Point and rear guard threw frags and followed up with a rapid assault, while the other two maintained a steady rate of suppressing fire. As soon as Fortis and Bender were in the enemy position, Ystremski and Woody followed.

"Contact ceased," Ystremski announced. "Muster on me."

After a quick debrief, they resumed their patrol with Bender as point man, followed by Fortis and Woody, with Ystremski as rear guard. The pace slowed and became more deliberate as they expected the contact call, but it never came. Instead, Ystremski called a halt, and everyone gathered by Bender.

"Better patrolling that time," the gunny said. "You were moving with a purpose, instead of walking along, waiting for the contact call." He checked his navigator. "There's a creek ahead. Let's switch it up again until we get to the other side. Captain, Bender, me, then Woody."

Fortis moved as the ISMC had trained him. Step, look, listen, step. He tried to reach out beyond his visual range and sense anything the forest might hide, but the team was alone. When he got to the creek, he called a halt.

"We're at the creek, Gunny."

"Lead us across, sir."

"Roger that."

The creek was only two meters wide, and Fortis discovered it was waist deep halfway across.

"Contact forward! Small force."

Fortis dove forward to gain the cover of the other bank and simulated hosing down the undergrowth. Bender splashed down next to him.

"Frag out!" Fortis shouted.

"Smoke out!" Bender called.

"Assault!" Ystremski ordered.

Fortis and Bender threw imaginary frags, and then the gunny and Woody splashed past them and up the opposite bank. Fortis and Bender scrambled to join them.

"Contact ceased."

"Good response," Gunny Ystremski told them. "Nobody expected the contact while we were crossing the creek, but everyone reacted like they were supposed to. Well done. Let's reset the patrol order again. I'll take point, Captain Fortis, Bender, and Woody."

During the last ambush scenario, the rain eased up, and dead silence settled over the forest.

Somewhere in the forest ahead of them, they heard a scream.

* * * * *

Chapter Fifteen

"What was that?" Bender asked.

The scream came again, and the anguish was palpable.

"Somebody's in trouble up that way." Fortis pointed. "Woody, lead us out. Standard patrol order, and be alert. This could be a trap."

They slipped through the trees as quickly as caution would allow. They heard the scream again, closer, followed by anguished wailing. Woody stopped and called Fortis forward.

"Four huts, Captain. That one on the left has a light on, and that's where I think the screams are coming from."

A new shriek confirmed Woody's suspicions. Fortis scanned the clearing and the surrounding forest, but the only heat signatures he detected were an indistinct cluster in the left-hand hut.

"What do we have, sir?" Ystremski asked as he kneeled down by Fortis.

"Four huts. Only the one on the left has any heat. The forest is clear."

Ystremski scanned the clearing and forest. "I agree, sir. What do you want to do?"

Another voice wailed, and Fortis heard muffled laughing.

"Woody, move up and see if you can get a look inside, and find out what's going on. We'll cover you. If there's any firing, get your ass back here, pronto."

Woody's recon armor made him almost invisible as he crept up to the hut. Light streamed out from an ill-fitting door made of sticks, and he peeked through the cracks.

"The fuckers are raping her," he said.

"What? Who?"

"Maltaani. Five of them. They're raping a Maltaani woman."

"I'm gonna check it out," Ystremski said and moved across the clearing next to Woody. After a few seconds, he called Fortis.

"We need to hit this hut, sir. Move up and let's do it."

Without hesitation, Fortis and Bender dashed across the clearing and joined their teammates.

"Two of them are holding the woman down in the middle of the room. A third is on top, and the other two are in the far left-hand corner, cheering. Their rifles are leaning against the wall on the other side."

"We'll go in patrol order," Fortis ordered. "Woody, cover the cheerleaders. Gunny, tackle the guy on top. Bender and I will split the other two. No shooting unless they reach for weapons."

The team stacked up at the door, and Fortis gave the go order. Woody was across the hut in three big steps and had his pulse rifle leveled in the Maltaani's faces before they could react. Ystremski launched himself at the assailant atop the female Maltaani and rode him to the ground. Fortis grabbed his target and dragged him away before he pinned him to the floor with a boot to the neck and a pulse rifle to the face. Bender was a half-step slower, and his target made a move toward the rifles, so the Australian giant butt-stroked the Maltaani behind the ear, and he went straight down on his face.

"Who are you?" Fortis' captive hissed. Fortis responded by pressing harder with his boot.

"Bender, search those guys," Fortis said, gesturing to Woody's pair of Maltaani.

Bender spun them around, patted them down, and then forced them to kneel facing the wall with their hands overhead. Fortis stepped back, and his prisoner got the same treatment.

"Woody, I'll cover them," Fortis told the medic. "See what you can do for her."

Meanwhile, Bender and Ystremski had the fifth Maltaani on his feet. Ystremski covered him while Bender searched, and the Maltaani made a break for the door. Without hesitation, the gunny slammed his rifle into the Maltaani's midriff, and he went down, retching and gasping. Bender finished his search, dragged the injured captive over by the others, and then deposited the unconscious Maltaani next to his comrades.

Meanwhile, Woody tried to examine the female Maltaani, but she protested in rapid-fire Maltaani and scrambled away from him.

"Gunny, Bender, watch these guys," Fortis said, and he went over to join Woody. He slung his rifle and held up his hands to reassure her.

"Little sister, this man wants to help you," he said in a calm, level voice. "You have wounds on your face."

The Maltaani woman stared at Fortis, and he smiled.

"Yes, I speak your language," he said. "*Some* of your language. Please, let us help you."

Woody approached her again, and this time, she didn't move away. She recoiled when his fingers touched her skin, but she allowed him to wipe away the blood and dirt from her face.

One of the Maltaani twisted around at the sound of Fortis speaking Maltaani. "I demand to know who you are!"

"Shut the fuck up, rapist," Bender said and slugged the Maltaani in the back of the head. Fortis knew Bender's history, and he knew he had to get the massive man away from the prisoners before he killed one.

"The others... next door..." Woody's patient whimpered.

"The next hut?" Fortis asked.

She nodded.

"Bender, I'll take over guarding these guys with the gunny. Go next door and see if there are others."

With a last long look, Bender exited the hut, and Fortis took his place. Meanwhile, Woody had cleaned and treated the injured female's facial wounds. He stood up and helped her to her feet.

"She's got a deep cut in her scalp, but the rest are scrapes and contusions," the medic told Fortis. "I can't... I mean... there's nothing... I'm not trained to help her down there," he said as his hand fluttered over his belt.

"You did just fine," Fortis told him.

Bender burst into the hut with his pulse rifle at the ready. He went straight for the prisoners, and before anyone could stop him, slammed one of them in the face with his rifle barrel so hard it shattered the Maltaani's teeth. He drew his rifle back for another strike before Fortis and Ystremski could wrestle him away.

"What the fuck, Sergeant?" Ystremski demanded.

"They killed them," Bender spat through clenched teeth. He lunged for the prisoners, and it was all Fortis and the gunny could do to hold him back.

"Who killed who?"

"Two more women. These bloody bastards killed two other women," Bender said. He relaxed, and they let him go. "The bodies are in the next hut. They killed them and cut their heads off."

"Show me," Ystremski said. "Captain, are you good?"

Fortis nodded. Three of the five Maltaani were unconscious or incapacitated, and the other two cowered from the enraged Bender. "I'm good."

The gunny and Bender disappeared, and the Maltaani who'd been demanding their identities spoke to Fortis.

"Sir? You are in charge of these humans?"

Fortis nodded but said nothing as he kept his pulse rifle trained on the captives.

"I'm Colonel Waadeen, and I'm a faithful royalist." the Maltaani said. "What's your name?"

"My name is shut the fuck up," Fortis snarled. "Be quiet."

"Please, why did you attack us? We're allies."

"Bender's right," Ystremski said as he reentered the hut. "Two dead Maltaani women. They stacked their fucking heads up on the other side of the hut."

"Where's Bender?"

"I told him to stay outside and cover us," the gunny said. "Otherwise, he's gonna kill these guys."

"What do we do, Captain?" Woody asked.

"I don't know," Fortis said. "I just don't know." He turned to the Maltaani woman. "Can you make it to safety? To your home, or somewhere else?"

She nodded. "Yes. My sisters and I live in the next village."

"Do you want us to walk you home?"

She shook her head. "No. I must go alone."

"I regret this happened to you, and I'm sorry we didn't get here soon enough to stop it," Fortis said as he escorted her to the door. When they got outside, Bender tried to take her arm.

"Let her go, Sergeant," Fortis said. "She's going to walk home."

"What about those bastards in there?" Bender demanded.

"We have to let them go."

"Let them go? What the fuck, Captain? They're rapists. They don't just get to walk away from this."

"Just calm down and listen to me for a second. One of them told me he's a colonel in the Maltaani military. We don't have any law enforcement authority, so we can't arrest them. Hell, I don't even know if rape is a crime here."

"We can make them disappear, mate."

"And what happens when that girl gets home and tells her story? They're going to wonder who the humans were that saved her. The Maltaani military are going to come looking for those five, and if they find them, then what?"

"Deny, deny, deny," Bender said.

"That's not gonna work, and you know it." Fortis put a hand on Bender's shoulder. "Look, I know why you feel the way you do, but these scumbags had nothing to do with Phaedra. If I had a choice, I'd let you tear them apart, but I don't. *We* don't."

Bender shook his head. "So they're going to walk away."

Fortis thought for a second. "No. Not exactly. You've already clobbered two of them. I'll give you one shot at each of the others. Bare-handed, no weapons. No killing blows, either. Deal?"

Fortis stuck out his hand, and Bender shook it.

"You're a good man, mate. For a wanker, I mean."

Fortis chuckled. "C'mon. Let's get this done and get the fuck out of here."

They reentered the hut, and Fortis gestured to the door. "Gunny, Woody, why don't you guys wait outside for a second? We'll be out in a minute, and then we'll go."

"What are you talking about?" Woody asked.

Ystremski read the tone of Fortis' voice and grabbed Woody by the arm. "C'mon, kid. Give me a hand with these rifles." The pair scooped up the Maltaani rifles and made for the door. "Not too long, sir."

"Nah, just a second."

When Ystremski and Woody were gone, Bender pulled the first uninjured Maltaani to his feet and spun him around.

"This one's for the girl," the hulking Australian hissed as he drove a massive fist into the Maltaani's face and knocked him out cold.

The second Maltaani protested and held his hands in front of his face. "That's not gonna help, mate." Bender delivered a powerful groin kick that crumpled his target and left him dry-heaving on the dirt floor. "That one's for the dead girls." He turned to Fortis. "I reckon they've got balls like us," he said in a lighthearted tone.

The Maltaani who'd called himself Colonel Waadeen drew himself up to his full height. "This is an outrage," he said to Fortis. "I intend to report this to the proper authorities. You will—"

Bender delivered a stiff-fingered strike to Waadeen's throat. His eyes bulged, and his fingers clawed at his neck as he fell to the ground.

"That one's for Phaedra."

"What the fuck?" Fortis demanded. "I said no killing blows."

Bender shrugged. "Sorry, mate. Kill them all, remember?"

"Not prisoners."

"Meh, fuck him. He was a rapist, not a prisoner."

Waadeen made thick, gurgling sounds, and his feet kicked as he fought to breathe through his ruined throat, but he soon fell silent.

"Come on," Fortis told Bender. "Let's get out of here."

They formed up in their regular patrol order and headed back south. Nobody spoke as a heavy rain pelted them, and it dogged them the entire way back to Camp Zulu-Five. When they got close, Fortis called for Red to open the gate, and they returned to the hangar, where Johnson and Varney waited.

"How did it go?" Red asked as the team stripped off their recon armor and stowed their weapons and gear.

"It went well," Fortis said. "We got some good training in, and I don't think we're going to have any problems when we do this for real tomorrow night." He looked at the team. "What do you guys think?"

"I agree," Ystremski said. "We're good to go."

"Yeah, mate. I reckon we're as good as any."

Woody just nodded.

Red smiled and pulled out a metal jug and a stack of mugs. "In that case, we need to christen our new team."

Fortis knew what was in the jug, but he asked anyway. "DINLI?"

"Not just DINLI, sir. The best DINLI I've ever had." Red poured equal measures for everyone and passed out the mugs.

They all lifted their mugs, and Fortis splashed out a bit for their fallen comrades everywhere. "To the dead and the living. And to Team Three."

"DINLI," they all said in unison as they tossed back their drinks.

Fortis expected the burn of raw alcohol, but he tasted a delicious sweetness that muted the scorching taste of traditional DINLI. From the looks on their faces, the DINLI surprised the rest of the team, too.

"They make it with a Maltaani fruit we get from the mama sans," Red told them. "It stands up to the distillation process, and it's got a ton of sugar to turn into alcohol."

"It's very good, and I hate to break up the party, but I need to report to Major Sokolov. Red, is Fender 454 available for a meeting?"

"Sure, Captain, but why? You don't need to—"

"Trust me, I need to. Meet me next door in a few minutes."

* * * * *

Chapter Sixteen

Fortis woke Sokolov to deliver the report on Team Three's training patrol, which annoyed the major. By the time Fortis finished making the report, he was furious.

"Are you out of your fucking mind? A Maltaani *colonel*?"

"He's a rapist and a murderer. They all were."

"We're not the fucking police!" Sokolov shouted as he stabbed a finger at Fortis. "We don't have any jurisdiction to do that shit, Captain." He slumped back in his seat. "What am I supposed to tell Anders?"

"Tell him the truth. Hell, I'll tell him if you don't want to."

"What am I supposed to tell the Maltaani camp commander? 'Hey general, some of my guys roughed up some of yours the other night, including a colonel. Sorry, our bad.'"

"Tell him the truth, too. 'His guys,' including a colonel, raped and beheaded two women, and were raping a third when we stopped them."

"Captain, your holier-than-thou, choir boy crap might sound good to you here in Camp Zulu-Five, but it's gonna blow up in your face when this story hits Division. General Boudreaux is going to take a giant shit on you from great altitude."

Fortis shrugged. "I don't care, Major. I have enough dirt on my soul without walking away from something like this. What if they were raping and murdering human females? Would you want us to walk away from that, too? 'Oh, well, we don't have jurisdiction.' Bull*shit*. We might not have jurisdiction, but we have a greater obligation to behave like human beings. If that means a couple Maltaani animals get beaten down, then too bad. You want to know why the locals support the nationalists? Look no further than the colonel and his rape gang."

Sokolov threw up his hands. "I need you to type up a patrol report, pronto, so I can send it up to Anders. Before you do, tell your team not to say a word about this to anyone, not even to each other. Not a word. We'll need some guidance from MAC-M on how to proceed, and I think we're going to get it in short order. Understand?"

"Yes, sir."

The major slammed the door shut behind him, and Fortis sat back in his seat and wondered what the major would say when he learned the colonel was dead. Someone pounded on the door, and he saw Gunny Ystremski waiting outside, so he waved him inside.

"What the fuck's going on, sir?"

"Sokolov gagged us until further notice. I have to give him a formal patrol report so he can send it up to Anders. That's where I'm headed. The rest of you can turn in."

"I don't mean that. What happened with Bender?"

"I told you to leave the hut so you wouldn't be held responsible for what was about to happen. If I tell you, then you can."

"Fuck that, sir. What happened?"

"There was no way those pricks were getting off scot-free, so I let Bender dole out some rough justice. One shot, barehanded."

Ystremski scoffed. "That's fair. Mighty big hands. Hell, that's better than they deserved for what they did."

"Yeah, but I think he killed the colonel. Stiff fingers to the throat. The colonel wasn't breathing when we left."

"Fuck 'em. The prick deserved it."

"Here's hoping the chain of command agrees. Sokolov isn't a big fan."

"Fuck him, too," Ystremski said, and they laughed.

Red stuck his head out of the cockpit. "Hey, Captain, I saw the major leave. Are you all set?"

"Yeah, Red, sorry about that. Shut it down; we're done for the night."

Maybe forever.

* * *

Sokolov paced while Fortis typed. He read over the captain's shoulder, but every time he did, Fortis lost his train of thought and had to stop.

Fortis finished the report and read over it. It was a recitation of fact, the unemotional account the ISMC preferred. He left out the part about allowing Bender to apply his brand of justice. If the question about what had happened to the colonel came up, Fortis would take the blame himself. It was wrong to lie on the patrol report, but he knew "just following orders" wouldn't be enough to shield the Australian, so it was better not to mention him at all. When he finished, the final product satisfied him.

Sokolov slid into the seat, and it was Fortis' turn to pace. The major read the report twice before he stood.

"Submit it. I'll write my endorsement and send it up to Anders."

"Do you want me to wait, sir?"

"That won't be necessary. Just turn it in. Nothing is going to happen with this until tomorrow. I doubt we'll hear much before midday."

"Major, I'm sorry about this, but we couldn't have done anything differently. *I* couldn't have done anything differently."

"Officially, I'm going to let the wolves feed on your ass if they come howling at the door over this. Unofficially, you did the right thing."

"Thank you, sir. Good night."

When Fortis entered the team bunk room, the lights were out, and he could hear soft snoring. He stripped off his dirty uniform, grabbed a towel, and headed for the showers. When he finished, Fortis slipped into his bunk and soon fell into a deep, dreamless sleep.

* * *

"Beck."

Beck jerked awake at the sound of his own name, and pain exploded in his left shoulder. It took several seconds for his sleep-addled brain to clear before he realized he'd been fast asleep on the forest floor. His body pinned his left arm under him, and a wave of nauseated agony washed over him when he tried to move it. That's when he remembered he'd wedged himself among the branches of a tree to sleep sometime the night before.

Did I fall?

He rolled over to stand up and came face to face with a gigantic serpent, bigger than the one that had eaten the hapless defecator at the Maltaani village. Its rope-like tongue fluttered in and out as if tasting the air, while glistening nostrils opened and closed as it sniffed the air. The beast was less than a meter away, and the malevolent beauty of its glittering eyes and slow, graceful undulations transfixed Beck.

"Fuck!" Beck screamed as he clambered across the ground to escape the snake. Abject terror overwhelmed the pain receptors in his shoulder with a flood of adrenaline, and he clawed and kicked his way clear before he stood up.

He ran through the forest, clutching his injured left arm across his chest with his right. The level ground gave way to a steep mountainside, and without his left arm for balance, Beck slipped and slid to his knees. He banged into a tree with his left side, and all the trauma masked by fear detonated in white-hot pain. He sobbed as the agony faded into a loud, unrelenting throb.

A low rumbling noise came to him, and at first Beck wasn't sure it was real. He shook his head to clear the pounding from his shoulder, and he heard it again.

A train!

Beck forced himself to his feet and scrambled down toward the sound. After two days wandering the mountains, first with the mercenaries, and then alone, he was desperate for rescue. When he caught sight of the railway through the trees, he wept with relief, until he realized the train sound was fading.

"No!" He jumped the last ten meters down to the tracks. The train was already a half-klick down the tracks and drawing away fast when Beck collapsed to the ground, defeated.

Every inch of his body hurt from his trek through the mountains, and the fresh injury to his shoulder compounded his misery. Beck was cold, tired, and hungry, and there was nothing he could do to solve any of those problems. He couldn't start a fire because the rain kept everything too wet to burn. He'd lost the rifle somewhere on his journey, but without a fire, he couldn't cook anything he shot. Somehow, his ingrained sense of survival had woken him up before the serpent could attack, but he didn't think he could ever sleep in the forest again.

After several long minutes of wallowing in self-pity, Beck settled his nerves and took stock of his situation. He was lost, but he was out of the forest. The railway was the most reliable way to travel from Daarben to Ulvaan, so he knew he'd see another train. He just didn't know when.

He knew the train he'd missed was eastbound. Walker had led the mercenaries from the cave across the tracks into the mountains, and he was certain the cave was south of the tracks.

Beyond that, he was clueless. He suspected Daarben was closer than Ulvaan; he didn't think the mercenaries had traveled very far east as they wound their way through the mountains. Daarben was the focal point of the Space Marine invasion, and there was bound to be more human activity in the west.

Beck turned his back on the distant train and headed west.

Several hours later, he spotted something unusual next to the tracks. As he got closer, he recognized the burned-out remains of a truck. Then it hit him.

Mitsui's truck.

When Beck had fled with Mitsui and Hahn, they'd traveled east along the railway in Mitsui's truck. A Space Marine hovercopter had strafed them and injured Mitsui. Beck and Hahn had carried the near-dead mercenary for a short distance before Walker and the other mercenaries had found them and taken them to the cave up above the railway.

Beck had the sudden idea of finding the cave. They'd left some dry firewood behind, and clean water seeped down through the rocks and pooled in several places. Food would be a problem, but he knew he could go a lot longer without food than he could without water and a good night's sleep.

He couldn't remember whether he and Hahn had carried Mitsui east or west. There was no sign of humans in the forest east of the destroyed truck. Beck decided they'd gone west, and not very far, either.

Beck was right. Less than a klick from the truck, he saw the familiar path that led up the mountain. The walk along the railway had dulled the pain in his injured shoulder, but the climb up to the cave soon reignited it. He almost gave up when the pain became too great, but he forced himself to keep going.

If you quit, you die.

After an exhausting climb, he reached the plateau that led to the cave and broke into a shambling run to reach it. When he got inside, Beck slumped against the wall, chest heaving with ragged breaths, his shoulder throbbing.

Safe at last.

* * *

Leighton's first attempt to enlist Space Marine assistance in the hunt for Dexter Beck was a failure. The MAC-M staffer who met with Leighton was a grizzled infantry colonel named Gunn, with tanned skin stretched over sharp cheekbones and dark eyes that seemed to look straight through Leighton.

After Leighton made his pitch, the colonel raised an eyebrow, a clear sign of his skepticism.

"You want me to send Space Marines out to search for one man?"

"Not just one man, Colonel. One of the men responsible for the war."

"Allegedly," the colonel said.

Leighton nodded. "We haven't convicted him of anything. Yet," he conceded.

"And where is this Beck character?"

"His last known location was a cave near the railway between Daarben and Ulvaan."

"Give me the coordinates, and I'll see about putting some boots on the ground."

"I don't have them."

The colonel's eyebrows knotted. "Then where would you have me send the troops?"

"Colonel, it's called a search. Send them into the forest along the tracks and have them look for the cave." Leighton allowed his frustration to show, and he braced himself for an angry response from the colonel. Instead, the man's face broke into a wide grin, and he threw his head back and laughed.

"You think I can just put Space Marines in the mountains somewhere, and they're going to find your cave, Mr. Leighton? Are you familiar with the terrain out there?"

Leighton left the meeting somewhat chastened. The colonel was right; Leighton didn't know what the terrain was like. His work as a criminal investigator had never taken him outside the city limits anywhere until now. The agent had naively assumed that finding the cave was a simple matter, but now he knew better.

He abhorred the thought of reporting his failure to Judon, so he did what he'd done his entire career: he scoured the evidence for clues he might have missed.

Hahn's interviews offered him no additional insight. She only knew they'd been somewhere east of Daarben when the Space Marine hovercopter had attacked their vehicle, and the cave was nearby. Mitsui had provided nothing useful, either. The pain and delirium of his leg wound had clouded his memory of their evacuation and attack. Beck was the only other survivor of the attack on the truck...

Find the truck, find the cave.

The idea hit him like a lightning bolt. Hahn and Beck couldn't have carried Mitsui very far, which meant the cave was close to the place where the Space Marines had destroyed the truck. The remains of the vehicle were somewhere along the tracks. Leighton just needed to find them.

Twelve hours later, Leighton sat in the darkened flight operations center next to the duty officer and watched the surveillance drone mission unfold.

"Daarben Flight Ops, this is Tophat. I've got a visual on the truck bearing zero seven one for five klicks. I just sent you a waypoint, over."

"This is Flight Ops, Roger. I see the waypoint, thank you."

At first, it seemed farcical to Leighton that the drone operator and duty officer spoke as if they were hundreds of kilometers apart instead of in adjacent rooms. When he asked about it, the duty officer told him the drone feed was available to MAC-M headquarters and the flagship orbiting Maltaan.

"This is Tophat, starting the first scan."

The duty officer removed her headset and turned to Leighton. "That's the exciting part, sir. We found your truck, or at least what we think is your truck. Now we wait for Tophat to complete the area scan and the computers to crunch the data."

"How long will that take?"

She shrugged. "Six hours. Maybe eight."

"Eight hours? Why so long?"

"Tophat can collect up to a petabyte of data on a typical mission," the watch commander said. "It takes time to download that much data after she lands. Then the computers go to work on it, and that takes time, too. We're just poor Space Marines. We don't have a bank of supercomputers like the flagship. But don't worry." She smiled. "When we're done, you'll be able to tell the eye color of a flea on a frog's ass down there. If your cave is in the scanned area, we'll find it. No problem."

* * * * *

Chapter Seventeen

Staaber looked at the faces of the easterners gathered around the hand-drawn map on the table in front of them. They were a hard lot, determined to push the humans and their royalist lackeys back to the west where they belonged.

"General, this map shows the layout of the spaceport under construction near the mines," a middle-aged Maltaani named Raabik said. "The positions of the buildings are accurate; I paced off the entire site this morning."

Staaber patted Raabik on the shoulder. "Fine work, my friend." He examined the map, searching for vulnerabilities and avenues of approach.

As soon as the GRC had received approval to reopen the helenium mines, construction crews began work on a massive new spaceport for the drop ships transporting ore to orbiting cargo vessels. They built it because the existing spaceport in Ulvaan was too small to handle the expected volume of traffic. Shipping the ore to the Daarben spaceport was impractical and would interfere with military operations there.

Since level, uninhabited ground for the new spaceport was scarce near the mines, GRC engineers had created some. They calculated how many hectares were necessary for the new facility, and then blasted the top off a nearby mountain to fit. They'd scraped the new surface with heavy equipment, which they stored in Quonset huts at night to protect it from the rain.

"Are there guards?" Staaber asked.

"There's a night watchman—a human—but the rain keeps him inside," Raabik said. "There are no lights or other security."

"Their arrogance will be their undoing," Staaber replied, and the group nodded in agreement. "They'll learn the high cost of stealing our mines and destroying our land, and then they'll run like whipped dogs."

Raabik had been the de facto leader of the cell since the ISMC had repatriated them from service in the west, so Staaber tried to stay in the background while the cell plotted their attack. It was important that he maintain a low profile to avoid human attention.

Their weapons and equipment were crude, and most had received little or no training before they went west to fight the royalists. Their plan reflected their lack of tactical proficiency, but Staaber still approved of the effort. They'd pour sand and rocks into the engines and transmissions of the equipment. When they finished, two of them would set fire to the fuel storage tanks while the rest escaped.

Staaber knew the attack was only vandalism, which the GRC would repair with little effort, but it was important for the cell to develop and take on more direct action. Their operations would grow in sophistication and the damage they caused, and the populace would have to take notice.

Despite his grandiose pronouncements about driving out the humans and royalists, a singular burning desire to avenge the damage done to his family home motivated Staaber. The sight of the human war machine at the spaceport in Daarben convinced him they'd remain on Maltaan as long as they chose to, but that didn't mean he had to tolerate the damage they'd done to his home and possessions. There were many other Maltaani like Raabik and his compatriots, and Staaber would use every one of them to satisfy his thirst for vengeance.

* * *

"Oy, Lucky." Bender's voice penetrated Fortis' sleep.

The captain sat up and rubbed his face. "What time is it?"

"Almost lunchtime, mate. Time to get up. There's something you need to see."

"What is it?"

"Get dressed and I'll show you."

The two men stepped outside into a light drizzle.

"The mama sans are asking for you," Bender said.

"Me? What do they want with me?"

"Beats me. I think the story of last night has gotten out. I can't understand what they're saying, since I only just got my implant. Me and Woody went out with the cooks, and the mama sans started bowing and kissing our hands. The cook said they were asking for you, too."

"Great. Where's Gunny?"

"He's in the gear hangar talking to the armorer."

The two old Maltaani women waited by the gate, and when they caught sight of Fortis, they nodded and rubbed their hands together.

"Hello, ladies," Fortis said.

"Thank you, thank you, thank you!" one of them said as the other took Fortis' hands and kissed them.

Fortis looked at Bender, who shrugged. "That's what they did with me and Woody, too."

The woman kissing Fortis' hands stopped and pulled him into a tight hug. "Attack tonight on the human spaceport," she whispered. Fortis pulled back and looked at her, but she and the other woman had continued to bow and thank him.

The mama sans turned and leaned on each other as they walked away, while Fortis and Bender stared after them.

"What did she say?"

"There's going to be an attack on the human spaceport tonight," Fortis said. "How would she know that? Our spaceport is in Daarben."

"Dunno, mate. Let's think about it over a big plate of braised rat, eh?"

They got their food and sat down next to Gunny and Woody. Ystremski gave Fortis a quizzical look.

"I figured you'd sleep until suppertime," he said.

"Fat chance. I had to get up for something else, and now that I'm awake, I'm hungry."

"What was it?" Ystremski asked.

"I'll tell you later," Fortis said as he looked skyward.

"You should have been a Fleet officer," Woody said. "Sleep until you're hungry, and eat until you're sleepy."

While he ate, Fortis caught the eye of Sokolov two tables over, and nodded, and the major nodded in response. Ystremski saw the exchange.

"Heard anything yet?"

Fortis shook his head. "Nothing yet."

"They can't be that mad, then."

"Don't count on it. They might be waiting for guidance from Terra Earth."

"Damn. I hadn't thought about that."

"It's all I can think about." Fortis saw Sokolov get up and head for the door. He stood and followed suit. "I need to catch the major. I'll link up with you guys later."

When he got outside, he saw Sokolov walking toward the flight line.

"Major. Major!"

Sokolov stopped. "What is it, Captain?"

Fortis lowered his voice. "Sir, I just had a strange encounter with the mama sans that I think you should know about. They were at the gate asking for me, and when I met them, one of them warned of an attack tonight on the human spaceport."

"What human spaceport? Did she mean Daarben?"

"She walked away before I could ask."

The major thought for a second. "The only spaceport we control is in Daarben. We use the one in Ulvaan for shuttles, but the Maltaani control it. Unless she's talking about the GRC one."

"The GRC has their own spaceport?"

"They're building one near the mines for transporting helenium," Sokolov said. "I heard they won't have a strip for shuttles, just pads for drop ships loaded with ore."

"Why would anyone attack there?"

"I don't know, Captain. Why don't you take your team out there tonight and find out?"

Sokolov's suggestion stunned Fortis. "You want my team to patrol?"

"You're not here to sit on your asses."

"What about last night?"

"What about it? I haven't heard from Anders or anyone else, so we're going to proceed UNODIR. If they want to stop you, it'll have to come from them."

UNODIR was an acronym for "Unless Otherwise Directed," and a junior used it to prompt a senior to decide, or prod them into action.

"You told them that, sir?"

"No, of course not. I don't want to poke the beehive, but I don't want to wait around for a decision, either. Get with your team, put a patrol order together, and submit it to me. What's the worst that happens? You squat in the fucking rain and stare at a spaceport all night?" On cue, the sky opened up, and rain fell in sheets. "Make it happen, Captain."

* * *

Fortis and the others gathered in the team room after chow to talk about their tasking. He'd given them the source of the intelligence outside, so they could discuss the nuts and bolts of the mission without disclosing the target.

Johnson proved to be adept at searching the many databases available to them, and they were soon staring at a holo of the region with the spaceport construction site marked in red.

"It looks like I can get you in here, or here," Red said as he pointed at the image. "Either is close enough to patrol in, but far enough away to disguise the insertion."

"I like this one better," Ystremski said. "This mountain will shield the noise from the target, but it doesn't look much farther than the other one."

"Any objections?" Fortis asked the team. Nobody answered. "That's Point Alpha, then. The other one is Point Bravo."

"What about extraction?" Bender asked.

"Plenty of room in this direction," Red replied. "There's not much on the other side, but there's no shortage of open areas. Pick one."

"Let's play the extraction by ear," Fortis said. "If nothing happens, there's no reason to hike five klicks away for pickup. If something happens, it's impossible to predict where we'll end up."

They agreed on four rally points and entered them into their navigators.

"Can you pull up an image of the target area?" Ystremski asked Johnson. An overhead shot of the spaceport construction site replaced the regional holo.

"This is dated five days ago," Johnson said. "It's the most recent one I can find."

The site was a large, flat area with Quonset huts and tanks clustered together in one corner.

"Not much to look at, is it?"

"No, but that makes our job easier," Bender said. "Less to cover."

"If we come in at Point Alpha and patrol around this way, we can take up positions here and here," Fortis said. "There's cover there and open lines of sight, too."

"Looks like another of those play it by ear deals, sir," Ystremski said. "All that stuff might be gone by now."

Fortis nodded. "You're right. Let's see how it looks, but this flank is our priority."

They'd launch just after dark, and after a couple faux landings to deceive any observers, Red would insert them at Point Alpha. The team would patrol in and take up positions where they could cover the spaceport unseen. Red would return to Camp Zulu-Five and monitor the satellite circuit. Fortis would decide when they'd seen enough and where to meet for extraction, and Red would recover them.

"Too easy, mate," Bender said and thumped Woody on the shoulder.

"Easy breather," the smaller man added as he winced and rubbed his new bruise.

"We'll travel light, same as last time," Ystremski said. "I'll bring a flare gun in case we need some illumination. Bender, bring some extra flares. Woody, is your med kit replenished?"

"Affirmative, Gunny. I restocked everything I used."

"Red, how's the bird looking? You said you had some maintenance to do last night."

"All set, Gunny. We've got sixty-two flight hours before major maintenance is due."

Ystremski turned to Fortis. "Captain, Team Three is ready to deploy."

Fortis smiled. "Roger that, Gunny."

* * *

It was dark when Varney rolled open the door and towed Fender 454 clear of the hangar. The rain had stopped, and the meteorologists predicted only a few passing showers until the following morning.

Fortis and the team belted into their seats with the doors pinned open and door guns deployed. Varney scrambled into his seat, and the engines whined as the hovercopter lifted off. After Red and Johnson completed post-takeoff checks, they began a wide, looping approach to Point Alpha. They simulated insertions in two other locations, hovering low to mimic troop debarkation before flying on to the next point.

"*One minute to Point Alpha,*" Red said over the intercom.

Fortis removed his headset and put his helmet on. "One minute."

The hovercopter slowed until they were in a hover, and a tiny red light over the door turned green. Fortis jumped the meter to the ground and angled off a few meters to his right. The rest of the team followed and established a perimeter as Fender 454 roared back into the night sky.

For several minutes, the team watched and waited for a reaction to their arrival, but the night remained quiet.

"Count off," the captain said in a soft voice, even though he could have shouted inside his helmet, and his voice wouldn't carry outside.

"One."

"Two."

"Three."

"Four. Okay, Woody, take us to the first waypoint, nice and quiet."

Without another word, the team rose and began their patrol.

* * * * *

Chapter Eighteen

An unsmiling second lieutenant ushered Leighton into Colonel Gunn's office and closed the door as she left. He flashed back to the humiliation he'd experienced during his first visit to MAC-M headquarters, and a knot formed in his stomach when the colonel looked up from his computer. Gunn rubbed his close-cropped white hair and sighed.

"What can I do for you this time, Agent Leighton?"

"I found the cave, General."

"You found it? How did you find it?"

"Well, *I* didn't. Tophat did. Daarben Flight authorized a scanning mission in the area where the suspects survived a strike on their vehicle, and we found it. It's in the system for your review."

Gunn located the mission report and pulled up the holo. It showed the railway, the mountainside, and the cave entrance.

"You're sure this is the right cave?"

"Not a hundred percent, but the parameters fit. It's close to the vehicle wreckage on the railway, and it's on a mountain about a klick from the wreck. Other suspects indicated they didn't travel far from the truck because of an injury to one of them. Tophat flew five-kilometer legs and detected nothing else that resembled a cave."

Gunn rubbed his chin as he reviewed the mission report on his monitor, and then studied the holo again. When he was done, he nodded.

"It looks like you've got yourself a mission, Agent Leighton. I'll send a company of Space Marines to investigate this cave first thing in the morning, weather permitting. Can you be at the spaceport at 0500?"

"Me? Uh, I wasn't planning to go, Colonel."

Gunn scoffed. "Okay, Agent Leighton, we'll handle the search ourselves. I assume you want Beck alive?"

"Yes, sir, alive. I'm very grateful for your help with this, Colonel. Thank you."

"That's what we're here for."

* * *

Team Three made good time on the patrol to the spaceport construction site, and it wasn't long before they were looking down on it from an adjacent hillside.

The spaceport was a rough rectangle with two long ramps built alongside for vehicle access. Mounds of boulders and other debris left over from blasting the mountain lined one side, and a row of dump trucks stood nearby, ready for loading when work resumed. The site appeared almost identical to the week-old imagery they'd viewed during mission preparations.

"What do you think, Gunny?" Fortis asked.

"It should be pretty easy to watch the whole place from this side or over there," Ystremski replied. "Let's split into two teams to cover more ground. I'll take Bender that way about fifty meters, and you and Woody move down this side. If something happens, we're close enough for mutual support, and we have a crossfire on the construction site."

"That sounds good."

The team moved into their assigned positions. Fortis and Woody found a spot in a jumble of tree trunks thirty meters from the site that provided suitable cover and some overhead protection from the rain they expected to resume at any time.

"Captain, why don't you shut down for a little while? I'll take the first watch. If anything happens, I'll wake you up."

Fortis' first instinct was to refuse the offer, but Woody wasn't just being generous. Fortis had gotten little rest after their post-lunch planning session, and the mission had only just begun. He'd be no good to the team if something happened and he wasn't clear-headed.

"Okay, Woody, I'll do that. Wake me up in two hours, and I'll take the watch. Hey, Gunny, did you copy that? Woody has the watch over here."

"*I copied. Posh officers sleeping on the job.*"

Fortis plunged into a deep, dreamless sleep, and it seemed like only minutes later that Woody nudged him awake.

"Two hours, Captain. You want more?"

"No, I'm good. Anything going on?"

"All quiet. Bender just took the watch across the way."

"Okay. I have the watch here."

Fortis looked out over the construction site and tried to stay focused. He wondered if he'd misunderstood the mama san's warning. Perhaps it was a psy-op or some other feint. He considered and discarded several other possibilities, each more outlandish than the last. Fortis gave up speculating and stared out over the darkened spaceport.

"*Captain, are you there?*"

"Go ahead, Bender."

"I've got movement in front of me. Looks like six, maybe eight Maltaani moving along the perimeter. They'll be at the corner in a minute."

Fortis looked where Bender indicated and caught sight of a shadow moving among the garages.

"I see one between the garages. Wake the gunny, and I'll get Woody up. Something's going down."

When the full team was awake, Fortis decided he and Woody would move closer, while Ystremski and Bender maintained overwatch.

"We need to get a better look at these guys. I didn't see any weapons, did you?" he asked Bender.

"Negative. I didn't get a good look at all of them, but the ones I saw appeared empty-handed."

"No shooting unless they engage," Fortis said.

"What are we doing with these guys, sir?" Ystremski asked. *"Are we going to ambush them?"*

"Let's figure out what they're doing first," Fortis replied. "We're not going to shoot them for trespassing."

Woody and Fortis slipped out of their hiding place and moved down toward the spaceport. Their recon armor rendered them invisible against the darkened jumble of logs and boulders, but they took care to remain in cover whenever they could. Five meters from the garages, they stopped and listened. Fortis heard muffled voices coming from a garage and the rattle of metal on metal.

"We've got eyes on you if you want to get closer," Bender said.

"I can hear them talking, but I can't make out what they're saying. It sounds like they're messing with the equipment in this garage. They're making too much noise to be trained troops."

"It might be kids, sir. Why don't we just scare them off?" Woody asked.

"*You must be joking, mate*," Bender said.

"No, I'm serious. Make some noise, shoot a flare, whatever. Let them know someone is here, and see what they do."

"That's not a bad idea," Ystremski said.

"Let's do it," Fortis said. "Gunny, you send up a flare, and we'll hold our position. If they come out shooting, we'll engage."

A few seconds later, a flare arced up into the sky and lit the spaceport in eerie white light. The Maltaani inside the hangar reacted right away. There was a loud *clang* and startled voices from inside the garages, and a group of Maltaani burst outside and ran down the embankment, straight at Fortis and Woody. The sergeant rose and tackled one of them, and the others veered away. Another flare zoomed into the sky while Woody and Fortis struggled to control their captive.

"*What the fuck's going on?*" Ystremski demanded.

"We grabbed one," Fortis said as he pinned the Maltaani's arms, and Woody laid across his legs.

"A full-grown one," Woody added.

Ystremski and Bender scrambled over to join them, and they had the prisoner subdued in a few seconds. They sat him up, and Bender crouched behind, ready to tackle him if he made a move.

Fortis took his helmet off so their captive could see his face. "What's your name?"

The Maltaani blinked in surprise at a human speaking his language, but he shook his head.

"We won't hurt you," Fortis said. He patted his pulse rifle. "If we wanted to hurt you, we'd have shot you and your comrades."

The Maltaani seemed to think for a moment. "Laaven," he said.

"Why are you here, Laaven?"

Laaven hung his head, so Fortis turned to Woody. "Climb up there and see what they were up to in the garage, would you?"

Laaven watched him go. "We were here to damage the trucks," he said.

"Why?"

"The mines. They belong to us, not you."

Woody slid back down to join them. "It looks like they were trying to sabotage the equipment. Some of the engine oil and transmission caps are open, and there are a couple bags of gravel and sand spilled on them, too."

"A labor dispute," Ystremski said.

Fortis stood and helped Laaven to his feet. "I told you we wouldn't hurt you. You're free to go. Remember to tell your friends that we're watching."

Laaven hesitated, and Fortis tipped his chin. "Go."

The Maltaani didn't need any more encouragement to hustle away into the darkness. Fortis put his helmet on and watched until Laaven disappeared.

A loud explosion ripped the night, and brilliant orange light lit the sky.

"What the fuck was that?" Bender asked.

The team scrambled up to the spaceport and saw several fuel storage tanks burning furiously. Flaming fuel spread in all directions and threatened to engulf the garages.

"Let's go!" The team raced across the smooth-scraped surface to escape the creeping flames, and Fortis saw a man with a flashlight running toward them.

"Get out of here!" he shouted, and the man jumped in surprise. Fortis remembered that the autoflage on their recon armor rendered them almost invisible, so he whipped off his helmet. "Go!"

When they were away from the flames on the far side of the construction site, the Space Marines pulled up and looked back.

"That was good shooting with the flare gun," Bender quipped. The team laughed.

The other man caught up with them and bent over, gasping for breath.

"Who are you guys?" he gasped.

"Space Marines," Fortis told him. "Who are you?"

"Paxton. I'm the night watchman. Why did you blow up the fuel tanks?"

"That wasn't us, mate."

Another explosion echoed across the construction site, and they saw the garages were blazing. More explosions, and the fiery hulk of a vehicle somersaulted high in the air.

"We interrupted some Maltaani who were vandalizing the equipment," Fortis said. "Where were you?"

Paxton pointed to a lone Quonset hut at the far end of the site. "I didn't hear a thing until the explosion. Maltaani, you say?"

"Yeah, Maltaani. We grabbed one of them. He told us they were unhappy about the mine ownership situation."

"Where is he?"

"We turned him loose," Fortis said. He pointed to the fires. "That was before this happened."

Paxton shook his head. "I told those cheap bastards we needed more security out here, but I didn't expect Space Marines."

"That's not us," Fortis said. "We were in the neighborhood, that's all."

The team left Paxton to figure out how he was going to report the destruction to his superiors and melted back into the woods around the construction site. Fortis called a halt so they could watch and listen, but there was nothing.

"At least we know the mama sans weren't bullshitting us," Fortis said. "Maybe we should have focused on the fuel tanks."

"Don't even start that, Captain," Ystremski said. "We had a clear line of sight to the tanks. They must have gotten to them when we were fucking around with the Maltaani."

Fortis decided to terminate the patrol early and call Red for extraction.

"There's no reason for us to hang around," he told the team. "The Maltaani are long gone, and there's nothing left here for us to worry about."

Fortis called Red, and they agreed to rendezvous with Fender 454 at the nearest rally point in twenty minutes. After a short, uneventful patrol, they took positions and awaited their ride. Red set the hovercopter down, they climbed aboard, and Fender 454 was airborne in seconds.

"How did it go?" the pilot asked Fortis as they flew back to Camp Zulu-Five.

"We interrupted an attack, but they got to the fuel tanks and garages. Total loss."

The rest of the ride home passed in silence. The mood was subdued as Fortis led the team into the gear hangar to store their weapons and equipment, and it surprised them when he told them to turn in.

"No debrief?"

"What debrief? You're all experienced operators. Does anyone have any lessons learned or critiques?"

They all shook their heads.

"Okay, then. You guys can go get cleaned up and turn in. I'll type up our patrol report and submit it to the major, and then I'll do the same."

It took Fortis almost two hours to finish the report. He emphasized how well the team had performed and took responsibility for the attack on the tanks. When he finished, the report satisfied the captain. He'd captured the narrative in complete and accurate detail.

He submitted the patrol report and debated whether to wake the major to brief him, but decided against it. The major would get the bad news soon enough.

* * * * *

Chapter Nineteen

"Beck?"

Beck jerked awake at the sound of his own name and flashed back to the serpent's attack in the forest. He cried out and tried to scramble backward, but his back was against the cave wall. A brilliant beam of light stabbed his eyes, and when he put his arms up to shield himself, his left shoulder exploded in pain.

"Are you Dexter Beck?" a voice behind the light demanded.

Beck slumped over on his right side and clutched his left arm to his chest.

"Sit up," the voice commanded. Hands grabbed his left arm, and Beck screamed.

"His arm's fucked up," another voice said. "Get Doc up here."

The spotlight moved off his face, and Beck could make out helmets and battle armor.

Space Marines.

Another Space Marine knelt next to him and doffed his helmet. "You've got an injury?"

Beck nodded. "Left shoulder."

"Were you shot?"

"Fell out of a tree."

"Huh. All right, I'm going to cut your shirt up the back so I can get it off, okay?"

The corpsman worked with practiced speed. When he finished, he put his face close to Beck's.

"I need you to sit up so I can examine you. Can you do that?"

Beck tried to push off with his right elbow, but he slumped back down.

"Let's try that again, but this time I'll get my hands under and lift."

Beck grunted and shook his head.

"Look, I know this sucks, and it hurts, but if you can't sit up on your own, I'll have to get a couple of these mouth-breathers to sit you up. Their bedside manner isn't too gentle. Do you want that?"

Beck shook his head again.

"Okay, then, let's do this together. Ready?"

Beck pushed with his elbow, and the corpsman lifted, and he forced himself to sit upright. His shoulder throbbed, but it wasn't the lancing pain like before.

"Let me cut the rest of this off and get a look." A few more snips, and Beck's shirt was gone. "Hmm. Uh-huh." Beck flinched when cool fingers touched the skin of his chest and shoulder, but they didn't prod or probe. The clammy cave wall was cold on his back, and he shivered.

"One more second and we're done," the corpsman said in a reassuring tone. True to his word, he completed his examination of Beck's shoulder a moment later.

Another Space Marine crouched next to the corpsman. "Whaddya got, Doc?"

"Dislocated left shoulder, maybe a fractured clavicle. Won't know for sure until he gets scanned, Gunny. He's dehydrated, and he's going into shock."

"Can he move?"

"Maybe to the mouth of the cave, but no further. Not under his own power. It would be best to carry him out on a litter once I get his arm immobilized and get him wrapped up in a survival blanket. We're going to need a hoist to get him off the mountain; he won't make it down the mountain on foot, and if we drop the litter, it might kill him."

"Okay, Doc. Do your thing and let me know when you're ready to move. I'll get a litter sent down. The lads are exploring way the hell down that hole, so we're going to be here for a while."

The corpsman turned back to Beck. "Mr. Beck, I'm going to wrap you in bandages to bind your left arm in place. You dislocated your shoulder, and I don't want to put it back in here unless I absolutely have to, okay?"

"Fuck no," Beck grunted through chattering teeth.

"I know you're getting cold. As soon as I get your arm immobilized, I'll wrap you in a survival blanket that'll warm you right up."

The corpsman wrapped a bandage around Beck's left wrist, and then around his neck, forming a sling. Then he wound several layers of bandages around his body to bind his arm to his chest. The manipulation made Beck's shoulder ache, but it also brought some relief, because his arm wasn't hanging free in the injured socket. Afterwards, the corpsman shook out a silver metallic blanket, wrapped it around Beck, and fastened it with several strips of tape.

"Just like last night's meatloaf," the corpsman quipped. While the corpsman worked, another Space Marine had delivered a litter, and he slid it over next to Beck. "Last step for you. I need you to swivel to your left, and then try to scoot onto this. After that, you can lay back, and we'll do the rest. You'll be at the hospital in no time."

Beck groaned in response, but he did as the corpsman bade and made it into the litter.

"Good job, Mr. Beck. Just relax. I'm going to elevate your feet, and then we'll get you on your way."

Beck heard a shout from somewhere deep in the cave.

"Hey, Gunny, grab the lieutenant and get down here. You're not gonna believe this."

* * *

Staaber met with Raabik in the morning to discuss the raid. When Staaber asked him how he thought it went, Raabik glowed with self-satisfaction.

"It was most successful," Raabik said.

"Your men panicked at the sight of a flare," Staaber said. "They dropped their tools and ran, and the humans captured you. How is that 'most successful?'"

"We destroyed the equipment and garages, General. They captured me, but I told them my name was Laaven, and they released me."

"What if they hadn't? What if they'd tortured you, or turned you over to their royalist lackeys? You might have told them everything you know about us."

Raabik didn't respond.

"As the leader, you must insulate yourself from the danger of capture," Staaber said. "Let your sergeants run the missions. How many went on the raid?"

"Six, plus me."

"How many were in the planning meeting? Ten? Eleven?"

Raabik nodded. "Eleven."

"You must limit the number of our compatriots who know of your plans to only those involved. The humans knew we were there. Somehow, they learned of our attack and sent Space Marines to guard the spaceport."

"We have a traitor?"

"You know them better than I do. Are any of them traitors?"

"No, General. I've known them all my life."

"Then someone accidentally spoke of the mission outside our circle. You must warn them not to speak to anyone. Our success—and perhaps our lives—depends on it." Staaber slapped Raabik on the shoulder. "Come, dear friend. It's a leader's burden to seek mistakes and correct them. The mission was a success, but we cannot allow ourselves more than a moment to celebrate our victory before we turn to the next mission."

"So soon?"

"Yes, Raabik. We must stay on the offensive and build on our success before the desire to be free of the humans and the royalists fades away. Even now, the men gather at night, and talk of returning to the forests and mines, and resuming our subservient existence. Is that what you want?"

"No, General."

"Then we strike again and again. Our numbers will grow with our reputation, and we will force the royalists to treat us as equals."

"What of the humans?"

Staaber scoffed. "The Space Marines are childish and simple to distract. They will soon tire of dying for the profits of others, and they will leave us alone to deal with those who have stolen the mines. The GRC."

* * *

Leighton couldn't stop smiling as he sat next to Dexter Beck's bed and watched the GRC executive sleep. The glow of victory he'd felt when Mitsui and Hahn had arrived at the Daarben spaceport had faded when their interviews were complete, but the news of Beck's capture had reignited it. His triumphant report to Judon had stoked it to a fever pitch.

When the hovercopter with Dexter Beck aboard made its final approach for a landing at the Daarben spaceport, it disappointed Leighton to learn that Beck was unconscious. As soon as the craft touched down, white-clad medical personnel raced out to meet it with a gurney in tow. When they had their patient strapped down, the medical team wheeled their cargo to the medical tent. Leighton followed and tried to be inconspicuous on the periphery of the action in the triage area.

"It's a good thing he's unconscious," the doctor said as the medical team sat Beck up to remove the binding around his body.

"Dislocated shoulder, possible fractured clavicle, dehydration, and shock," another one read the electronic chart the corpsman had sent with Beck. "His vitals are stable. Let's get scans on that shoulder, and then we'll get an IV in him."

Leighton waited while the medical team scanned Beck's shoulder and treated him for dehydration. Beck remained unconscious throughout, and they immobilized his shoulder again.

"No fracture, but he's going to need surgery to repair that shoulder," the lead doctor announced when the scans were complete. "He's stable, so let's get him ready for the shuttle to *Solicitude*."

Leighton stepped forward. "Excuse me, Doctor?" He held up his credentials for the doctor to read.

"What can I do for you, Agent Leighton?"

"This man, Dexter Beck, is in the custody of the Ministry of Justice, and I can't allow you to send him to *Solicitude*."

"What?" Confusion darkened the doctor's face. "This man's injuries require treatment we can't give him here in a field hospital."

"You just said he was stable. Is his life in danger?"

"No, but he needs an orthopedic surgeon, which we don't have on staff down here. The nearest orthopedist is aboard *Solicitude*, so that's where I'm sending him."

"Doctor, I appreciate that under normal circumstances, transferring Mr. Beck to *Solicitude* would be the logical choice. However, these aren't normal circumstances. Mr. Beck is a dangerous criminal, and I can't allow him to travel to *Solicitude*."

The doctor wasn't used to being second-guessed, especially by a civilian, and his confusion turned to anger.

"Agent Leighton, if you don't stop interfering with our duty of care for this man, I'll call for the military police and have you removed from this facility. I'm sending Mr. Beck to *Solicitude*. My decision is final."

"Doctor, if you do that, I'll bring you up on charges for interfering with a UNT security investigation. I don't want to do that, but you would leave me no choice. However, things don't have to reach that point." He pulled out his communicator. "I'd be happy to call MAC-M headquarters and have General Boudreaux explain the situation to you."

"MAC-M?"

"Yes, MAC-M. That's who I coordinated with to capture Mr. Beck, and the general is well aware of the security implications of this investigation. Doctor, please understand that I'm as concerned about

Mr. Beck's health and well-being as you are, but I can't allow you to transport him off Maltaan."

The doctor considered Leighton through narrowed eyes, but Leighton knew he'd back down. He'd bluffed when he'd invoked MAC-M; Leighton didn't know whether the general was aware of the hunt for and capture of Beck or not. In fact, the agent preferred he wasn't. The fewer senior officers and government employees who got involved in the case, the better. Regardless of who knew, he couldn't permit Beck to leave Maltaan.

"Okay, we'll do it your way, Agent. Know this: if Mr. Beck suffers any complications because you interfered with his care, the responsibility is yours."

Leighton nodded. "That's a risk I'll have to accept, but I'm grateful for your cooperation, Doctor. Thank you."

The agent made the same arrangements for Beck that he'd made for Mitsui—an isolated bed in a distant corner of the medical ward, out of sight and earshot of the other patients. Leighton had moved the mercenary leader to a confinement tent as soon as the doctors had cleared him, and he'd do the same with Beck, shoulder or no shoulder.

* * * * *

Chapter Twenty

"I don't think your team could fuck things up any worse if you tried," Sokolov told Fortis as he gave the captain a one-eyed glare. "You knew the attack was coming, you had your team in position to disrupt it, you even captured one of them, and the place *still* went up in flames. And you don't have shit to show for it."

"Major, I know I screwed up, but I don't think it's as bad as you make it sound. We knew 'the attack' was coming at 'the spaceport,' but we didn't know what kind of attack or which spaceport. Our confidence in the intel was so high that we deployed one four-man team to stop it.

"Also, when we got there, we discovered the GRC site security comprised of a single watchman on duty in a hut on the other side of the site. There were no security lights, and they didn't even have a fence. The GRC have no grounds to complain about us. If they're not concerned about security, then I'm not, either. Had we seen someone near the fuel tanks, we couldn't have stopped them without engaging, and the rules of engagement don't cover trespassing.

"I realize none of that excuses what I did with the prisoner, but what was I supposed to do? Bring him back here and turn him over to the Maltaani so they could torture and kill him for vandalism? From what he told me, those guys aren't part of an insurgency. They just want their jobs back."

"And you believed him?"

"Why not? The construction site doesn't have any military value, and it belongs to the GRC, not the royalists."

"I'm sorry to disagree with you, Major, but my team didn't fuck anything up. We inserted into unfamiliar territory, we patrolled into the target without detection, and we extracted without incident. What happened with the prisoner is on me, but the team performed well."

Sokolov leaned back and crossed his arms, then rolled his eyes and shook his head. "I can't believe I'm saying this, but you're right. We're not responsible for securing GRC facilities. Those bastards have an army of mercenaries who can pull guard duty. They'll get some kind of special war zone tax exemption and write off their equipment, too." He snorted. "It wouldn't surprise me if they *make* money on the deal."

"Has there been any word from Colonel Anders about the other patrol report?" Fortis asked.

"No, there hasn't. I'm thinking MAC-M wants to pretend it doesn't exist."

"What about the dead Maltaani colonel?"

"Captain, I had the displeasure of serving as a liaison officer with the royalists when we planned the invasion, and one thing I can say for certain: there's no shortage of Maltaani colonels. There must be five colonels for every lieutenant in the Maltaani military, and most of them are political appointees. I thought some of our senior officers were bad, but they have nothing on the plumage and preening I saw on the Maltaani flagship. Unless that colonel had political connections, they won't miss him. Speaking of colonels, Anders wants to meet with us tomorrow. You, me, and Gunny Ystremski."

"Yes, sir. Any idea why?"

"He didn't say. Maybe to talk about dead Maltaani colonels. I want Team Three to stand down tonight. Tell Red to have Fender 454 gassed up and ready to go at first light. Weather permitting, Anders and Wagner will meet us in Daarben at 0900, and we'll travel together to the MAC-M headquarters."

"MAC-M? That sounds serious."

"I don't know what it sounds like. I'm out here on the pointy end of the kukri, just like you. Hell, maybe we're all getting court martialed."

"General Boudreaux seemed like a reasonable man when I met him back on Terra Earth."

"He seemed pretty normal to me, too, but that was before the invasion commander dropped the MAC-M job in his lap. Boudreaux's division did most of the fighting on D-Day. Did you know that?"

Fortis nodded. "Yes, sir. Gunny Ystremski and I led a 2nd Division recon company. We went in before the main drop."

Sokolov shook his head again. "Why doesn't that surprise me, Fortis? Is there anything you *haven't* done?"

Fortis laughed. "I haven't paid off my student loans yet, sir."

The major's expression was proof of his confusion. "What the fuck are you talking about?"

"It's nothing, sir. Just an old joke."

"Well, get all the joking out of your system before we go see Anders."

"Roger that, sir."

* * *

First Lieutenant Wilhelm "Chug-A-Lug" Vogel and his platoon struggled to offload their cargo from the hovercopter onto the tarmac in Daarben. The pallet was heavy, and the driving rain didn't help. After they wrestled it to the ground, one of the ground crew arrived with a forklift.

"What took so long?" Vogel asked in his heavy German accent. "It's raining."

"Sorry, sir," the forklift driver replied with a smirk. "I left the keys in my dry coveralls."

"Bah! Never mind that. Let's get this inside."

The Space Marines trotted behind the forklift as the driver led them to an empty cargo hut. There was less than a centimeter of clearance between the load and the doorjamb, but the driver set the load down and backed out.

"*Danke*," Vogel said as he waved at the driver. "Thank you."

"Now what, LT?" the platoon sergeant asked Vogel.

"We find someone to give these to, then we get a beer," Vogel said.

The platoon laughed. Every job always ended with Vogel telling them it was time to get a beer. His nickname wasn't Chug-A-Lug for nothing.

"Lieutenant Vogel?" A white-haired female civilian stood in the door. Several other civilians peered around her.

"*Ya*, I am Vogel."

"I'm Doctor Longfellow from the MAC-M staff. I understand you found something interesting."

Vogel waved his arm, and his Space Marines pulled back the tarpaulin that covered their cargo.

"The skeleton."

Longfellow and her companions gasped. "The skeleton" was in fact a skull at least five times larger than a human skull, perched atop a pile of oversized but otherwise recognizable bones.

"Is it complete?" Longfellow asked in a muted voice.

"All but one. The, eh," Vogel tapped his thigh. "This one."

"Femur."

"*Ya*, femur. All but one femur. Don't know where it went."

The enormous skull looked somewhat human, with two eyes, a nose, and teeth. That's where the similarities ended. The back half of the skull was bulbous, like an enormous button mushroom. The lower jaw jutted forward well beyond the upper, and the teeth were rows of pointed fangs.

"My God, Doctor. What kind of creature is this?" one of the civilians asked.

The Space Marines moved aside as the civilians swarmed the fossilized remains and assembled the skeleton on the cargo hut floor. When they finished assembling the skeleton, they stared in awe. The creature would have stood almost five meters tall, with thick bones and a heavy skull.

"That's how we found it," Vogel said. "In the cave."

"Do you remember where you found it?" Longfellow asked.

"*Ya*. I have the coordinates here." Vogel held up his navigator.

"Oh, thank God," Longfellow said.

"What is it?" the lieutenant asked. "Maltaani?"

"No. It's a species we've never seen before."

* * *

Raabik had known about the village bartering with the Space Marines since it began, and had himself partaken in the delicacies the humans traded for simple Maltaani fare. His mother-in-law was involved in the barter, and his family enjoyed an enhanced social status from sharing the largesse.

It seemed harmless, but Staaber objected because it allowed the humans to insinuate themselves into Maltaani society and weakened their resolve to drive the invaders out.

"We can't allow them to be seen as anything but the enemy," the general told him. "If we tolerate their presence, we'll soon tolerate the yoke of royalist oppression. The cooperation must end."

Staaber's pronouncement put Raabik in a difficult position, so he investigated the situation for himself. He positioned himself near the Maltaani camp and watched as the old women pushed the cart full of food to the gate of the human compound. Some humans met them at the gate, and the two groups exchanged smiles and greetings. One human was much larger than his companions and looked familiar. When they turned and walked away, Raabik realized where he'd seen the human before.

The spaceport.

When the humans had captured Raabik, the one who'd held him down was much larger than the others, just like the one he watched during the food exchange. He couldn't be certain, but he hadn't seen another human that big anywhere else.

Also, the young woman from the village who'd been rescued by humans from the royalist marauders who'd raped and murdered her friends had described one of her rescuers as enormous.

It has to be him.

The behavior of the Space Marines confused Raabik. The humans had saved the girl from their royalist allies, and they'd captured him and released him during the raid on the human spaceport. These weren't the actions of the blood-thirsty enemies Staaber made them out to be, and yet they aligned themselves with the royalists.

As he turned to follow his mother-in-law and her companion back to their hamlet, Raabik's head swam with disjointed thoughts and half-formed ideas. If Raabik was right, and the massive human was one of his captors, how had they learned of the raid? Had his mother-in-law passed the information on to them? Raabik hadn't felt the need to keep his activities secret from his family.

Am I the leak?

* * *

Corporal Vincent escorted Dalia Hahn to a different tent and left her there without a word of explanation. This tent was larger than the one she'd been living in, with a small bedroom area partitioned off by curtains. Instead of a single cot, the bed was comprised of two cots pushed together, and Hahn's hopes soared. No sooner had she seen the bed than the tent flap opened, and Saito Mitsui hobbled in.

"My love!" Hahn cried and rushed into Mitsui's arms.

"Easy, darlin'," Mitsui said as he tried to balance on his good leg. "I'm tender as a newborn foal."

After a long, tearful embrace, Hahn led the injured man to the bed and sat down next to him.

"I don't know how much time we have," she said as she tugged at her clothes.

"We have all the time in the world," Mitsui said. He stopped her from undressing. "This is where we're going to live. Together."

"What?" Hahn sat up. "What do you mean?"

"Yeah, that's what one of those Justice fellas told me. We're being held pending judicial proceedings, and they decided we'd be happier together."

Hahn sat bolt upright. She looked around, jumped to her feet, and paced.

"What's wrong, little lady? Aren't you happy?"

Hahn returned to the bed and pushed Mitsui back. "Of course I'm happy, my sweet." She cupped his face and kissed him all over, starting at his lips and working her way across his cheeks until her lips brushed his ear.

"They're listening," she whispered.

Mitsui jerked, but Hahn held him down and peppered his neck with smooches. She worked her way under his chin and up to his other ear. "They want us to talk."

The Asian cowboy closed his eyes and nodded. "Baby, I love it when you do that," he murmured.

Hahn grabbed his earlobe between her teeth. "You mean this?"

Mitsui chuckled, and she kissed his ear again. "They might be watching, too."

He winced as he rolled her over until they were facing each other. "Baby, when I get healed up, I'll show you a high time. I sure am sorry, but right now I need to take it easy. Makin' love to you might kill me."

"What a great way to die."

"It would be, wouldn't it?"

She snuggled up to him, and he wrapped his arms around her. They lay like that for a long time and reveled in their nearness.

* * * * *

Chapter Twenty-One

Beck hugged his left arm to his body and strained his ears to hear what was happening in the medical tent beyond the screens that surrounded his bed. After his harrowing two-day ordeal alone in the Maltaani wilderness, Beck craved human company. Since he'd woken up, he'd seen two people: His doctor and the orderly who brought his meals and assisted him with the bedpan. Neither was talkative. The doctor only offered short answers to Beck's questions, and the orderly communicated by appearing with a food tray or the bedpan. He closed his eyes and tried to teleport himself anywhere but there.

"Knock, knock."

Beck opened his eyes and saw a civilian with mousy brown hair and a big smile. The smile widened when he saw Beck's eyes open.

"Oh, good, you're awake. We were afraid you were sleeping again."

Behind the civilian stood a Fleet major with a serious expression on his dark features. The civilian pulled a chair next to Beck's bed, while the major stood at the foot.

"I'm Supervisory Agent Thomas Leighton with the UNT Ministry of Justice. This is Major Jean-Paul Bisset of the Fleet Legal Counsel Office. I'm here to interview you about your activities here on Maltaan as an employee of the GRC. Do you mind if I record this?"

"No." Beck knew he didn't have an actual choice. Either Leighton would use an open recording, or he'd use a surreptitious recording device. By agreeing to the recording, he would at least appear cooperative.

"Great, thanks." Leighton turned on a portable holo generator and set it on Beck's bedside table. "This is Supervisory Agent Thomas Leighton with the UNT Ministry of Justice, along with Major Jean-Paul Bisset of the Fleet Legal Counsel Office." Leighton noted the time and date, then he advised Beck of his rights. "Do you understand these rights, Mr. Beck?"

"I understand."

"I'm here to get some information about the transfer of Precision Crafted Soldiers, or PCS, from the GRC to the Maltaani, Mr. Beck. Are you willing to answer my questions with the truth, to the best of your ability?"

"Of course. I'm here to help."

"Super." Leighton flashed that smile again, and Beck struggled not to snap at him.

Beck was stuck. He wasn't getting out of this predicament, and Leighton's absurd cheerfulness seemed to taunt him.

Leighton nodded as if he could read Beck's mind. "So, why don't you tell me about your involvement with the PCS program?"

"From when? Here on Maltaan, or the beginning?"

"Start at the beginning. It'll help add context to your activities here, I think."

"Okay. The GRC developed technology to create expendable soldiers for the UNT by cloning humans. I oversaw product testing for the first generation of PCS. The GRC gave them rudimentary military training, and then scheduled a test for them in a real-world scenario against a bug infestation. We went to Pada-Pada because the bug colonies there are well-documented. The ISMC had sent a company of Space Marines to observe and assist the tests. During the testing, we triggered a swarm of bugs much bigger than any we'd seen before. The bugs killed all the Space Marines and the PCS. I and four other GRC employees were the only survivors."

"Wow. That was fortunate."

"Yes, it was. Seven years later, we tried again, with the second-generation PCS. Once again, the ISMC sent troops to observe. During the course of the testing, they convinced themselves that the PCS were a threat, so they attacked our camp. I only survived because I took refuge in the jungle and waited until Fleet drop ships arrived to evacuate the Space Marines."

"I remember that. There was a lot of fallout because of that, wasn't there?"

"Yes. There were accusations and allegations. They never filed charges, nor was the GRC ever found at fault in any court, but the officer in command of the Space Marines was court martialed. Still, the financial impact was devastating, and the conglomerate suffered significant losses. They shelved the PCS program and assigned me to other duties."

"When did you go to work for Weldon Krieg?"

"Mr. Krieg was my boss throughout my time working in the PCS program. He is the director of Military Sales and Affairs, after all."

"How did you end up here on Maltaan, Mr. Beck?"

"When Terra Earth and Maltaan established diplomatic ties, it opened up new opportunities for human businesses positioned to take advantage of them. The GRC won several service contracts for the embassy, including executive protection, secretarial support, and maintenance. The Military Sales and Affairs Directorate administered those contracts."

"Mr. Krieg?"

"Correct. Mr. Krieg. He offered me the opportunity to resurrect my career with the GRC and assigned me to be the lead GRC representative to the embassy and the Maltaani government."

"That's quite a vote of confidence, considering how things went for you with the PCS," Leighton said. Beck tried to read the agent's face to detect whether it was a barb or an innocent remark, but his face was a cipher. Instead, he scoffed.

"Don't be so sure. He assigned his daughter, Dalia Hahn, as my executive assistant and his spy."

Leighton shook his head. "That's tough."

Beck nodded. "Her assignment presented some challenges."

"Let's talk about transferring PCS to the Maltaani. What do you know about that?"

"The original deal I struck with General Staaber of the Maltaani military was for ten thousand PCS. In exchange, he agreed to assign the GRC mineral rights to several areas in the east. Mr. Krieg later amended this deal, without my knowledge, to one hundred thousand PCS for the mineral rights and clearance to build a spaceport suitable for drop ships to haul away the ore."

"Were you aware that transferring military technology to the Maltaani required prior approval?"

"Yes, but the PCS were not military technology. The 'S' in PCS is a holdover from our days developing warriors for the UNT. The GRC didn't militarize the PCS we planned to transfer to the Maltaani. I got permission for the transfer from Ambassador Brooks-Green, just in case."

"Written permission?"

"Hmm, no, I don't think so. The ambassador gave me verbal authorization during a meeting. Ms. Hahn may have followed up with a memo or something from her office. I didn't get it in writing."

"Why would a Maltaani general want a hundred thousand human clones if they weren't soldiers?"

"Krieg told me Staaber's family controlled several inactive helenium mines, and he required a large pool of labor to get them working again." Beck read the skepticism on Leighton's face. "There's something about Maltaani society that you have to understand. Despite our common origins, their ideals vary from ours. Maltaani government officials use their official positions for personal gain. Krieg explained it as a deal between the GRC and a private individual, who was also a general."

"And you went along with that?"

"Why wouldn't I? I had no reason to believe the Maltaani could or *would* use the PCS in an unauthorized manner. They weren't supposed to be militarized."

"Was the order changed?"

"Yes. After the first delivery, Mr. Krieg once again amended the order without my knowledge and increased it to two hundred thousand PCS."

"Two hundred thousand PCS arrived on Maltaan without your knowledge?"

"No. I learned of their arrival after the deal was done. Krieg and Staaber made the deal without my knowledge, facilitated by Hahn."

"Do you know Saito Mitsui?"

"You know I do. I evacuated with him when the invasion started."

"What did you know of him before the invasion?"

"He was in charge of the trainers hired on by the GRC to assist the Maltaani with their purchases. I met him, and he nominally answered to me, but I didn't know him well. I knew he and Hahn had a romantic relationship, which I disapproved of on professional grounds."

"They have an ongoing romantic relationship. They cooperated with my investigation, so I placed them in conjugal pretrial confinement after I completed their interviews," Leighton said with a smile.

Beck nodded. "Brilliant. I suppose you wired their love nest so you can listen in when they talk about the case?"

Leighton cleared his throat, a sure sign to Beck that he was correct.

"Look, Agent Leighton, I've seen enough tricks to recognize an obvious one like that, and you can damn well bet Dalia Hahn has, too. I may not be a choir boy, but she's a barracuda—cold, ruthless, and ready to bite. She's no fool."

Leighton shook his head, annoyed. He hadn't thought his ploy would be that obvious. "Let's get back to the questions, shall we? What can you tell me about Mitsui's activities?"

"Like I said, he was the head trainer. After that, he accepted a position in the Maltaani military as a colonel in command of the PCS."

"You agreed with that?"

"No, of course not. The situation between the royalists and the nationalists was growing worse by the day, and we were caught in the middle. I thought the move was an unnecessary provocation, but mercenaries do that sort of thing all the time. It was about that time that I learned the PCS had received basic military training before the GRC transferred them."

"What did you do with that information?"

"What was I supposed to do, round them up and send them back? Notify the embassy? Call the Ministry of Justice? Events were swirling out of control, Agent Leighton. There were massive riots at the embassy. The Maltaani military was shooting protestors. There was talk of evacuation and abandoning the embassy. Do you think anyone cared about a bunch of untrained human clones?"

"Human clones intended to help repel our invasion," Leighton said.

"Did they fight?"

"I don't know, Mr. Beck, I'm not a military man. If they did, they were ineffective, because the Space Marines won without too much effort. Who told you the PCS had received military training?"

Beck shrugged. "I don't recall."

Leighton gave him a skeptical look. "The most important piece of information about the illegal transfer of military technology, and you don't recall?"

"It wasn't illegal at the time."

The agent consulted his notes. "Why didn't you evacuate with the rest of the humans from the embassy?"

"It was Krieg's desire that we continue to service the contract with Staaber, so we stayed. General Staaber promised us safe passage as GRC employees, so Hahn and I traveled to a base east of Daarben, where Mitsui had his headquarters. We stayed there until the invasion, then we headed east."

"Where did you go?"

"We planned to try for the spaceport in Ulvaan to arrange a GRC shuttle, but a hovercopter strafed our truck and wounded Mitsui. We found a group of mercenaries living in a cave near the railway, so we joined them. A few days later, Hahn and Mitsui disappeared, and the mercenaries went in search of food. I followed them for a couple of days, and then returned to the cave, where the Space Marines captured me."

"Interesting stuff, Mr. Beck."

"I got lucky."

"Indeed. Here's your situation. You're in the custody of the Ministry of Justice. The doctor tells me your shoulder will heal, but without surgery, you'll end up with a 'trick' shoulder, so you'll spend the rest of your life popping it back into the socket after it pops out. They say you get used to the pain." Leighton gave an exaggerated shiver. "The nearest surgeon capable of repairing your shoulder with surgery is orbiting above us on the hospital ship *Solicitude*. The doctor here wants to send you up there, but I can't allow that."

"Why not? I need surgery!" Beck said.

"That may be, but once you're aboard *Solicitude*, you'd become the responsibility of the Ministry of Health and Wellness, which means Justice would lose custody of you. Health could send you back to Terra Earth and let you go, and then I'd have to go through the trouble of tracking you down again. Do you see my quandary?"

"You can't do this!"

Leighton chuckled. "That's where you're wrong, Mr. Beck. As long as the UNT considers Maltaan a war zone, the rules regarding your treatment are in my favor. Here's what I want you to do. Take some time over the next day or so and think about our conversation. I'll come back, and we'll talk again. That will be your chance to better explain what happened, and maybe add some detail. When we're finished, if I'm satisfied, I'll arrange for the proper surgeon and operating team to come here to repair your shoulder."

Beck scowled but said nothing. He'd held nothing back, so he wasn't sure what Leighton was after.

"Cheer up, Mr. Beck," Leighton said as he turned off the holo generator. "Perhaps tomorrow, you'll see things my way." Leighton reached out as if to touch Beck's shoulder, and Beck flinched. "The key to your recovery is cooperation."

* * * * *

Chapter Twenty-Two

Fender 454 took off at first light and made good time, pounding through wind-driven rain. As they approached Camp Romeo-Nine to refuel, Red came over the intercom.

"*Major Sokolov, Romeo-Nine has requested that we pick up four pax for transfer to Daarben. Three medicals and a VIP.*"

"Who's the VIP?"

"*They didn't say, sir.*"

"If we can carry the weight, let's do it. Are they ready to go?"

"*Yes, sir. They were supposed to leave two days ago, so I imagine they're more than ready.*"

"Okay, thanks."

Red set the hovercopter down with a gentle bump, and a ground crewman ran out and connected the fuel hose. When refueling was complete, he disconnected the hose and signaled to a group of people waiting just off the landing pad. They picked up two litters and trotted for the hovercopter. It surprised Fortis to see Liz Sherer follow the litters aboard the hovercopter.

"Liz!"

The reporter sank down onto the web seat next to him. "I've never been so happy to see you, Abner. Except the other day."

"Ma'am, they said four passengers," Varney said.

Sherer shook her head. "One of them didn't make it."

"What happened, Liz?" Fortis asked as Varney closed the doors and Fender 454 lifted off. "Why are you still here?

"The weather happened. After you dropped us off, the clouds opened up. We've been waiting for a bird ever since."

Sokolov had leaned into the conversation, so Fortis introduced them.

"Liz Sherer, this is Major Sokolov, my commanding officer. Major, this is Liz Sherer, reporter for the Terra News Network."

"I'm a big fan of your reporting, ma'am."

"Stow the ma'am stuff, Major. Call me Liz."

Sokolov chuckled. "Okay, Liz."

Liz pointed to Gunny Ystremski, who was sound asleep on the other side of Fortis. "Is that Petr?"

"Yeah, it's me," Ystremski replied as he sat up. "Just a working stiff trying to get some shuteye."

"He's getting grumpy in his old age," Liz told Fortis.

"He's like that if he doesn't get his nap."

"Nice to see you again, Liz," Ystremski said as he twisted around in search of a comfortable position.

"May I ask how you know Captain Fortis?" Sokolov asked.

"9th Division embedded me with his platoon on Balfan-48," Liz said. "Or should I say, his division?"

Sokolov held up his hands. "I don't want to know."

Fortis and Sherer exchanged knowing smiles.

"Where are you headed this time, Abner?" Sherer asked.

"Daarben, same as you. How's the news biz?"

"I don't know. The weather trapped us at Camp Swampy. What's new at Zulu-Five?"

"Rain, followed by rain, with the chance of more rain," Fortis said. "Trying to stay dry."

"Hmph. Why don't I believe you?"

Fortis grinned. "Liz, after all we've been through, would I lie to you?"

She gave him a narrow-eyed look but didn't respond.

"*Major, Daarben just issued a turbulence warning for the airspace between here and the spaceport,*" Red announced over the intercom. "*Tighten your belts. It's about to get sporty.*"

The next thirty minutes were the most frightening of Fortis' brief ISMC career. The hovercopter lurched up and down between slams back and forth as the Maltaani atmosphere fought against their progress. He kept his eyes squeezed shut except for brief peeks around the cabin after an especially hard slam. Even Ystremski, who was still feigning sleep, was gripping his seat frame with white knuckles.

"*Final approach.*" Fortis heard the tension in Red's voice. "*This might be a rough one.*"

As Fender 454 touched down, a gust of wind pushed it sideways. Even the gunny sat up and looked around after that one. After one more strong gust, the hovercopter settled onto the landing pad.

"*Welcome to Daarben,*" Red said as he cut the engines.

"Good flying," Sokolov replied.

Ystremski stretched and looked around the cabin. "We're here?"

Everyone laughed, and the fear and tension that had gripped everyone dissipated. The hovercopter doors slid open, and white-clad medical personnel collected the litters. The rest of the passengers followed them through the driving rain into an empty hangar, where a triage team waited.

Liz touched Fortis' arm. "Abner, I'm going to see if I can find the Public Information Officer so he can feed me the usual bullshit party line. Maybe we can meet up later, and you can give me the real scoop?" She looked at Sokolov and laughed at his expression. "I'm only teasing, Major. Abner is the most taciturn source I have." She hugged Fortis and disappeared back out into the rain.

"Now what, sir?" Ystremski asked.

"We're early," Sokolov said after he checked the time.

"I can go over to the air ops tent and see if the shuttle from *Mammoth* is due in soon," Ystremski said. "They might not be coming at all in this weather."

"Don't say that," Sokolov groaned. "I don't want to be here any longer than necessary." He nodded. "Go ahead, Gunny. We'll wait here."

The medical teams had taken the two casualties away, leaving Sokolov and Fortis alone in the hangar. They took turns checking the time and staring outside at the rain that buffeted the spaceport until Red, Johnson, and Varney dashed in.

"Daarben Control just suspended all flight operations until further notice, sir," Red told Sokolov. "Me and Johnson are gonna go talk to the weather guessers and find out when this is going to break."

"Okay, Red. Tell them to make it today, all right?"

Red and Johnson passed Ystremski on his way back from the air ops tent.

"Don't tell me," Sokolov said. "No shuttle, because they suspended flight operations, right?"

"No, sir. The shuttle from *Mammoth* will be on the ground any minute now. *Then* they'll suspend flight ops."

"At least they'll be here. Gunny, do you think you can work some magic at the motor pool and get us a ride to MAC-M?"

"I'll see what I can do, sir."

Two minutes later, Fortis heard the unmistakable sound of shuttle engines as the craft landed and taxied to the hangar. Moments later, Jerry Wagner and Colonel Anders dashed into the hangar.

"Welcome to Daarben," Sokolov said as the newcomers brushed off the water.

"Lovely weather you have here, Major," Wagner said as the group shook hands. "We heard they suspended flight ops?"

"Affirmative. Red and Johnson are getting a weather update, and Gunny Ystremski is organizing a ride to MAC-M."

"Mech convoy to MAC-M leaves from the motor pool in ten minutes," Ystremski announced from the door. "I got eight seats."

"Eight?" Anders asked.

"Five of us, plus three aircrew," Ystremski said.

Just then, Red and Johnson returned from the weather office. "Hiya, Colonel, Mr. Wagner. Weather guys say this storm is here for the next five hours, minimum. There's a high-pressure system pushing through, and once it gets here, things should clear up for a day or so."

"Good," said Wagner. "Red, you and your crew might as well stay here in case the rain clears out sooner than expected. If that happens, we can catch a ride with you from MAC-M back here before you head home."

"Roger that, sir."

Wagner turned to Ystremski. "Gunny, which way to the motor pool?"

* * *

The sergeant in charge of the motor pool told them the convoy commander had delayed their departure for a few minutes, so the group waited in the garage next to their mech. The constant rain sharpened the stink of grease and oil that hovered in the air inside the garage, so Fortis stood by the open door and watched the rain. Anders joined him.

"How are things going in the east?" Anders asked.

Fortis gave a wry smile. "You've read our patrol reports?"

"I have."

"Not the results we were hoping for."

"Your team stayed alive and returned home unhurt. Those are victories."

"I hope the rest of the chain of command agrees."

"How are Bender and Woods working out?"

"Great. Both are outstanding Space Marines. Did you know Woods before this?"

Anders shook his head. "No, but when I told Bender to bring someone along for the team, he didn't hesitate to nominate Woods, so I knew he was good. I'm glad to hear they're working out."

"They're a squared-away bunch, that's for sure."

"Okay, gentlemen, if you want to load up, we'll get this thing on the road!" the sergeant shouted. They followed Wagner up the ramp and buckled into their seats as the mech engines roared to life.

"*We're the third mech of four in the convoy,*" the mech commander announced over the intercom. "*We're not expecting any trouble, but this is still a war zone. If you hear any firing, stay in your seats and let us handle it.*"

"Are convoys still necessary?" Wagner asked the mech crewman seated by the ramp.

"I dunno, sir. I've been on this milk run about a hundred times since we got here and haven't heard a shot fired in anger yet. The war is over, I think."

The trip to the MAC-M compound was uneventful. Mech suspensions were stiff, and the ride was rough, but after the beating they'd taken in Fender 454, it felt like the gentle rocking of a crib. The crewmen kept the hatches closed against the rain, and the atmosphere inside became stuffy. Fortis stifled an enormous yawn and earned dirty looks from his companions as the reflex became contagious.

When they arrived at MAC-M headquarters, the mech squealed to a stop. When the ramp dropped, fresh air flooded the mech and woke everyone up.

"All ashore," the crewman quipped as they disembarked. The rain had stopped, and a sergeant named Cooper waited for them at the bottom of the ramp.

"Colonel Anders? Mr. Wagner?" he asked as he threw up a crisp salute.

"That's us," Wagner said.

"Follow me, please."

Cooper led them to a Quonset hut with a large sign over the door that read "MAC-M Headquarters." It surprised Fortis to see none of the bustle he expected from headquarters, and Cooper seemed to read his mind.

"Everyone is out back enjoying a quick breath of rain-free air," Cooper said. "It's rained for six days straight, and we're all going stir crazy." He motioned for them to follow him. "This way, please."

They arrived at a door marked "Commanding General," and Cooper ushered them inside. General Boudreaux rose from behind his desk and cracked a wide smile.

"Come on in, gents."

* * * * *

Chapter Twenty-Three

Staaber watched from his hiding place as the convoy rolled through a driving rain squall along the road to Ulvaan. There was an armored escort vehicle in the lead, one in the rear, and another ten trucks full of PCS in a tight formation between. He estimated four mercenaries in each escort, plus one driver for the other vehicles.

Eighteen humans.

The Maltaani ambush squad numbered nine members, plus Staaber, but they'd have the element of surprise on their side, and Staaber was confident of success. Humans wouldn't expect an ambush in the rain, and their vigilance would be low.

As the lead escort passed a pile of branches and rubble, the improvised explosive device—or IED—concealed within detonated with an ear-splitting *boom!* The Maltaani had shaped the charge to direct the energy at the vehicles on the road, and the force of the blast tumbled the vehicle three times before it came to rest on its roof and burst into flames.

As soon as the first explosion went off, four Maltaani gunmen concealed in the forest opened up on the rear escort. They killed the turret gunners, and then the shooters shifted their fire to the driver's windows and windscreen. Maltaani ballistic rounds couldn't punch through the heavy, bullet-resistant glass, but the noise distracted the occupants long enough for another Maltaani to dash up to the vehicle from behind and throw a satchel charge underneath.

The detonation lifted the vehicle two meters straight up, and it slammed down onto the road. Black smoke billowed from inside the vehicle, and the gunners mowed down the humans as they tried to escape.

Meanwhile, the remaining Maltaani engaged the truck cabins up and down the convoy. The lighter armor on the trucks didn't protect those inside, and the shooters killed several of the drivers before they could react. The rest of the Maltaani shifted their fire to the trucks, and they soon reduced the vehicles to steaming, smoking wrecks.

When Staaber saw the humans were all dead, he signaled his team to approach the destroyed convoy and free the PCS. The Maltaani kicked and punched at the PCS to get them out of the trucks, and the clones huddled in uncertain groups on the road. The Maltaani shouted and fired their weapons in the air, and the PCS reacted as Staaber had expected. Panic swept over them, and the clones scattered in all directions. The general smiled in grim satisfaction as he watched the PCS disappear into the forest or run down the road toward Daarben.

Staaber signaled his troops to return to their vehicle, and he allowed them a moment of self-congratulations and laughter as they surveyed the wreckage of the convoy.

"Excellent work," Staaber told them. "We killed all the mercenaries, and the Space Marines will have their hands full, chasing their clones through the forest. Let's mount up and return home before the humans discover us."

The likelihood of detection by the humans was very low. The heavy cloud cover would shield them from their satellite systems, and the high winds of the rainy season kept their aircraft grounded. Still, Staaber didn't want his men to become complacent. When the weather cleared, the humans would reassert their dominance of the airspace, and they had to be prepared. Until then, he wanted to strike as often and as hard as he could. The question was, where?

As the driver slowed at the approach to the railway crossing, Staaber got a sudden inspiration.

* * *

The communicator encryption light turned green, and Leighton heard the familiar voice of Associate Minister of Justice Judon.

"Hello, Thompson. I'm glad you were there to receive my call," she said.

Leighton went on alert. Senior Justice personnel didn't address their juniors by first name.

Unless it's bad news.

"I'm happy to hear from you, ma'am."

"There's been a major development in the case, and I wanted you to hear it from me before it breaks on the news," Judon said. "The solicitor general has dropped all charges against Weldon Krieg and his associates."

"What the fuck?" Leighton blurted out. He cleared his throat. "Pardon me, Minister. She did what?"

Judon laughed. "I had the same reaction. More subdued, but the same. It's true. Solicitor General Gomez called a meeting to review the case, and after we presented the evidence we have so far, she decided that there's not enough to get a conviction."

"But we're not finished," Leighton said. "I've only interviewed Beck once."

"I read your interview report, and you did a noteworthy job with him. The problem is, his answers do nothing to advance our case. The GRC and Mr. Krieg claim the PCS they transferred weren't supposed to be militarized. Even if they were, the GRC received approval for the transfer from the ambassador herself, since the military attaché position was vacant. At its core, they characterized the deal as an administrative foul-up, and Gomez agreed."

Leighton was stunned by what Judon told him. "And we believe them?"

"Not necessarily, no, but we can't prove otherwise. There are no electronic records of the meeting between Mr. Beck and Ambassador Brooks-Green, and if there was a paper trail, it disappeared when they destroyed everything during the embassy evacuation."

"This is outrageous!"

"Once again, we agree, but there's nothing we can do about it."

"Give me permission to take another run at Beck. This time I'll use a needle to prod his memory."

"To what end? We don't have any evidence to back up anything he might reveal. If his testimony ever got to court, his attorneys could force us to admit that we extracted his statements under duress, not to mention that we denied him medical care for his shoulder until he cooperated."

Her description of Beck's treatment wasn't a hundred percent accurate, but Leighton knew not to argue with her. "What about Hahn and Mitsui? They might corroborate, with the right motivation."

"You can dope them all and get confessions to whatever you want, but it won't matter. It won't be enough to convict anyone."

Leighton shook his head. "I can't believe this."

"Let me explain what's going on with this case. Yesterday, Krieg's defense team filed twenty-one motions. Almost a thousand pages. The Ministry has to analyze each one and respond in a timely manner. While we're doing that, the defense will generate another wave of motions, and we'll all go blind as we choke on paperwork for the next two years.

"Another consideration is that the defense minister has announced his intention to lift the Maltaan war zone declaration by the end of the week. When that happens, we'll have to return Beck, Hahn, and Mitsui to Terra Earth, where their defense teams will churn out paper, too.

"Last but not least, the GRC and UNT have struck a deal for the PCS. The Space Marines are rounding up the PCS, and the GRC are transporting them to the helenium mines to work. The government has been relieved of a massive headache, and they want nothing to sour the deal."

"Like convicting Krieg of treason."

"Supervisory Agent Leighton, I've done the best I can to explain the circumstances of this case. Like it or not, the solicitor general, our big boss, has dropped the charges and ended the investigation. Our job now is to wrap up loose ends, generate an accurate summary of the case that no one will ever read, and move on to the next case."

It's Supervisory Agent again.

Leighton thought for a long second. "Okay, ma'am. What do you need me to do?"

"Arrange for Beck, Hahn, and Mitsui to travel to Ulvaan to catch the next GRC shuttle up to *Vast Expanse*, the GRC transport in orbit. The war zone declaration is still in effect, so don't allow them to move around without escort. They're still our responsibility, and if anything happens to them, it won't go well."

"Anything else?"

"You've done a magnificent job, Thompson."

Now it's Thompson again.

"No matter how this case turned out, your investigation was thorough, and your interview technique was superb. You figured out how to find Beck, which was nothing short of brilliant. Take care of those three, and then why don't you take some time off? Head over to Eros-69 to unwind and blow off some steam."

Leighton blushed, and he was thankful it wasn't a video call. "Thank you, ma'am. It was a pleasure serving on your team, and I hope to do so in the future. As for Eros-69, it's not for me, but thank you for the offer."

Judon promised to send written authorization for the release and transport of the trio of GRC employees, and then signed off.

Leighton leaned back in his chair and laced his fingers behind his head. He'd watched arrogant GRC executives break the law and escape punishment all his life, and this case had represented one of the few chances to hold any of them accountable. The decision to drop the charges against Krieg and his confederates was infuriating, and Judon's conciliatory tone and praise did little to mollify him.

He imagined the reactions of Beck, Hahn, and Mitsui when they learned of their charges and pending release, and his stomach soured. The claim by the defendants that they didn't militarize the PCS before the transfer was dubious, and it didn't matter that the PCS had played almost no role in the Maltaani military resistance during the invasion. Whether or not the criminals succeeded, the criminal intent was there. Now, instead of the punishment the trio deserved, they'd receive no punishment, and return to their lives scot-free.

A sudden idea popped into his head, and the more Leighton thought about it, the more it amused him.

No kid glove treatment from me.

Ten minutes later, he shoved aside the privacy screens that surrounded Beck's hospital bed. Two unsmiling Space Marines flanked him, and Beck looked up with a mixture of surprise and fear.

"Mr. Beck, come with me please," Leighton said.

"What is this?"

"No questions, Mr. Beck. Just come."

"But my shoulder—"

Leighton gestured to the Space Marines. "If you won't come along, I'll have them bring you."

Beck groaned as he swiveled his legs off the bed and slid his feet into the hospital-issue slippers. "Where are you taking me?"

Without a word, Leighton led Beck to the tent door. Outside, a light rain swirled around on a blustery wind.

"I can't go out in that," Beck protested as Leighton stepped out into the rain.

"This way, Mr. Beck."

The Space Marines loomed over Beck, and he followed Leighton. Leighton watched with grim satisfaction as Beck slipped and almost fell as he struggled to keep his footing, and mud and rain soon soaked his hospital gown. Leighton stopped at the tent where Hahn and Mitsui lived and held the tent flap open.

"Inside."

Leighton followed Beck into the tent and saw Hahn and Mitsui standing by the bedroom partition.

"What's this?" Hahn asked. Then she recognized the bedraggled man with Leighton. "Beck!"

"That's right," Leighton said. "It's your old boss and coconspirator. Say hello, Mr. Beck."

Instead, Beck sank onto a folding chair and sat, dripping.

"I brought Mr. Beck here because I have important news for all three of you," Leighton said.

One of the Space Marines entered the tent and held up a folding cot. "Where do you want it, sir?"

"Right there is fine," Leighton said. "These three will figure out where to set it up. Thank you."

Mitsui limped over and sat on a chair next to Beck. "What is this?"

"I brought you together to inform you that the Ministry of Justice has dropped all the charges against Weldon Krieg."

Hahn gasped, and Beck snapped out of his lethargy to stare at Leighton.

"They've ordered me to transport you three to Ulvaan to meet a shuttle to the GRC transport *Vast Expanse*. From there, you'll be free to go."

"Why Ulvaan?" Beck asked. "Why not here?"

"Because this is a MAC-M spaceport, and the GRC doesn't operate from here. They ordered me to take you to Ulvaan, so you're going to Ulvaan."

"When are we going?"

"After I get you settled in here, I'll arrange transportation and let you know. You'll have to take ground transportation, since the flight situation is so uncertain because of the weather."

"What do you mean, 'settled in here?'" Hahn asked.

"Now that you're not in formal custody anymore, the Ministry has to reimburse MAC-M for any costs related to your stay here. As a cost-saving measure, I'm housing the three of you here, together."

"You can't do that!"

Mitsui banged his crutches on the tent floor. "What the fuck?"

"I can," Leighton said. "In fact, Justice regulations say that I could house up to eight individuals in a tent this size. Would you like me to find five more to join you?"

"I'm not staying here," Beck said as he got to his feet. "This is ridiculous."

"Sit down, Mr. Beck. You're not a detainee, but until you climb aboard the shuttle in Ulvaan, you're still in my safekeeping. I've decided that this is the safest place for you, so you will stay here." Leighton looked at Hahn and Mitsui. "That goes for you two as well. The two gentlemen who escorted Mr. Beck here will ensure you remain here. For your own safety." He walked to the door. "Enjoy your reunion," Leighton said with a smirk.

"Any chance I can get some real clothes?" Beck asked. "Maybe some pants with an elastic waistband? I'm tired of my ass hanging out of this gown."

Leighton stared at him for a long second before he went outside. He couldn't help smiling as he trudged through the rain to the motor pool to check on space in the next convoy headed for Ulvaan. Leighton knew they'd file a complaint the first chance they got, but he didn't care. He'd do everything he could to make their remaining time under his control as miserable as possible.

I can't wait to hear what they're talking about.

* * * * *

Chapter Twenty-Four

"Good to see you again, Jerry. How are things on the flagship?" Boudreaux shook their hands as he greeted them. "Colonel, my pleasure. And you must be Major Sokolov. Good to meet you."

"Yes, sir, my privilege," Sokolov said.

Boudreaux's smile widened, and his eyes twinkled when he got to Fortis. "Captain Fortis, you magnificent bastard, get in here!" Boudreaux shook Fortis' hand and then pulled him in for a quick embrace and pat on the back.

Fortis' face reddened at the attention. "I'm happy to see you again, General." Before he could continue, Boudreaux turned to Ystremski.

"And you have to be Gunny Ystremski." Boudreaux gave him the same treatment he'd given Fortis. "I still owe Betty Kline a favor for you, and she doesn't miss a chance to remind me, either. The best damn favor I ever had to owe." He gestured to the chairs arrayed in front of his desk. "Sit down, please." The general looked at Cooper. "Sergeant, how about fixing these men up with some coffee?"

"Yes, sir." Cooper pulled the door shut behind him.

"While we're waiting for Cooper, Captain, tell me about your D-Day mission. I read the report, but I want to hear the no-shit story from you and Gunny Ystremski."

For the next ten minutes, Fortis and Ystremski recounted Tango 2/2's recon mission, from the drop on Island Ten to their rescue from the embassy roof. Boudreaux smiled when they described how they'd destroyed the jamming tower and the Maltaani weapons in the warehouses, and he laughed aloud and clapped when they talked about the nuke explosion at the spaceport.

"That's the goddamnedest thing I've ever heard," Boudreaux exclaimed as he slammed his hand on his desk. "Sheer brilliance. Saved the entire invasion."

Fortis finished with a summary of their casualties, and the general grew somber. "Hell of a price to pay," he said as he shook his head, "but you saved a lot of lives."

"We did our duty, sir," Fortis said.

"DINLI," Ystremski added.

"DINLI, indeed," Boudreaux said. Wagner, Anders, and Sokolov nodded.

Cooper had delivered coffee during their tale, and the general waved at the mugs. "Drink up before it gets cold, boys, and I'll tell you why I asked you to come here."

They did as they were told and waited for Boudreaux to begin.

"I'm not complaining. Every day in the Corps is a holiday, but a lot of things are moving in the wrong direction here on Maltaan, and it's turning into a shit sandwich," Boudreaux said. "Our mission is supposed to be to provide military assistance to stabilize the place and give the royalists a chance to get on their feet and reassert control. As it stands right now, the royalists don't seem interested in ever taking over."

"What about King Taalbin?" Wagner asked. "What's he doing?"

"Shit." Boudreaux sneered. "That boy is as useless as tits on a boar." He looked around the group. "Let me start at the beginning to get you all up to speed. I had my intel folks put together a timeline of everything that's happened since we got involved here so I can send it up the chain. Y'all know what went on before the embassy evacuation, so I'll start there.

"After we evacuated, the nationalists and royalists squared off and started killing each other. The royalists were holding their own until the nationalists assassinated Queen Aarfak and Foreign Minister Gafaard. Her youngest son, Taalbin, murdered his two older brothers and claimed the throne, which caused half the Grand Council to resign in protest, along with many of their senior military officers. The nationalists took that as a signal to attack, and they drove Taalbin and the remnants of his government into exile aboard the Maltaani fleet in orbit. The *only* Maltaani fleet, I might add. That's when we showed up and made a deal with him. They give us Menard-Kev and the helenium mines, and we defeat the nationalists and restore royalist control."

"What's Menard-Kev, sir?" Sokolov asked.

"It's a water planet way the hell out in the middle of nowhere," Boudreaux said. "We could've just taken it, but I guess the government was feeling generous. Anyway, we invaded, and the nationalists collapsed. The problem now is, King Taalbin's gotten comfortable on his flagship and doesn't want to return to the surface. It seems like he wants nothing to do with the place, which makes it damned hard to get anything done. Nobody wants to make decisions without royal approval, and he doesn't give a shit. So now, we're the de facto government."

"I should think that would simplify things for you, sir," Anders said. "You can get a lot more done without having to dance around the Maltaani government."

Boudreaux shook his head. "Simple isn't a word I'd use to describe this situation, Colonel. We're Space Marines, not civil engineers and urban planners. We're not trained or equipped to do everything this place needs. We can't perform the functions of the government when our alleged royalist allies seem to work against us.

"For example, we processed every Maltaani nationalist soldier we captured, trying to weed out the real bad guys. We interviewed them, photographed them, and issued them official government ID cards. Royalists monitored the process to vet out high-ranking officers and other leadership, and when we finished, we shipped them all back east. You want to know how many officers we found among the thousands of prisoners we took?"

Nobody responded.

"Two. We found two officers, a colonel and a lieutenant. Now, I might be just a simple boy from the backwoods and bayous, but I know you can't run an entire army with one colonel and one lieutenant. We investigated and determined that our royalist allies fucked us. We trusted them to identify the officers, and they passed them through.

"Now all those soldiers are back east with their leadership intact, including the head general named Staaber. We've received reporting that they're organizing again, and the insurgency is building momentum. It's shaping up into the same them-versus-us we were in before the war started. There are a lot of pissed off Maltaani in the east, and it's a wonder they haven't started an open rebellion again."

"What's got them so angry, sir?" Sokolov asked.

"For starters, we're here, and their government isn't. Enter the GRC. Our government gave the GRC full control of the helenium mines, and they don't plan to hire the Maltaani miners who just got home from the war. Instead, they're going to use the same test tubes they sold to the Maltaani before the invasion. The GRC convinced our government that Space Marines should round the damn things up for them, too. They have the east-west highway jammed with test tubes so bad that we can't get supply trucks through."

"What about the railway, sir?" Wagner asked.

"That's another debacle. The train makes a round trip from Daarben to Ulvaan over two days and undergoes maintenance on the third. We have to take good care of it, because we only have twelve cars and two engines to pull them."

"Why so few?"

"Some overzealous sonofabitch called down a Black Hole strike on the rail yard in Ulvaan and destroyed all the rolling stock, except what we captured on this end. Nobody here can manufacture replacements, and it's gonna be a couple months before we get some built and sent from Terra Earth."

"Fuck," Ystremski said with a grunt.

"Fuck is right, Gunny, and it gets worse. Crops from the last growing season rotted in the fields because the nationalists ran the royalist farmers off, so there's no food to send east. That's another reason they're pissed off. We've set up soup kitchens to feed them, but I'm having trouble getting enough supplies through to keep our own troops fed, because the rainy season keeps our aviation forces grounded. I might have to redeploy those troops back here, at least until the rainy season ends.

"In summary, their feelings are hurt, their bellies are empty, and there's no work to keep them occupied. And now they have a leader to organize them."

"What can we do, General?" Anders asked.

"That's what we're here to talk about, Nils. Remember I mentioned the Maltaani general, Staaber?"

"I do, sir," Anders said. "In fact, I remember when General Staaber came to the embassy."

"Should have shot the bastard then and saved us a lot of trouble," Boudreaux replied. He leaned forward and lowered his voice. "What I'm about to tell you cannot leave this room." The general's eyes flicked from face to face before he continued. "We have a source who's close to Staaber. I don't know who it is or how reliable he is, but our spooks swear he's solid. The word I got was that the insurgency was almost nonexistent until Staaber showed up. Now it's alive and growing, and we have to snuff this thing out, and fast. We want Staaber dead."

Fortis knew the UNT had outlawed assassinations a long time ago. Anders shifted in his seat.

"Does that bother you, Colonel?"

"The UNT Human Rights Charter prohibits assassination," Anders said.

"The Maltaani aren't human," Fortis said.

"They're not humane, either," Ystremski added.

"How does that make a difference?" Anders asked. "We can do whatever we want to the Maltaani because they're not human? They're pretty damn close, if I read the Inter-Species Congress report correctly."

"Sir, have you ever seen what they do to prisoners?" Ystremski asked. "They're animals."

"I was on the street next to Admiral Kinshaw when the Maltaani murdered him," Anders retorted. "I know what they're capable of."

Boudreaux raised his hands. "Gentlemen, please. Colonel, I acknowledge your objections. If your conscience won't allow you to be a part of this mission, you're free to go. All I ask is that you keep it confidential."

"Sir, my only concern is that our civilian leadership has sanctioned this at some level. I mean no offense to you or your authority, but military history is replete with good ideas gone wrong because the right people weren't involved in the decision making."

Boudreaux nodded. "Colonel, I promise you—I promise all of you—that people at a much higher level than anyone in this room made this decision. Elected officials, not political appointees."

"Roger that, sir. Thank you."

"The concept of the operation is straightforward. Staaber moves a lot, so we won't have a lot of lead time to set up a hit. Therefore, I want Captain Fortis' team ready to go at a moment's notice, day or night. When we get tipped to Staaber's location, we'll pass it on to Major Sokolov, and also to you, Jerry. While the team is spinning up, I want your cell to do whatever you can to confirm the information.

"Captain Fortis, this is going to involve a lot of improvised action for your team. You're here because you think on your feet, and I like what I've seen from your operations so far. You'll have as much external support as we can give you. I'll have a Black Hole bird dedicated to your team, and drone support, too, if the weather cooperates."

"General, how will we recognize Staaber?" Fortis asked. "I've been dealing with the Maltaani as long as anybody, and I also saw the general at the embassy, but I haven't learned a reliable way to tell them apart. Is he still wearing a uniform?"

"I doubt it, but he carries a sword. It's a family heirloom, and our source saw him wearing it on the streets of Ulvaan. If you surveil a target location and see a Maltaani wearing a sword, hit him."

"What do we tell the rest of the team, sir?" Sokolov asked.

"Tell them as much as you have to. How much, I'll leave up to you. The fewer people who know what we're up to, the better, but it's their ass, too. Anybody have any more questions?" Nobody spoke up. "That's all I have for you. Jerry, if you and Colonel Anders would stick around for a minute. The rest of you, thanks for coming."

Sokolov, Fortis, and Ystremski waited next to Cooper's desk.

"Any word on flight ops?" Ystremski asked the sergeant.

"No change, Gunny. It's still clear here, but the weather has the spaceport socked in. You ought to go outside and enjoy some fresh air you don't have to swallow before it starts up again."

"Yeah, I need to look into the ground transportation situation. Where's the motor pool?"

"Out the door, turn left. Second hut on the left."

"Thanks." Ystremski looked at Sokolov. "Hey, Major, I'm going to see about our ride back to the spaceport."

Ystremski left in search of the motor pool.

"Captain Fortis, you commanded Tango Company on D-Day, didn't you?" Cooper asked.

"I had Tango. Why?"

"I had a bro in Tango. Seamus O'Reilly. We went to boot camp together."

"Corporal O'Reilly? Big kid, red hair?"

"Always talked about getting laid. That's him."

Fortis laughed. "That was O'Reilly."

Cooper's face grew somber. "How did he get it, sir?"

Fortis had faced Cooper's question many times, but it never failed to catch him by surprise. It embarrassed him that he couldn't recall how O'Reilly had died.

"He died when we blew the nuke at the spaceport," Fortis lied. "We couldn't get far enough away."

"Damn. Hell of a way to die."

"DINLI."

"Yes, sir. DINLI."

* * * * *

Chapter Twenty-Five

When Ystremski returned from the motor pool, he had a large package under one arm.

"The sergeant at the motor pool told me to have Cooper call him when we're ready to go," he told Sokolov and Fortis. "He's got a two-mech convoy ready to roll."

"What's in the box?" Sokolov asked. "Did you do some early Christmas shopping while you were gone?"

"No, sir. I stopped at the supply tent and asked about Bender's new boots. Since we're assigned to MAC-M and not a division, I figured supply would route anything we ordered through here, and then lose it, too. I was right. The logistics folks here didn't even know who we were, so I educated them."

Just then, Wagner and Anders emerged from Boudreaux's office. Ystremski nodded to Cooper, and the sergeant called for their convoy.

They made the ride back to the spaceport in silence. Fortis spent the time searching his memory for anything about Corporal O'Reilly and how he died. He didn't know why it bothered him so much that he couldn't remember, but it did.

Red greeted them when they got back to the hangar.

"Good news, Mr. Wagner. The air boss has authorized shuttle flights. Winds are straight down the runway, so the shuttle pilots can pull their nose up and head for space. It's still too turbulent for hovercopters, though."

"Thanks, Red." Wagner turned to Sokolov. "Are you guys all right to get back to Zulu-Five?"

"Yes, sir, we're good. We just need a weather window."

"Okay, then, we'll get going back to *Mammoth*. I've got some additional tasking from the general that I'll send to you after we get our end sorted out."

After a round of handshakes and well wishes while they waited on the shuttle, Wagner and Anders waved goodbye, climbed aboard the craft, and roared into the air.

"Varney, stow this in the bird," Ystremski said as he handed the package to the sergeant. "Don't lose it. Bender's new boots are in there." He turned to Fortis. "Hey, Captain, why don't you come with me to the motor pool and see if we can catch a ride to Ulvaan? I might need some captain's bars to throw a little weight around."

Fortis looked at Sokolov, who shrugged.

The two men leaned into the wind-driven rain as they trudged to the motor pool.

"Are you okay, sir?" Ystremski asked.

"Yeah, why?"

"I dunno. You seem preoccupied."

"Eh, I'm just thinking about Corporal O'Reilly."

"What about him?"

"I can't remember how he died. He was with us on the street by the spaceport, and then... nothing."

Ystremski stopped and stared at Fortis. "You're not cracking up on me, are you?"

"What? No. I can't remember, that's all."

"You can't remember because a house landed on your head when the nuke went off," the gunny said. "We found him under the rubble after the blast buried you across the street."

"Are you sure?"

"I'm not in the habit of lying to you, sir. C'mon, let's get moving."

"Damn, I thought I was lying when I told Cooper that he died in the nuke blast. I must be losing my mind," Fortis said as he followed Ystremski.

"Just your memory." Ystremski pointed to a large sign that read "Motor Pool." "Here we are."

The sergeant behind the desk was apologetic when the gunny inquired about east-bound convoys. "I have nothing moving that way, Gunny. The GRC took over the highway to move test tubes, and we can't get anything through except in an emergency." He nodded to Fortis. "Begging the captain's pardon, but you don't look like an emergency."

"There's gonna be an emergency if I have to sit here and stare at the rain for much longer," Ystremski said.

Fortis laughed. "Thanks, Sergeant." He patted Ystremski on the back. "C'mon, Gunny. Let's go wait for a break in the weather."

"Hey, Captain, have you heard about the train?" the sergeant asked.

Fortis and Ystremski exchanged glances. "No, what about it?"

"It runs between here and Ulvaan a couple times a week. It's not as fast as flying, and you'd have to find your own way from Ulvaan, but if you're in a hurry, that might be your answer."

"Which way to the train office?"

"Right next door, sir. The Transportation Office controls the train and the motor pool."

They thanked him and went next door.

"Next eastbound train is in three days, sir," the Transportation duty officer told them. "It went east this morning, and it won't be back until tomorrow night. Then we do maintenance for a day before we send it out again. Sorry."

"This fucking rain better clear up," Ystremski grumbled as they walked back through the rain. "I'm not waiting three days for the train."

Ystremski stopped Fortis as they walked back to join the others.

"What are you going to tell the rest of the team about our mission?"

"Everything. Like the general said, it's their asses, too."

The gunny nodded. "Good."

When they got back to the hangar, Sokolov shook his head at the news about ground transportation.

"Red, fix the weather," he said.

"Yes, sir, I'll get right on it," the pilot responded with a smile.

"Let's go find some chow," Sokolov told the group. "Then we'll check the weather and start thinking about somewhere to bed down for the night."

* * *

"What's the story with you two?" Beck asked Hahn and Mitsui after Leighton left the tent.

"No story," Hahn said. "The Space Marines captured us, and Leighton interrogated us. Then he put us in here. What happened to your arm?"

"After you two left the cave, I—" Hahn stopped him with a finger over her lips and then pointed to the ceiling. Beck nodded and cleared his throat. "I went down the mountain to find some food and got lost in the forest. I fell out of a tree and almost got eaten by a giant fucking snake before I got back to the cave. That's where the Space Marines found me. How's your leg?" he asked Mitsui.

"Sore as hell, but I'm getting around better. I'm not a fan of the Space Marines, but their doctors did a good job fixing me up."

"I wish I could say the same," Beck replied. "The doc says I need surgery to repair some damage to my shoulder, but the nearest surgeon is on a hospital ship in orbit. Leighton wouldn't let me go for surgery unless I cooperated with him. Now, I guess I'll have surgery back on Terra Earth. Prick."

"Geez," Hahn said. "I'm sorry to hear that, boss."

Beck snorted. "'Boss?' What world are you living in, Ms. Hahn? I'm not your boss anymore. I'll be lucky to have a job after the last couple months on this miserable rock."

"Oh, please, Mr. Beck. Why would the GRC let you go?" Hahn gave him an exaggerated wink. "You did nothing wrong. None of us did. How can they hold us responsible for what the Maltaani did?"

"All this talkin' is making my leg hurt," Mitsui said as he stood up. "I'm gonna lay down."

"I'll join you." Hahn took his arm and guided him to their bed behind the screens.

"Before you go, can you help me out with this thing?" Beck asked and pointed to the folding cot. "I don't know if I can set the cot up one-handed."

Hahn set up the cot as far away from her bed as possible and unfolded a spare blanket. "I hope you're comfortable, because that's all we have."

The cot was far less comfortable than the hospital bed he'd just left, but Beck found a position that minimized his discomfort. Fatigue tugged at his eyelids even though it was the middle of the afternoon, and he'd drifted when Leighton returned.

"Sorry to bother you," the agent said in a loud voice. "Hahn, Mitsui, can you hear me?"

"We can hear you."

"Good. I've arranged passage on the next train bound for Ulvaan," he said.

"When is that?" Beck asked.

"Three days."

"Three days? Are you serious?"

"I can't control the weather, Ms. Hahn. There are no flights, and your fellow GRC employees have jammed the road with PCS headed for the mines. That leaves the train, which only runs twice a week."

"What are we supposed to do for three days?" Beck asked.

"The same thing you've been doing," Leighton said. "Nothing." He held up a box. "There's an additional condition to your, eh, stay here with us."

"What's that?"

"It's an ankle monitor, Mr. Beck. The Ministry of Justice can't afford to lose one of you, so we've decided that each of you will wear one of these until you board the shuttle in Ulvaan."

"Bull*shit*!" Mitsui announced from behind the screen. "I'm not wearing a fucking tracking device. We're not inmates or safari animals."

"It's for your own safety," Leighton said as he pulled back the blankets from Beck's feet and slipped the monitor around his leg. "It's painless and non-intrusive. If you don't believe me, ask Mr. Beck."

"I'm not doing it," Mitsui said.

"That's up to you, Mr. Mitsui." Beck watched Leighton walk around the screen to Hahn and Mitsui's bed. "If you won't wear this, I'll have you shackled to your bed for the next three days. Either way is fine with me."

He emerged a few seconds later. "Thank you for your cooperation," Leighton threw over his shoulder as he went out the door.

* * *

When they got to the chow hall, Fortis bumped into another Space Marine. He mumbled his apology before he recognized the other man.

"Chug!"

"Fortis!"

Wilhelm "Chug-A-Lug" Vogel was a classmate of Fortis' from Officer Basic and Advanced Infantry School. Chug had earned his nickname because he encouraged struggling classmates by shouting, "Keep on chugging!" in his thick German accent. He also drank prodigious amounts of beer on the rare occasions the staff granted them liberty. Chug was the younger brother of Captain Stefan Vogel, Fortis' commanding officer when he served with Lima Company.

The two Space Marines laughed and bro-hugged.

"What are you doing here?" Fortis asked. "I thought 4th Division was back east?"

"*Ja*, we are. They assigned my company to search for a fugitive in the mountains by the railway."

"Did you find him?"

Chugs nodded. "We did. He was hiding in a cave." Chugs looked around and lowered his voice. "That's not all we found. We found bones."

"You found bones? I don't understand." Fortis half-smiled, expecting a punch line.

"Bones. You know, a skeleton. A *big* skeleton."

"Maltaani?"

"No, no, not Maltaani. Bigger. Four meters tall, at least."

"Wow!" The news surprised Fortis. "If it wasn't Maltaani, what was it?"

His friend shrugged. "I don't know. It wasn't human or Maltaani, that's for sure. My platoon brought it here and gave it to some doctors from *Mammoth*. Now we are stuck by the damned rain. Why are you here? How did you make captain already?"

Fortis gave him a self-conscious grin. "These bars aren't real. 2nd Division needed an officer to command a recon company for the invasion, so I got brevetted to captain. My CO is here for a meeting at MAC-M headquarters, so he brought me to hold his horse. Now we're stuck, too."

Fortis looked and saw Sokolov and Ystremski waiting.

"Hey, Chug, it's been great to see you, but the major is waiting for me. DINLI, and tell your brother I said hello."

"*Ja*, DINLI. Keep on chugging."

Fortis laughed and rejoined the major and gunny.

"Sorry about that, sir. That was one of my classmates from Officer Basic. He's with 4th Division."

Sokolov nodded. "If you're finished greeting your adoring fans, I'm starving. Let's eat."

The food was typical chow hall fare: 3-D printed meat and vegetables served on battered aluminum trays.

"This looks delicious," Johnson said with a heavy dose of sarcasm. "Way better than the food in camp."

Red speared a piece of meat and held it up. "It beats the hell out of rehydrated ham and limas, but I'll never understand how they get everything to look and taste the same. Don't they pack the ingredients to give it color and flavor?"

"It could be worse," Ystremski said with a grin.

"It could be raining," they all said in unison and broke into uproarious laughter.

* * * * *

Chapter Twenty-Six

After chow, Sokolov led the group through the light rain back to the hangar, where Fender 454 waited.

"Major, we're going to stop in the weather office and see if there's any change in the forecast," Red said. "It feels like things have improved since this morning."

"Roger that, Red. We'll be with the bird."

When they got to the hangar, they discovered two canvas-covered pallets waiting beside the hovercopter.

"What's all that stuff?" the major asked.

"Stuff for the camp, I guess," Varney said. He pulled the canvas off and read the labels. "Pig squares, canned rations, and two boxes of boots."

"Boots?"

"Size 14 boots," Ystremski said. "Twenty pairs, ten per box. I guess they decided Bender needed a few new pairs."

"Take that shit back to the supply office," the major said.

Red and Johnson ran into the hangar.

"What the hell's all that?" Red asked as the pilots scrambled into the hovercopter.

"Camp supplies," Varney said. "What's going on?"

"Open the hangar door and get that crap loaded. We've got a launch window, and it's first come, first served."

The group scrambled to load the supplies while Red and Johnson went through the pre-flight checklist, and Varney shoved the hangar door open. Ystremski left the two boxes of boots beside the door.

"We're not taking that bullshit with us," he said, and nobody argued.

They were still strapping down the cargo when Varney flagged down the ground crew with their yellow gear to tow Fender 454 to the launch spot. They finished as Varney scrambled aboard, and everyone secured their harnesses as the engines wound up.

"*We're cleared for takeoff,*" Red announced over the intercom. In seconds, the hovercopter was climbing through the cloud cover on the way to refuel at Romeo-Nine for the last leg home.

* * *

Staaber stood atop a tall hill during a rare break in the rain and evaluated his location as the site to ambush the train. The tracks climbed for five kilometers before they made a sharp turn and began the descent down the other side. The train would slow as it climbed the hill and approached the curve, and the slower speed would simplify timing the blast that would start the attack. There was suitable cover on both sides of the tracks for the shooters, and the spot was far enough from Ulvaan that no one would hear the attack.

The plan was identical to the one they'd used on the truck convoy. A large IED would derail the engines, while concealed gunmen would engage the human crew and passengers. Once they dealt with the humans, his men would steal as much of the cargo as they could and fire the rest. Their priority would be weapons and ammunition, followed by food.

The humans relied on the train to resupply their troops in the east since the rainy season started. Staaber considered ripping up the tracks, but any damage they did could be readily repaired. The humans only had two engines they used in tandem, and he believed if he destroyed them, he'd force the humans to use the road. Shifting to the road would interfere with transferring the clones to the eastern mines. Truck convoys would be both less efficient and more vulnerable to attack; a single shooter in the forest could disable a truck and force convoy security to react, which would slow them down. It might even force the humans to withdraw their forces from the east until they could resume their regular flight schedule. In any case, it would complicate their operations in the east.

After careful consideration, Staaber ordered all Maltaani in the Ulvaan area to stop interacting with the humans.

"General, there's no food," Raabik had protested. "Who will feed the people? Many of them rely on the humans for food since the crops failed."

"The people will do as they've always done in lean times," Staaber said. "They'll tighten their belts."

"But won't they be angry with us?"

Staaber had poked Raabik in the chest with his finger. "The humans are robbing them of their dignity with every mouthful," he hissed. "The people are trading their souls for a few scraps of food. The humans feed them like farm animals."

"We *have* to eat. If there's no food, how will we live?"

Staaber had then questioned Raabik's dedication to their cause, and his lieutenant could only hang his head in response. The general knew his personal zeal for the fight was unmatched, and it disturbed him to see his people grovel at the feet of the humans and their royalist lackeys.

Until he was certain his followers were trustworthy, Staaber had decided to keep the details of impending operations to himself. He regretted that he couldn't share his plan with his fellow insurgents, but the Space Marines' presence at the spaceport the night his cell attacked was too much of a coincidence, and he suspected news of their plan had somehow gotten to the humans. Raabik was of particular concern because his family traded with the humans.

His bomb maker only knew that Staaber required a much larger blast this time, and Staaber had intimated that they'd use it against a human mech. The shooters had been gathering in the forest daily to practice marksmanship. On the day of the rail attack, they'd assemble as usual, but instead of shooting practice, they'd travel to the ambush site.

After another look around, he turned and began the long walk back to his family mansion, which had become the headquarters of the insurgency.

* * *

It was dark when Red set Fender 454 down with a gentle bump, and the engines wound down as the Space Marines climbed out. Fortis stretched, glad to be free of the cramped hovercopter cabin, despite the light rain that fell on him.

"Let's get this thing unloaded and go get some of that good Zulu-Five chow," Sokolov said.

The six of them had the hovercopter unloaded in minutes, and several other Space Marines showed up to move it from the landing pad to the logistics hut. Ystremski tucked Bender's new boots under his arm and went in search of the hulking Australian.

The atmosphere in the chow hall was subdued, and when they got in line, Fortis saw they had standard chow hall food instead of the delectable Maltaani dishes they'd been eating.

"What's this?" Sokolov asked the server.

"Sorry, Major. The mama sans stopped delivering. The supply sergeant went up to the village to find them, but they wouldn't talk to him. So now it's normal rations until we run out, and then pig squares until the next supply hit."

"Damn."

Ystremski joined them a few minutes later.

"Bender and Woody were having a little siesta in the bunk room," he said with a wink. "Now he's breaking his new boots in. What's with the chow?"

Sokolov repeated what he'd been told, and Ystremski shook his head. "We need to get our hands on some recipes. How hard can it be to shoot rats in the trees?"

After chow, Red, Johnson, and Varney headed for the hangar, while Fortis and the rest of the team went in search of Bender and Woody. They found the pair hard at work swabbing the already-gleaming deck of their bunkroom.

"Welcome back," Bender said. "Have fun in Daarben?"

"Yeah, it was a blast. Maybe you can go next time."

"I'd rather stay here and dance with a swab, thanks." He pointed to Fortis' captain's bars. "You're still a captain, so they couldn't have been that mad about that colonel."

"It never even came up," Fortis said. He looked at Ystremski. "In thirty minutes, I want everyone to muster in Fender 454. Time for a team pow-wow."

"We're fucked, mate," Bender said to Woody.

An hour later, Fortis finished briefing the team on their new tasking.

"That's our tasking? To kill this bastard general?" Woody asked.

"Yes, but it's more complicated than sniping an officer on the battlefield. Staaber is a civilian, and targeted assassination is illegal."

"So, if he died in an airstrike on a suspected insurgent position, that's okay, but if we hunt him down, it's not?" Woody said.

"I can't explain it any better than I already did," Fortis said. "If we get a shot at him, we'll take it. You just need to understand that some armchair warrior somewhere with a law degree might cause a fuss if it gets out that we targeted Staaber personally."

"Kill 'em all. Problem solved," Bender said.

Fortis chuckled. "That's one way to handle it."

* * *

The next morning, General Boudreaux was at his desk reviewing a report about the ambush of a PCS convoy when Sergeant Cooper knocked on the door and poked his head in.

"Excuse me, General? Doctor Longfellow is here to see you."

"Good morning, General. Thank you for making time to see me," the doctor said as she approached. They shook, and the general waved her into a chair.

"I always have time for the Medical Corps." Boudreaux smiled. "What can I do for you?"

"It's the most extraordinary thing," Longfellow said as she dug a data stick out of her pocket. "Could you bring up the image on this, please?"

Boudreaux did as she asked, and a holo of a skeleton appeared over his desk. To the general's untrained eye, it looked human, except for the skull. He leaned in and examined the bulbous skull and rows of fangs in place of teeth.

"What the hell is this, Doc?"

"We don't know, sir. Advance the holo, please."

Another skeleton appeared. This one had a normal human skull, but it was one third the size of the first.

"That's a nominal two-meter human skeleton for size comparison," Longfellow said.

"That son of a bitch is five meters tall!"

The doctor cleared her throat, and Boudreaux's cheeks flushed.

"Pardon my language, Doctor, but that's incredible. Where did this come from?"

"Space Marines discovered it two days ago in a cave along the railway, General."

"This is a real creature?"

"To the best of my knowledge, yes. I'm not a forensic anthropologist or paleontologist, but I believe it is. I searched every database available on the flagship and found nothing close. It's like nothing seen before on Terra Earth. It's a new species."

"I appreciate you showing me this, Doctor. We never know what we're going to encounter on strange planets."

"General, one more thing. Before I ship these off to Terra Earth to collect dust in a museum somewhere, I'd like to send these holos to the Interspecies Scientific Congress. The Maltaani scientists there may have some information or research experience with this creature that'll aid our understanding."

"Be my guest, Doc. You don't need my permission for that."

"This is still a war zone, which means we can't disseminate information without authorization," Longfellow said.

"I appreciate your adherence to the regulations. I wish more people observed them with the same diligence. Please, be my guest to send whatever information you like about those fossils to anyone you choose."

"General, they're not fossils. They're bones. We can't date them until we get them back to Terra Earth, but they don't appear to be all that old."

"This thing could have a brother wandering around in the mountains?"

"It could have an entire tribe out there somewhere, or it might be the last of its kind. We don't know."

"Hmm. I haven't seen any reports of encounters with a monster like this, so maybe they're extinct. Go ahead and confirm with the Maltaani, and keep me posted, Doctor."

"Thank you, sir."

After he showed the doctor out, Boudreaux went back to the ambush report. He read through it twice more before he picked up his communicator and called Colonel Gunn.

"Hey, Gunner, did you see this ambush report from the GRC?"

"Yes, sir, I did."

"What do you make of it?"

"It looks like a well-executed op, sir. They destroyed both escort vehicles and killed all the truck drivers, too. I guess somebody doesn't want the test tubes to reach the mines."

"You notice anything strange about it?"

"I'm curious why they allowed a bunch of the test tubes to escape into the mountains."

"Yeah, that's what I saw, too. Why would someone ambush the convoy to stop the test tubes from getting to the mines, and then let them run off? Why not shoot them, too?"

"I don't know, sir. Saving ammo?"

"Huh. Well, the GRC has requested help in rounding up the test tubes, and they want us to provide convoy security, too. We already have the job of collecting the clones. The damn things are a menace when they run wild like that. I won't commit resources to riding shotgun on their convoys. They've got plenty of mercenaries who can do their trigger pulling for them."

"I agree, General."

"I think it would be a good idea if we assigned some Space Marines to the train, though. Just in case."

"Do you have a particular company in mind, sir?"

"No, not a company. There'd be no room for supplies. A platoon can cover it."

"I'll make it happen, sir."

"All right, Gunner, that's all I have. DINLI."

"DINLI."

* * * * *

Chapter Twenty-Seven

Two days later, Jerry Wagner entered the 2nd Division intelligence suite and found Colonel Anders seated at a holograph terminal.

"Any news on Staaber?"

"No, no updates. We haven't heard from our source for almost twenty-four hours now."

"Is Team Three ready to go?"

"Yes. I talked to Sokolov again this morning, and he confirmed they were standing by at Zulu-Five, ready to deploy as needed."

"Good. Here's hoping we can get this done clean and quiet."

"If anyone can do it, Fortis can," Anders said.

"Nils, did you see the report about the GRC convoy that was ambushed outside Ulvaan?" Wagner asked.

Anders shook his head. "No, sir. When did it come in?"

"It's dated yesterday. We weren't on the original distro list, but General Boudreaux forwarded it to me this morning."

"Anything interesting?"

"The circumstances were unusual. Unknown gunmen attacked a convoy of PCS with explosives and firearms, killed all the mercenaries, and turned the PCS loose."

"What did they take?"

"Nothing. That's what's strange. The convoy carried PCS only."

"Any theories on who did it?"

"The obvious choice is Maltaani insurgents intent on stopping the PCS from arriving at the mines, but they released the PCS instead of shooting them. The general thinks it might have been a Maltaani criminal gang looking to loot a supply convoy, and they hit the wrong one."

"That might explain why they let the PCS go free."

"That's a definite possibility. MAC-M has directed that from here forward, Space Marines will provide security for all trains."

"Jerry, did you read the press release from the Ministry of Justice? They've dropped all charges against Weldon Krieg."

"I haven't read it yet. Any surprises?"

"It's about what we expected. The Ministry of Justice dropped the charges, and he walked, along with all his subordinates."

"You're not suggesting there were external pressures applied to the solicitor general, are you?" Wagner said with a wry smile.

Anders shrugged. "The GRC's never been shy about using political influence to achieve their goals, but I doubt they had to use much to change the solicitor general's mind. The treason charge would never stick, anyway. Not against a GRC executive with Krieg's connections. I think the treason charge was a knee-jerk reaction to the discovery of two hundred thousand PCS under nationalist control."

"I'm sure you're right. The news made a lot of people angry."

"I don't blame them. The sale might not have been illegal, but it stank."

"Things would be different if the PCS had played a significant role in the invasion. As it stands, some in the Grand Council are calling for the breakup of the conglomerate."

"Interesting times we live in, Jerry."

"That's our curse."

* * *

Sergeant Phineas Letterkenny laughed so hard that tears leaked down his cheeks as he watched his platoon commander, Lieutenant Vogel, stumble and almost fall. The officer kept his feet and completed his lap around the hangar, but not before the flame from the burning toilet paper clenched between Vogel's ass cheeks scorched the hair from the back of his leg. The rest of the platoon cheered when Vogel crossed the finish line and slapped at the flame.

"Is this Charlie Company?"

Letterkenny turned around and saw a female captain in starched utilities surveying the scene with undisguised disgust.

"Uh, yes ma'am, 1st Platoon, Charlie Company. That's us."

"Which one of you animals is Lieutenant Vogel?"

"Lieutenant Vogel is… well… the ass… uh, let me get him for you, ma'am."

Letterkenny waded through the Space Marines crowded around Vogel and said something in the lieutenant's ear. Vogel's eyebrows shot up, and he struggled to pull up his trousers.

"DFA is over!" Letterkenny shouted. The platoon protested until he gestured to the captain standing by the door.

"Lieutenant Vogel, reporting," Vogel said when he approached the captain, whose nametape read Miller.

"What do you think you're doing, Lieutenant?" Miller demanded.

English wasn't Vogel's first language, which meant that sometimes he misunderstood the context of what people said. Like now.

"The Dance of the Flaming Asshole," Vogel replied.

Miller scowled. "I can see that, Vogel. What makes you think this is the time and place for horseplay like that?"

"My apologies, ma'am. We have been stuck here for days because of the rain."

Miller thrust an envelope into his chest. "Not anymore. You have orders."

"*Ya?*" Vogel fumbled to tear it open.

"Report to the Transportation Office on the double."

"Yes, ma'am."

"And Vogel, for God's sake, button up your trousers."

When she was gone, Letterkenny walked up to Vogel. "Trouble, sir?"

"No. A mission." The lieutenant tore open the envelope, read the document inside, and passed it to Letterkenny. After Letterkenny read it, he handed it back.

"You want me to tell the men, sir?"

"*Ya*, do that."

"Listen up, 1st Platoon. You've got five minutes to gear up. We're going on a train ride."

* * *

Leighton entered the tent without knocking. Beck sat on his cot, Mitsui sat next to him, and Hahn stood at the sink.

"Get your things," Leighton said without introduction. "The train is leaving in thirty minutes, and we'll be on it."

"We?" Beck asked.

"I'm riding with you to Ulvaan," the agent replied.

"Wonderful." Beck's voice was heavy with sarcasm. He stood up. "Okay, I've got all my things. Let's go."

Mitsui snickered and stood up next to Beck. "Cut this damn anklet off, and I'll be ready to ride, too."

"Nothing doing," Leighton said. "Anklets stay on until just before you get on the shuttle."

Hahn joined Beck and Mitsui. "I guess I'm ready to go, too." She looked around the tent. "I'm gonna miss this place. Especially the microphones."

Leighton reddened, and he gestured toward the door. "Enough chitchat."

The trio followed Leighton outside. A soft rain was falling, but they didn't object. After three days trapped in the tent together, Leighton figured they would've walked through a hurricane to get off Maltaan. He hadn't arranged ground transportation to the train to penalize them for the failure of his eavesdropping plans. Despite Beck's accusation that Leighton was listening in on Mitsui and Hahn, the agent was desperate to capture an unguarded comment that would be enough to get the criminal charges reinstated. For three days, they'd talked about everything and anything but their case. Hahn's remark confirmed Leighton's suspicion that they avoided the topic on purpose, which only intensified his loathing for them.

When they reached the train station, Leighton made them wait outside while he checked in. He came out and pointed to the waiting train.

"The passenger car is the first car behind the engines."

While they helped Mitsui aboard, Leighton saw several Space Marines seated throughout the car. He nodded to a lieutenant as he slid into the seat across from him.

"I'm Lieutenant Vogel," the officer said. "My platoon has been ordered to secure the train."

"Great. I'm Supervisory Agent Leighton, Ministry of Justice. I'm escorting dangerous prisoners to the spaceport in Ulvaan."

Vogel looked at the rain-soaked trio huddled together in the back of the car. "They're dangerous?"

"They caused this entire war," Leighton said in a low voice.

"Huh. Well, if there's any trouble, I have men in both engines, and the cars, too."

"Okay."

Leighton leaned against the window and closed his eyes, hoping the Space Marine would take the hint and leave him alone. The train lurched into motion, and it didn't take him long to fall asleep to the comforting *click-clack* of the wheels as the train sped east.

* * *

Staaber moved his troops into their ambush positions piecemeal, and it surprised and excited each group to discover the others. As veterans of the attack on the trucks, they knew what was required of them without being told, and they explained their role to the few new members of their band.

The idea of attacking the train excited them. The iron behemoth was a symbol of royalist power, and they laughed with nervous excitement as the afternoon wore on and the ambush drew closer. They knew the train arrived in Ulvaan in the evening, so they knew the attack would come soon.

Wind-driven rain slashed the forest, and Staaber took it as a good omen. If the humans on the train sent a distress call, the weather would prevent air support from responding, either to attack his men, or deliver more troops.

"General, all is ready," Raabik reported.

"Very well."

Raabik appeared as surprised as the rest of the shooters when they arrived at the ambush site and discovered they weren't in the forest for marksmanship training. Staaber had observed him but had seen no sign that his exclusion from the ambush plan had disturbed the other Maltaani.

"This is a bold move, General."

"Our success depends on boldness," Staaber replied. "The humans and their royalist dogs are confident in their material and technological superiority. That confidence makes them careless, and the best way we can take advantage of that is to strike hard where they're most vulnerable."

Raabik nodded, but Staaber knew he'd wasted the words on the miner. Raabik had no formal education, and little experience outside the mines, so any discussion beyond the basics was beyond his comprehension.

Off in the distance, a train whistle wailed.

* * *

"Did you see that?"

The excited shout jerked Leighton from his slumber, and he sat up, disoriented. The Space Marines gathered at the windows on the right side of the car, along with Beck, Mitsui, and Hahn.

"That big bastard was close enough to touch," one of the Space Marines said.

"What was it?" Leighton asked.

"An elephant," the Space Marine replied. "That's what they call those six-legged animals running around out here. I have a bro in 3rd Division who told me he heard a guy in another company got pulped by one when it ran into his mech and flipped it."

"There's an authoritative source for you," Beck said.

The Space Marines laughed at the expression on their friend's face, and the red-faced Space Marine stood up and walked back to Beck's seat.

"What did you say?"

"Nothing," the GRC executive said. "I pointed out that there's no more reliable source of information than the rumor mill."

"Are you calling me a liar?"

"No, not at all. I have no reason to."

"Gibson, lock it up," Letterkenny called from the front of the car.

Gibson, the offended Space Marine, glared at Beck for a second before he rejoined his companions at the windows. Now that they'd seen one Maltaani elephant, they were eager to see more.

Mitsui leaned forward and put his face close to Beck's ear. "You might not want to pick fights with Space Marines, pardner. At least not until you get your arm healed up."

"Bah. Those guys are all talk. I'm surprised he realized I was mocking him. The average Space Marine is no more intelligent than—"

Boom!

Razor-sharp shards of glass sprayed the car as the right-side windows blew in. The force of the blast hurled everyone across the car and rocked it over on its side. Glass shredded the Space Marines, and their torn and bloodied bodies flew across the car and piled up on the far side.

Beck and Mitsui screamed in unison when the trio of GRC executives landed in an unceremonious jumble of bodies. Beck fell on his injured shoulder, and agony exploded throughout his body. Mitsui's injured leg tangled in the bench he'd been sitting on and bent behind him. Blood streamed from a deep gash on Hahn's forehead and added a coppery tang and horrifying slickness to the scene. Their individual struggles to free themselves only increased the misery of the others, and they wriggled and wrestled until automatic weapons fire tore into the car.

* * * * *

Chapter Twenty-Eight

The explosion toppled the two engines and killed the crew members inside. The passenger car tipped halfway over, twisted by the engines in front, but was kept standing by the boxcars that remained upright behind it. Maltaani shooters poured fire into the engines and passenger car, and Staaber realized most of their bullets were doing only minor damage as they hit the underside of the train. Confident that nobody could have survived the blast in the engines or passenger car, he ordered them to stop firing and advance.

To his horrified surprise, the boxcar doors rolled open, and the Space Marines concealed inside engaged his fighters. The shock of the counterattack caused many of the untrained Maltaani to freeze, making them easy targets for the humans. Pulse rifle bolts tore through the shooters, until a few returned fire and suppressed the Space Marines.

"Concentrate your fire!" Staaber shouted. "Shoot at one car at a time."

The nearest shooters followed his order and silenced the firing from the front three boxcars. They shifted their fire further back, and soon the only sound was the Maltaani rifles.

"Cease fire!" Staaber ordered. "Check those cars for survivors."

Maltaani dragged dead Space Marines from the boxcars and dumped their bodies on the ground. Two of the humans were still alive, and the Maltaani dispatched them with bullets to the head.

The Space Marines surprised and infuriated Staaber. He'd been unaware that the humans defended the train, and he suspected that somehow, someone had leaked his plan to the humans despite his security measures.

How else would they know to put Space Marines aboard the train?

The Maltaani began to unload the boxcars. They threw the boxes on the ground and tried to decipher the labels, separating obvious foodstuffs for transportation to Ulvaan. Meanwhile, Staaber went to inspect the passenger car.

"General!"

One of his troops called to him from inside the passenger car, and when he boosted himself up to peer through the window, he saw a handful of humans cowering in the corner. A blood-drenched female held her hands up in supplication, and it shocked Staaber to hear her begging in Maltaani.

"Please don't kill us. We're friends of General Staaber."

"Get them out of there," Staaber ordered.

The Maltaani dragged the humans out of the passenger car and lined them up. There were eight total, four civilians and four Space Marines. Two of the Space Marines were obviously dead, while the two others knelt and bled in silence. One civilian, a male, whimpered and clutched his arm, while another groaned as he rubbed his leg. Yet another man sat and looked around in confused silence.

The blood-soaked female pleaded in Maltaani. "Please, we are GRC. We're friends." She gestured to the man with the injured leg next to her. "This is Colonel Mitsui, of the PAM. The Space Marines wounded him during the invasion."

Staaber recognized Mitsui.

"What is your name?" he demanded.

"My name is Dalia Hahn, and this is Dexter Beck," the woman replied. "We're business partners of General Staaber."

Although Staaber couldn't recall what Beck or Hahn looked like, he was certain the one man was his former confederate Mitsui.

"Why are you here?"

"That man," Hahn replied as she pointed to the confused-looking human, "he's our captor. He's taking us to the spaceport in Ulvaan to meet a shuttle and return to Terra Earth."

Without warning, there was a loud *crack* and the shriek of metal tearing as the coupling between the passenger car and the boxcars ripped apart. The engines and passenger car, held in mid-tumble by the weight of the boxcars, tumbled free and crushed several unwitting Maltaani who were looting the engine compartments.

Gravity seized the boxcars, and they rolled down the hill. Panicked Maltaani jumped clear, and one foolish Maltaani on the ground next to the tracks grabbed a door handle and dug his heels in, as though he alone could stop two thousand tons from rolling down the hill. His feet caught in the ground, and he tumbled head-over-heels before he landed with his legs across the tracks. He screamed as the wheels severed his legs above the knees, and thick gouts of blood spurted from the wounds. Before his shocked comrades could respond, he was dead.

Staaber watched in stunned silence as the boxcars careened down the five-kilometer hill and derailed at the bottom with a tremendous *crash*. Even at this distance, he could see cargo fly in all directions. Something inside the general snapped.

"Aargh!" He yanked his sword from the scabbard, raised it high overhead, and brought it down in a powerful stroke that decapitated one of the captive Space Marines. The body slumped sideways as blood sprayed the other captives, and his head bounced across the ground and came to rest in front of Beck. Beck shrieked and tried to get away, but he fell over on his injured shoulder, and his shriek of fear became a squeal of pain.

The other Space Marine surged to his feet. Staaber struck him across the head with the flat side of his blade. As the injured man went down to his hands and knees, Staaber beheaded him, too.

The general slammed his sword into the scabbard and pointed at the four remaining humans.

"Bring them."

* * *

Colonel Anders had just turned in for the night when his communicator beeped.

"Nils, it's Jerry Wagner. I need you down here now. There's been another ambush."

Five minutes later, Anders entered the intelligence suite and found Wagner and a worried-looking woman poring over a map of the region around Ulvaan.

"Colonel, this is Associate Minister of Justice Wanda Judon. Minister Judon, this is Colonel Nils Anders."

Anders nodded. "What's happening, Jerry?"

"Someone ambushed the supply train west of Ulvaan," Wagner said. "It was overdue and didn't answer on comms, so the yardmaster sent a search party down the line to look for it. Thirty minutes ago, they found the engines derailed about eighteen klicks west of the city. The boxcars are gone."

"Any casualties?"

"So far, they've recovered the bodies of seventeen Space Marines assigned as security on the train. They're still searching."

Wagner's words hit Anders like a punch to the gut. "Fuck."

"Minister Judon, do you want to brief him on the others?"

"My senior supervisory agent on Maltaan boarded the train in Daarben, along with three GRC executives. The search party didn't find them."

"Huh. And who are these executives?"

"Saito Mitsui, Dalia Hahn, and Dexter Beck."

Anders' eyebrows shot up in surprise. "Dexter Beck? Isn't he—"

"Mr. Beck and the others were being held in pre-trial confinement at the spaceport in Daarben," Judon said. "Thompson Leighton, my missing agent, completed their interviews last week, and they were awaiting trial when Solicitor General Gomez dismissed the case against Weldon Krieg. We had no reason to hold them, so Leighton was escorting them to the spaceport in Ulvaan to catch a GRC shuttle to *Vast Expanse*."

"Do you think they escaped?"

"Possible, but unlikely. Mr. Beck has a severe shoulder injury, and Mr. Mitsui can't walk without crutches."

"Someone kidnapped them."

"That's where things get a little complicated," Wagner said. "It looks like the attackers decapitated two of the Space Marines. Who do we know that carries a sword and has reason to attack humans?"

"Staaber."

"Just before I called you, General Boudreaux told me our source reported Staaber led an attack today. He didn't specify where or what they attacked, but we've received no reports of any other attacks. The attack on the train followed the same basic plan as the ambush of the PCS convoy. A large explosive device destroyed the train engines, and the attackers killed the Space Marines with small arms fire."

"You think Staaber attacked the train and kidnapped the GRC people?" Anders asked.

"I don't know what to think right now," Wagner replied. "They may have gone with him on their own."

"Supervisory Special Agent Leighton didn't go with the Maltaani insurgents on his own," Judon interjected. "He's a loyal human. He was hand-picked for this assignment, in part because of his loyalty."

"I'm sorry, Minister. I didn't mean to imply anything about Agent Leighton. The past relations between the GRC and General Staaber is what I was getting at."

"Minister, you said they were on their way to Ulvaan to catch a shuttle and leave Maltaan?" Ander asked. She nodded. "Therefore, it's unlikely this was a rescue attempt. There would be no reason for them to require rescue by Staaber. In fact, they had every reason *not* to want to be rescued by Staaber. They were on their way home."

"We can worry about the whys and wherefores later. Right now, the high probability of Staaber's involvement in this attack makes this our baby," Wagner told Anders. "The general made that clear in our call."

"As soon as we get some solid location data, we can unleash Fortis and his team."

Wagner smiled and looked at Judon. "Would you like to explain?"

"Colonel, Agent Leighton required Beck and his group to wear ankle monitors until they left the planet. They're the same monitors we use to keep track of criminals on Terra Earth."

Anders blinked in surprise. "We're tracking them?"

"That's what we were discussing when you got here," Wagner said. "Minister Judon's people have tracked the monitors to a location five klicks northwest of Ulvaan. It's in an area that we haven't gotten around to mapping yet. It is—or was—a low-priority residential zone. If the weather clears, we'll get an air asset overhead to get some imagery.

"The plan is to merge the three Zulu-Five teams, with Fortis in command. They'll forward deploy to the rail yard in Ulvaan and stand by for mission tasking. As soon as we get confirmation of the whereabouts of the humans, we'll send them in."

* * *

The bunkroom door opened, and the lights flickered on.

"Captain Fortis, Major Sokolov wants you and your guys in the team room ASAP."

Fortis swung his feet off his bunk and rubbed his face as the others groaned and cursed.

"Let's go," Fortis said as he reached for his utilities. "It sounds like they're giving us a mission."

The adrenaline surge in the room was almost palpable as the Space Marines scrambled to get dressed. When they were ready, Fortis led them through the driving rain to the team room, where they found Sokolov and Team One. They sat down just as Team Two arrived.

"Listen up," Sokolov said. Every eye was on him, and nobody said a word. "You've just received tasking from MAC-M. The three teams from Zulu-Five are now joined under the overall command of Captain Fortis and will proceed to the ISMC detachment at the Ulvaan rail yard. When you get there, report your arrival to MAC-M and await further orders."

"What's the mission, sir?" Fortis asked.

Sokolov shook his head. "I don't know. All they told me was that you'll be under direct MAC-M command. There'll be a truck ready to leave in fifteen minutes."

"A truck, sir? What about the hovercopters?" the Team One pilot asked.

"Nobody's flying right now," Sokolov replied. "Hovercopters and crews will remain here. If the weather breaks, we'll notify Captain Fortis and MAC-M."

"Are we going to stage to the spaceport up there when the weather clears?" Red asked.

Sokolov shook his head. "Negative. The Ulvaan spaceport isn't much more than a flat spot long enough to handle shuttles. If you fly up there and the weather closes in again, you'll be stuck for who knows how long, without support. If the weather is flyable, you can launch from here and be overhead the rail yard in a few minutes." He saw the questioning looks from the teams and shrugged. "That's the best we can do right now."

"How long will we be gone, Major?" Ystremski asked.

"The mission is open-ended, Gunny. Take as many pig squares and hydration packs as you can, because I don't know what the food situation is up there. This is a high-priority mission, so you'll get more support than you know what to do with. You should be ready for extended operations in the field." He looked around the group, but nobody else spoke. He pointed to Fortis. "Captain, it's your show."

"You guys know as much as I do," Fortis said. "Until we get specifics on our tasking, I think we should operate like three platoons in the same company to maintain the integrity of the teams. We'll need a new comm plan, and if we get the opportunity, we'll do some combined training. Otherwise, let's keep it simple. Are there questions?" Heads shook around the group. "Okay, then, you heard the major. Grab your gear and supplies, and let's mount up."

* * * * *

Chapter Twenty-Nine

Beck, Hahn, Mitsui, and Leighton huddled together in the back of a canvas-covered truck that bounced along a dirt track through the forest. They'd fashioned a makeshift bandage to staunch the blood flowing from Hahn's head wound, but the blood had soaked through and dribbled down her face. There was one Maltaani with a rifle seated near the front, but he paid them no attention.

"What are we doing?" Beck hissed.

"We're going where the Maltaani with guns tell us to go," Hahn said.

"I mean with Staaber."

"We're playing along with him until we see an opportunity to escape."

"You don't think he's angry with us? With the GRC?"

"Maybe. Stick with our story, and he might not see us as the enemy. We're prisoners, and Mr. Brain Dead is our captor."

When they loaded into the truck, Beck had seen an angry purple-black knot on Leighton's left temple. Since the explosion, the agent hadn't made a sound, and his eyes lolled around as though on gimbals.

"What fucking difference does that make?" Beck struggled to keep his voice at a whisper. He was terrified, and Hahn's matter-of-fact demeanor about their predicament angered him.

"Unless Staaber reads TNN, he doesn't know what's been happening with the GRC, my father, or us. As far as he's concerned, the GRC fired us, and the UNT government arrested us for supporting him. Leighton and the Space Marines were transporting us to Terra Earth to stand trial."

"He won't buy that." Beck thought for a second. "Will he?"

"He'll buy it." Mitsui groaned as he sat up. "Why else would we be under guard?"

"You better hope Leighton doesn't wake up."

"Did you see his head? His brain is mush. He's not going to wake up soon. Now, shut up. You're giving me a headache."

The trio lapsed into silence as the truck bounced along the forest track. Beck fretted in the dark until he couldn't take it anymore.

"This won't work. He's going to figure it out."

"Beck, I told you to shut the fuck up. Staaber won't figure it out unless you keep panicking. Stop whining and show some gratitude that he rescued us."

Beck sank back in his seat and hugged his left arm to his chest. The bouncing of the truck reverberated from his injured shoulder through his entire body, and his mind raced with the dire possibilities that awaited them.

Wherever we're going.

* * *

Fortis waved to First Lieutenant Abdullah from Team One and Warrant Officer Heggie from Team Two to sit next to him in the truck. Ystremski huddled with the other team sergeants, and the other six Space Marines sat together in the back.

"This ride is my best chance to learn about your teams. First question, do you both have medics?"

Abdulla and Heggie nodded. "I've got two," the warrant said.

"I've got one," Fortis said. "How about demo guys? Do you have engineers?"

They both nodded again.

"I have two," Fortis said. "How about snipers?"

Heggie shook his head, and Abdullah shrugged. "Just me."

"You're the team sniper?"

"I grew up hunting with an antique ballistic rifle to feed my village. A pulse rifle is easy."

"Good to know."

"What do you think this mission is, Captain?" Heggie asked.

"I meant it when I said you know as much as I do about what's going on. Sokolov didn't tell me anything else before we left. If I had to guess, I'd say Fleet intel got wind of a big move by the insurgents, and we're being sent to interdict them. That's the only thing I can think of that would require all three teams merging like this."

"Why so hush-hush, sir?" Abdullah asked.

"Major Sokolov claims the Maltaani can hear every word we say in the camp. Perhaps MAC-M doesn't want to tip our hand."

"Maybe the royalists are involved," Heggie said. "It wouldn't surprise me. I don't trust any of those fuckers."

"I bet we have a spy in the insurgency," Abdullah said. "That would be worth all this cloak-and-dagger bullshit."

"There are a lot of possibilities," Fortis said as he tried to steer the conversation away from Abdullah's accurate speculation. "We'll find out when they want to tell us."

Abdullah and Heggie nodded, and the conversation waned for a moment.

"Have either of you been to the rail yard?" Fortis asked.

"My battalion captured it during the invasion," Heggie said. "Then our idiot XO destroyed it with Black Hole."

Fortis chuckled. "What happened?"

"There were some Maltaani hiding out among the trains, and I guess we missed one when we cleared the place. He took a shot at the battalion XO, and the XO flipped out and called an emergency Black Hole strike down on the whole fucking place."

"Where was your CO?"

"He died on the first day, so the XO, Major Innskeep, had command."

"Wait a second. Innskeep? That name is familiar."

Heggie patted his stomach and rubbed his head. "Fat guy. Balding. Came straight to the battalion from Personnel. I guess he was trying to make colonel."

"Oh, shit. I know him. I mean, I ran across him in Junior Officer Assignments." Fortis shook his head. "He was a piece of work, for sure."

"No, sir, Major Innskeep wasn't a piece of work. He was a piece of shit. He got a lot of guys killed for no reason before he blew up the train station. If the division commander hadn't relieved him, the guys would have fragged him for sure."

"Huh. It's a damn shame it cost so much to get rid of him."

"Too many REMFs are using this war to get ahead," Abdullah said. "REMF" was an acronym for Rear Echelon Mother Fucker, a term of derision used by field Marines to refer to Marines who avoided front line service.

All three officers nodded and lapsed back into silence. Fortis had encountered his fair share of headquarters officers who seemed to take great pleasure in standing in the way of mission accomplishment. It sickened him to think of the loss of a single Space Marine because of the incompetence of rank-hungry REMFs.

The ride smoothed out, and the truck sped up as they left the narrow road that led through the hamlets and entered the streets of Ulvaan. Fortis knew they were close, so he tapped Heggie and Abdullah to rouse them. When the truck squealed to a stop, Fortis jumped out into a light rain and found a master sergeant waiting under a narrow overhang.

"Captain Fortis?"

"That's me."

"Master Sergeant Heinz. I'm the yardmaster. Come on, I'll show you to your quarters."

Fortis waved, and the rest of the team followed as Heinz led him to their quarters, a dingy-looking garage.

"It's not much to look at," Heinz said as he rolled the door open. "In fact, it's not much of anything at all."

Dust coated the inside of the garage, and rusted equipment littered the dirt floor.

"What a shithole," Ystremski said.

"Hey, Gunny, DINLI. If it's not up to your standards, you're welcome to find a hotel. Or sleep outside, since there are no hotels."

"It's fine, Master Sergeant," Fortis cut in. "We'll clean it up a little, and it'll be just like home."

"Captain, I'm sorry, but this is what we have. We don't get too many overnight guests. Me and my guys have been living in a derelict boxcar since we got here. I think the Maltaani used it to haul livestock, because it smells like shit. You're welcome to join us, but there's twenty-six guys sleeping in shifts."

"Don't worry about it. We'll be fine. Is this secure? Can we leave our supplies in here?"

"Yes, sir, nobody will steal a thing. You have my word on that. You didn't bring any food, did you?"

"Pig squares and hydration packs. Why?"

"Hmm. Pig squares might be a problem. Fucking tree rats are everywhere, and they get into everything. Especially food."

"Why don't you get rid of them?"

Heinz shook his head. "The Maltaani used to hunt them for food, but they stopped coming to work. Since then, the rats are coming back in a big way."

"Shoot them. They taste good."

"Fuck that, sir. I'm not eating a rat."

"Where can we store our food?"

"We've got a cache you can share. Unload your truck in here for tonight, and we'll get it sorted out in the morning."

"Okay, ladies, you heard the man," Ystremski announced. "Let's get the truck unloaded, and then we'll clean this shithole, er, these accommodations."

"Don't let Gunny Ystremski bother you," Fortis said when the rest of the team was outside. "He's happy sleeping in a hole, as long as no one is shooting at him."

"Why are you here, Captain? Are you gonna hunt down the bastards who ambushed the train?"

"I haven't heard about an ambush. What happened?"

"The train was late arriving from Daarben earlier today, and they weren't answering comms, so I sent a platoon to look for it. They found the engines all blown to hell, and the security force killed. The boxcars were gone."

"Insurgents?"

"Probably." Heinz shook his head. "Fucking Maltaani. That train carried food, which we've been feeding to the locals so they don't starve, and they blew it up. Who does that?"

Fortis shook his head in response, but one name stayed in his head.

Staaber.

"Anyway, that's why I figured you guys were here. To find the pricks and kill them. Kill them all."

"All we've been told is that we're supposed to stage here and stand by for orders, but I hope you're right. We need to kill them."

Heinz told Fortis how to find the boxcar where he slept, and then the captain helped the team unload the truck. When they finished, they set to cleaning and organizing the garage.

Fortis located the satcom set and stuck the antenna outside so he could report their arrival in Ulvaan to MAC-M. The strength of the connection surprised him, considering the weather. The voice on the other end of the circuit instructed him to maintain a 24-hour comms watch.

"What's our status, Gunny?" Fortis asked when his check-in was complete.

"The floor is dirt, but we found a wooden turntable to set up on. It could be worse."

"What's a turntable?"

"It's used to turn train engines around, sir. See the tracks? The engine rolls on, and they turn it around. What's the word from MAC-M?"

"Set a comms watch and stand by for orders," Fortis said. "There are twelve of us, so it should be pretty easy duty."

"We should run two Space Marines per watch, sir," Ystremski said. "The comms watch and a security rover."

"Sounds good to me. It seems pretty quiet around here, but all that can change." He told Ystremski what Heinz had said about the train. "That might be why we're here."

"Could be. In the meantime, I'll get the duty roster posted, and then I'm gonna check out this dump. Maybe there's something useful stuck away in here."

They stacked their supplies in the center of the turntable and set up sleeping accommodations around the rim. One of the team turned up a pile of musty, moth-eaten blankets, which they shook out and laid out on the deck. It wasn't a feather bed, but it was better than nothing. The Space Marines flaked out and tried to get some sleep.

Ystremski set up the comms watch by the door near the antenna. The rover's presence upset the tree rats living in the garage, and their chittering protests followed him as he made a circuit around the building.

"I should have brought a poodle shooter," Abdullah said. "We could have fire-roasted rats with our pig squares. Pulse rifles won't leave much to eat."

A poodle shooter was a sound-suppressed, low-caliber pistol. It wasn't an official ISMC weapon, but covert operators often carried them to deal with sentries and guard dogs.

Fortis didn't think he'd be able to sleep, but he was out almost before he closed his eyes.

* * * * *

Chapter Thirty

Excited voices woke Fortis, and he opened his eyes in time to see Abdullah hold up a tree rat in one hand, and a makeshift slingshot in the other.

"Nice shooting, LT," one of the Space Marines called.

The rat was the size of a large Terran house cat, with a thick, rope-like tail and sharp claws. The smiling officer approached Fortis and dangled the dead beast in front of him.

"Sorry to wake you, Captain, but this little bastard and his buddies were trying to get to the food. I found a piece of bent metal and threw together this slingshot. One shot, one kill."

Fortis sat up. "What time is it?"

"0620, sir," said Ystremski as he sat down next to Fortis. "You were asleep for two hours before this circus started."

The Space Marines formed a hunting party. Bender and Woody beat their way around the warehouse to flush out the rats, while Abdullah trailed with his slingshot at the ready. Two other Space Marines armed with metal bars followed him as a backstop. The rest of the team watched with amusement and offered crude suggestions on how to improve their odds.

A tree rat broke cover and tried to escape across the barn. Abdullah aimed and fired in one smooth motion, and the stone hit the animal in the head. It was still wriggling when a backstop charged forward and dispatched it, and the Space Marines cheered. Abdullah laid it next to the other one and grinned at Fortis.

"A couple more, and we'll have breakfast!" He chuckled.

Ystremski shook his head as the lieutenant rejoined the hunt. "Why are all officers crazy?"

Before Fortis could answer, the comms watch called from the door.

"Captain Fortis, MAC-M wants to talk to you."

Fortis nodded his thanks and took the handset.

"This is Captain Fortis."

"*Fortis, this is General Boudreaux. I've got a mission update for you.*"

"I'm ready to copy, sir."

"*Maltaani insurgents, led by Staaber, attacked the supply train west of Ulvaan. They butchered the Space Marine platoon assigned to guard it, destroyed the engines, and kidnapped three and maybe four civilians. Staaber himself beheaded two captured Space Marines.*"

"Bastard."

"*Agreed. We tracked the hostages throughout the night, and it looks like the Maltaani are holding them in a location about five klicks northwest of Ulvaan, about six klicks from you. It's an area we don't have maps for, but we believe it's a low-density residential area. Jerry and Nils are doing everything they can to get some imagery of the area, but the damn weather isn't cooperating.*

"*We're going to monitor the location throughout the day to make sure they don't move the hostages. Tonight, after dark, your tasking will be to move to the target location undetected and conduct surveillance on it. I'll decide how we're going to proceed. Questions?*"

"How are we tracking the hostages, sir?"

"*That's one wrinkle in this story. Three of the hostages are GRC employees who were being held in pre-trial confinement in Daarben. The Ministry of Justice ordered them released, and one of their agents was escorting them to the spaceport in Ulvaan. They're wearing ankle monitors like criminals back home do, so we can track them."*

"Ankle monitors? Who are they?"

"That's another wrinkle. It's Saito Mitsui, Dalia Hahn, and Dexter Beck."

Beck!

"We're going to rescue Dexter Beck from his Maltaani allies?"

"Not rescue. Surveil."

Fortis was silent.

"Captain, Anders told me all about your experiences with Beck. I say, tough shit. Do your fucking duty. DINLI." Anger tinged Boudreaux's voice.

"Sir, I wasn't questioning your orders. I'll do my utmost to carry them out. I'm surprised that we're going to rescue a traitor from his allies."

"Good." Boudreaux's tone softened. *"This whole situation is one great big unknown, which is why I need you to find out the ground truth. For all we know, Beck and the other two are with Staaber by choice, and those GRC pricks are plotting a new deal with him. That's the information I need to know. I'll have forces ready to move on your report."*

"What about Staaber, sir? Does our original tasking stand?"

"Affirmative. If you get the chance, and it won't endanger the hostages, drop the bastard."

"Yes, sir. One more thing?"

"Shoot."

"You said they kidnapped three or maybe four civilians. Who's the fourth?"

"The Ministry of Justice agent. He's not wearing a monitor, but they didn't find his body at the ambush. Until we know otherwise, we're assuming he's with

the other three. I'll try to send the locating data to your navigator. If it doesn't work, I'll get you the coordinates over this circuit."

"Roger that, sir. I'll brief the team, and we'll be standing by."

"Outstanding."

* * *

When Fortis told Ystremski that Beck was a hostage, the gunny snorted.

"Beck tried to kill us on Pada-Pada. Let them have the fucker," he said.

"Not a bad idea, but not our mission," Fortis said. "DINLI."

"Yeah, DINLI. What about Staaber?"

"If we can do it without endangering the hostages, we've got a green light."

"Okay, sir. Give me a minute to get these guys together. The lieutenant shot enough rats for everyone, so we'll be eating good this morning."

"Sounds delicious."

"Come on, Captain. What's the worst that could happen?"

There were grumbles from the team when Fortis told them of the dead Space Marines on the supply train, but they otherwise listened to his brief in silence. They understood the mission was a basic sneak-and-peek, complicated by the lack of maps and the possibility of hostages. Otherwise, it was like other missions they'd all conducted before. There were no comments or questions, so Fortis dismissed them.

Abdullah set to cleaning the tree rats while others gathered wood scraps for a fire. They soon had the rats roasting over the flames, and the smell of cooking meat filled the barn.

"What's that smell?" Heinz asked when he entered the barn.

"Rat," Bender said as he brandished a rat splayed open on a homemade spit. "Hungry?"

"Ah, shit." Heinz put a hand to his stomach. "I thought you were kidding about eating those things."

"They're good. Try some." The Aussie held out a roasted leg, but Heinz waved it away.

"I'll stick with pig squares."

"What can we do for you this morning?" Fortis asked Heinz.

"I came by to show you where the food cache was so you can store your rations there." He nodded to the spits over the fire. "I didn't realize you brought yours on the hoof."

"Lead the way, Master Sergeant," Fortis said as he climbed to his feet. "I could use a break from these maniacs, anyway."

The food cache was a metal trailer in a barn across the compound from Fortis' quarters.

"It doesn't lock," Heinz said, "but it's dry, and the rats haven't figured out how to open the door latch."

"It looks fine," Fortis said. "When we move out, you're welcome to whatever we leave behind."

"Excuse me, Master Sergeant?" A corporal joined them by the trailer. "Uh, sorry, Captain." He handed Heinz an envelope. "We just got this from MAC-M. I figured you'd want to see it ASAP."

Heinz gulped when he read the front page.

"Two companies? Where in hell are we going to put two companies?" He looked at Fortis. "Looks like you're getting some roommates, Captain." Heinz flipped to the second page, and his face grew somber. After a minute, he handed it to Fortis. "Casualty list from the train ambush.

Fortis meant to scan the list, but he didn't get past the first name at the top, and he got a sick feeling in his stomach.

First Lieutenant Wilhelm Vogel.

Chug-A-Lug!

"A lot of good Space Marines on that list, sir."

Fortis swallowed the lump in his throat. "Too many."

"DINLI."

"Indeed."

Before they went back out into the rain, Heinz grabbed Fortis' arm and stopped him.

"Captain, I know you can't tell me why you're here or where you're going, but when you get there, kill those fuckers, would you? I lost some good Marines, and some good friends, on that train."

Fortis scowled. "I can't promise anything, but if I ever cross paths with the Maltaani who hit that train, they're as good as dead."

Heinz thumped him on the shoulder, and they trotted across the yard.

* * *

Staaber descended the steps into the basement of his family home, where he'd had the four humans confined since they'd arrived from the train ambush the previous evening. He wrinkled his nose in disgust. Empty wrappers from foodstuffs plundered from the boxcars littered the floor. The room was damp and airless, and the odor of unwashed human bodies made it almost unbearable.

Filthy humans.

The injured female stirred, and when she saw Staaber, she got to her feet.

"General, we are—"

"Silence!" Staaber's voice roused two of her companions, including Mitsui. He pointed to the injured human. "Bring him."

Staaber climbed the stairs, and his guards followed with Mitsui supported between them. In the main room, they deposited Mitsui in one chair, while Staaber took another. He nodded at the human.

"Colonel."

"General."

The former confederates stared at each other for a long moment.

"What happened to your leg?"

"A Space Marine hovercopter strafed my truck as we withdrew to the east. We hid in a cave, but the humans captured us a few days later. I had a nasty infection, and it forced the doctors to operate to save my leg." Mitsui spoke in broken Maltaani, but Staaber understood what he said.

Staaber remained stoic, but he'd formed a strange attachment to the human during their service together. He didn't trust the humans, but Mitsui was one of the very few Staaber had encountered who hadn't betrayed him or failed him at a critical moment.

"How did you come to be on the train?"

"The man with us works for the Terran Ministry of Justice. They confined us at the spaceport in Daarben since our capture, and he was escorting us to Ulvaan to travel back to Terra Earth to stand trial. The weather forced us to take the train."

A question formed in Staaber's mind. "Why Ulvaan? Why not Daarben?"

Mitsui hesitated before he replied. "The, uh, the Space Marines won't permit them to use Daarben."

Staaber felt a twinge of suspicion at Mitsui's answer. He didn't understand the internal politics of the humans, but Mitsui's explanation made little sense.

"What of your trial?"

The human shrugged, a gesture Staaber associated with deception.

"You saved us from that, General. What now?"

Staaber stood and waved the guards forward to help Mitsui to his feet. "I'll speak with all of you and determine how you can best continue to serve our cause."

"We look forward to it," Mitsui said as they carried him to the basement steps.

In the basement, Staaber gestured at Hahn.

"Where are you taking her?" Beck demanded.

Mitsui put his hand on Beck's shoulder. "It's okay, Beck. Just an interview."

Upstairs in the main room, Hahn made a show of adjusting the bloodstained bandage wrapped around her head.

"What news of your father?" Staaber asked.

"The humans charged him with treason for his dealings with you."

Staaber grunted and nodded, which Hahn took as a cue to continue talking.

"My father honored his contracts with you, General, as did Mr. Beck, Mr. Mitsui, and myself. We remained faithful to our agreements despite the invasion—"

"Silence!"

For the second time in as many conversations with her, Staaber shut her up. She seemed to view every conversation as a sales opportunity, a human practice Staaber found especially vulgar.

"Your company betrayed me," he spat at her. "They seized the helenium mines and stole the PCS to work them."

"General, when the fortunes of war changed, the GRC betrayed me like they betrayed you."

"Why did the humans send you to Ulvaan?"

"I guess the weather is better for shuttles in Ulvaan," Hahn said.

Staaber hadn't believed Mitsui's story, but Hahn's was inconceivable. There was more to the story, but he let her remark pass unchallenged. He'd pose the same question to Beck and weigh all three answers.

He motioned to the guards. "Return her to the basement and bring up the third one."

Staaber knew Beck didn't have a translator implant, so he called for one of the other Maltaani who'd spent considerable time with the humans before the invasion to help with interpretation.

Beck shuffled in and slumped in the chair, hugging his arm to his body.

"Why are you here?" Staaber asked.

"You rescued us from the humans," Beck said.

"Why go to Ulvaan? Why not Daarben?"

"I don't know."

Staaber remained stoic in the face of Beck's lie.

"What are you going to do with us?" Beck asked.

"I don't know."

Beck smirked at the irony of Staaber's answer.

"We can be useful," Beck said. "When the Space Marines leave, we can negotiate with the GRC for you."

Staaber laughed, and Beck recoiled from his expression.

"There will be no negotiations with the GRC," he snarled. "When we drive the Space Marines from Maltaan, there will be no GRC to negotiate with."

Beck didn't answer, and Staaber knew he'd get no useful information from the human.

"Take him back downstairs," he ordered the guards.

* * * * *

Chapter Thirty-One

"Staaber's not buying it," Beck whispered to Hahn and Mitsui, who sat together in the corner. "He doesn't know what to do with us, and pretty soon, he'll decide we aren't worth the trouble to keep around."

"Relax, Beck," Mitsui said. "Staaber won't make a hasty decision. He's not impetuous."

"Not impetuous?" Beck's voice was almost normal volume, and Hahn and Mitsui shushed him. "You saw what he did to those Space Marines at the train. What do you call that?"

"Those guys were dead before the Maltaani dragged them out of the train car. The Maltaani don't tolerate prisoners, remember?"

"Yeah, I remember. *We're* prisoners, though. Right?"

"Calm down, Beck. Panicking won't make things any better. Now, what did you see upstairs?"

The trio compared notes of what they'd seen during their brief trips to the main room. The stairs led to a kitchen with a door that looked like it led out the back of the house. Hahn had paced off the hall to the main room and estimated it was ten meters from the kitchen to the main room, and another five from there to the front door. They hadn't seen an organized sentry force; each had seen Maltaani moving in and out, but the only guards were the two who'd escorted them up and down the stairs. And dogs.

"I saw two of them," Mitsui said. "I'd heard they were big bastards, but I hadn't realized how big until tonight." Mitsui pointed at the stairs. "They keep the door up there locked, and they might lock the back door, too."

"I'll go up and inspect the lock," Hahn said. "Maybe they don't have guards on duty because they don't think we can get through it."

"They weren't planning on human prisoners." Beck swept his good arm across the basement. "No showers, and the toilet is a bucket."

"That might help us," Mitsui replied. "If they're not accustomed to holding prisoners, they might get careless."

"Or impatient," Beck said as he drew his forefinger across his throat. He looked at the insensate Leighton. "What about him?"

"What about him?" Hahn said. "If he can't move when the time comes, we leave him. Maybe the Ministry of Justice will send someone to look for him."

Beck scoffed. "That's pretty fucking noble."

"Survival of the fittest, Beck. I won't die doing the right thing by a man who wanted to send me to prison. Don't tell me you like him?"

"Of course not, but he's a fellow human being, and you'd leave him for the Maltaani."

"If that's what I have to do to survive, then yes, I will."

"Remind me not to hit my head around you, then."

* * *

The tension in the barn built as the day wore on, despite the usual banter and grab-assing. The beaters had flushed out every tree rat in the barn, and Abdullah had slaughtered them all. Fortis alternated between pacing and standing at the door, watching the rain. He checked with the comms watch to see if MAC-M had called, but the answer was always the same. No.

"Captain, do you want to take the watch?" Bender asked after Fortis inquired for the third time in an hour.

Fortis didn't answer, but he took the hint and stopped asking. Several minutes later, Bender called him over.

"MAC-M, mate," the Aussie said without a trace of irony as he passed the handset.

"This is Captain Fortis."

"*Captain, this is Colonel Gunn, MAC-M. I just transmitted the latest locating data; verify you received it on your navigator.*"

Fortis checked and saw updated positions. "I got them, sir."

"*Our source verified Staaber was there this morning. The goddamn weather isn't cooperating right now, so we don't have any imagery for you. The weather guessers say there's a high-pressure cell building over Ulvaan, so it might clear up for a few hours after midnight.*"

"That's good news. The general said we'd have a Black Hole bird, sir. Is it still available?"

"*Affirmative. Do you have something in mind?*"

"No, sir, just keeping my options open."

"*Okay, good. No change to the timeline. Move out after dark, patrol to the target location, and surveil the area. Two companies from 4th Division will stage at the rail yard and wait for your report.*"

"Roger that, sir."

"*Good luck, and get it done.*"

Fortis gathered the teams together, ensured everyone had the current locating data in their navigators, and verified the team comm frequencies.

"Patrol order will be Team One, Team Three, Team Two," Fortis said. "Colonel Gunn said the weather might clear around midnight, so I want to be in position before it does. We're gonna have to play the rest by ear." He checked the time. "It'll be dark in about two hours; be ready to move out."

* * *

Fortis munched a pig square and washed it down with a hydration pack. He wasn't hungry, but he didn't know when he'd have time to eat again. Ystremski walked over and sat down next to him with his own food.

"How's it going, Captain?"

"Good. How about you?"

"Same here. Begging your pardon, but you're acting a little strange, sir. Quiet, I mean."

Fortis stopped chewing. "I saw the casualty list from the train ambush. One of them was an officer I trained with."

"Damn. Sorry to hear it." Ystremski shook his head. "Do this long enough, and it's bound to happen."

"I know. I've seen plenty of Space Marines die, but this guy was different. Even as a trainee, he seemed larger than life."

They chewed in silence for a minute before Ystremski spoke.

"You're good for tonight?"

"Yeah, of course. DINLI, right?"

"DINLI."

The last hour before dark lasted forever, and relief washed over Fortis when it was dark enough to jump off.

"Is everyone ready?" Fortis asked over the team circuit, and he got waves and thumbs up from everyone on the team. "Lieutenant Abdullah, lead us out."

The rain had picked up since the last time Fortis had been outside, and he welcomed the additional cover it provided. Anything that would keep Maltaani inside and off the streets could only help their mission.

Team One set a quick pace as the team moved through the dark streets of Ulvaan. The target was only six klicks from the rail yard, but Fortis wanted to get to the target area as quickly as possible to take advantage of the weather and maximize their time surveilling the target.

After twenty minutes, Fortis called their first planned halt. Abdullah, Heggie, and Ystremski joined him for a quick huddle.

"We're making excellent time. Is everybody good?"

"Do you want to pick up the pace?" Abdullah asked.

"No. We're almost halfway there, and I don't want to run into any surprises between here and there because we're in a hurry."

Abdullah called another halt moments after they restarted.

"Fortis up."

When Fortis got to the front of the patrol, he saw a wide creek across their direction of travel. There was a narrow footbridge that crossed the creek, but bare ground surrounded the approaches for ten meters on either side. A small lamp threw weak yellow light on the scene, and Fortis could see water rushing under the bridge.

"What do you think, sir? Do we cross here?"

"No choice. The water is moving too fast to wade across, and we don't know how deep it is, anyway. One at a time, and move fast. First man across, break the lamp."

Fortis passed the word over the team circuit, and then Team One's point man, Sergeant Karlaftis, sprinted across the bridge and took cover on the far side. The light was still burning.

"*It's pretty creaky,*" he reported. "*I missed the fucking light because I almost fell in.*"

The second Space Marine went next. He slowed at the bridge and smashed the light as he crossed.

Abdullah was next, followed by the last member of Team One.

"*All secure over here,*" Abdullah reported.

Woody, Team Three's point man, was next. Ystremski was right behind him. Just before the gunny reached the bridge, his feet slipped out from under him, and he skidded toward the creek. Fortis, who was next in line, dashed out and helped Ystremski to his feet.

"Fucking mud," Ystremski grumbled as he crossed the bridge with Fortis at his heels.

Bender followed, and then Heggie led Team Two across. They waited for several minutes to see if there was a reaction to their crossing, but the only sound was the rain.

"Let's move," Fortis said.

Almost immediately, Karlaftis spoke up. "*Down. Take cover.*" A few tense seconds passed. "Three Maltaani heading for the bridge."

Fortis felt his pulse quicken as he waited for them to pass. Even though he was well-hidden in the bushes, and his autoflage made him invisible, the possibility of discovery ratcheted up the tension.

The Maltaani continued along the road, shoulders hunched against the heavy rain. They crossed the bridge and disappeared, and Fortis took a shaky breath. They'd never know how close they'd come to death on this rainy night in Ulvaan.

After another brief delay, Fortis ordered the team to move out. They went to ground twice more when Maltaani passed them, headed for the bridge. After the second stop, Fortis ordered Sergeant Karlaftis to scout fifty meters to the left and right of the road they were on in search of another way to their target.

"*I didn't find another road going north,*" Karlaftis reported when he returned. "*The brush is too thick to the west, and there's a bunch of houses to the east with walls and gates.*"

"Okay. Let's double the interval between the point and the main body, then, and we'll drop the rearguard back some more, too. We're two klicks out, and I don't want any surprises."

They continued north, but encountered no more Maltaani. Fortis was about to order a halt a half-klick from the target when Karlaftis shouted over the circuit.

"*What the fuck was that?*" Ystremski demanded.

"*Moving up,*" Abdullah said. After several interminable seconds, he spoke again. "*Fortis up.*"

When Fortis got to the front, he saw Team One's medic crouched next to Karlaftis. Three Maltaani bodies sprawled in the street. One of them was headless.

"Fuckers came out of nowhere," the wounded sergeant said through gritted teeth as he pointed to a small gate set back into a wall next to the road. "I bumped into the first two, and before I could get a bead on them, they tackled me. I drew my kukri and killed them, but the third one clobbered me with his rifle before I could get up."

"He was drawing a bead on Karlaftis when I got here," Abdullah said as he brandished his kukri. "I chopped at his shoulder, he dropped his weapon, and then I whacked his head off."

"Give me a hand to get these bodies off the road," Fortis said. They dragged the three bodies into the brush, and Abdullah kicked the head in behind them. Karlaftis got to his feet and insisted he could continue.

Abdullah rearranged his team with a new point man and put Karlaftis in the rear.

"We're ready to move, Captain," the lieutenant reported.

"We'll move a hundred meters to get clear of the bodies and halt," Fortis said. "Then I'll go forward and scout the target."

The team took cover further down the road, then Fortis stopped to update his navigator. There was no change to the monitor locations.

"I'm going to take Gunny Ystremski and move to the target," Fortis told Abdullah and Heggie. "We'll get the lay of the land and figure out how to position the teams. If anything goes wrong, if there's any shooting, this is the rally point. If you don't hear from me in twenty minutes, assume the worst and fall back."

Fortis and Ystremski snaked their way through the brush and climbed over a low wall as they approached the target.

"Lights," Ystremski said. Fortis peered through the trees and saw a large, two-story house with lights burning in several windows, upstairs and down. It was a grand-looking place, with tall columns and a long porch across the front. A wide gravel drive connected the house to the road the Space Marines had followed there, and four Maltaani trucks squatted in the side yard.

"That's got to be it," Fortis said after he consulted his navigator. There were no other buildings nearby. "Let's move around to the right and get a look at the back."

They circled around the house, careful to keep a thick screen of underbrush between them and the target. The side of the house was nothing but windows, and on the back, they saw a small porch with a door.

"There's somebody on the porch," Ystremski said. Fortis looked and saw a Maltaani on a chair tilted against the wall.

"Sentry?"

"I don't know. I don't see a weapon."

As if the Maltaani had heard their conversation, he shifted in his chair, and they saw a rifle leaning against the wall next to him.

"Sentry," Fortis said. "This is the place."

They slipped back to the team, and Fortis scratched a diagram in the mud.

"Team One, you take sniper overwatch on the main entrance." He pointed to Karlaftis. "Are you okay?"

"Yes, sir. Just a little headache."

"Good. Team Two, you've got the north side of the house. We didn't look at that side, but I doubt it's much different from the south. Just windows. I'll take Team Three around the back and watch the back porch. We saw one sentry, so plan on there being more. We didn't see any patrols, but they might have one, or they might have dogs, or both. Be ready."

* * * * *

Chapter Thirty-Two

The rain had stopped by the time the teams surrounded the house. Fortis, Ystremski, and Bender took up positions along the back of the house, while Fortis posted Woody where he had a clear view of the south face. The sentry they'd seen on the back porch was still there, leaning against the wall. After everyone reported they were in position, Fortis settled in to watch and wait.

Shadows moved behind the curtains in the windows, and at one point, Fortis saw a Maltaani pause in front of an uncovered window upstairs, but it was impossible for him to estimate how many were inside. He didn't see any humans, so they couldn't determine if they were in there, or what their status was. The anklets were battery powered, so there might be a pile of trackers in the house, and the humans were elsewhere. They might even be dead.

They watched for thirty minutes to get a feel for the place before Fortis keyed his mic.

"I've got one sentry seated on the back porch and no other movement."

"*We've got three up front,*" Abdullah said. "*Two on the porch, and one on the balcony. I think the two on the porch are asleep, and the one on top is leaning against the rail.*"

"Woody, are you clear?"

"*Affirmative, Captain. No movement.*"

"Move up to the house and see if you can get a look in the windows on your side," Fortis said. "We're looking for numbers of Maltaani, whether they're armed, and if there are humans inside. Everyone else, stand fast and watch for a reaction."

"*Roger that, sir.*"

Fifteen minutes later, Woody reported.

"*There are two rooms on this side of the house. One of them looks like a sitting room, and I counted six Maltaani with rifles stacked in the corner. There was nothing in the other room but two Maltaani dogs. I also saw two windows at ground level that might open to a basement, but they're boarded up from the inside. I didn't see any humans or Maltaani with a sword.*"

"Good work, Woody. Team Two, send someone to peek in the windows on your side if it's clear."

"*Yes, sir,*" Warrant Heggie said.

A few minutes later, Fortis heard someone cursing on the circuit.

"*There's a living room and dining room on this side. That's all I had time to see, because those damn dogs came right to the window. I bailed before I could see any more; I thought I was caught.*"

"Does anyone see any reaction?"

"*Negative on the front,*" Abdullah said.

"*Not here,*" Woody added.

"It's all quiet back here as well. We'll give it some time, and we'll try again."

A soft rain began to fall as Fortis settled back into his hiding place to monitor the back of the house.

He heard a faint commotion inside.

"Something's happening."

The back door banged open, and a man raced outside and jumped off the porch.

* * *

Staaber sat alone and considered his options regarding the human captives. He had to decide soon. Too many of his troops knew he had them, and he suspected it wouldn't be long before the humans knew. The longer they remained in the basement, the greater the chances the humans would discover his headquarters.

He could kill them. The Maltaani despised prisoners and executed them, so it wouldn't be without precedent. Still, these humans were different. They weren't soldiers; they were important members of the GRC. While Staaber didn't expect to do business with the conglomerate in the future, anything was possible.

Another option was to release them to face trial on Terra Earth. Their future in the human justice system wasn't his concern, but he discarded that idea out of hand. The move would appear weak to his fellow Maltaani, and he couldn't afford to appear weak.

He could offer a prisoner swap, but he didn't know if the humans held any of his fellow nationalists, or whether they'd be worth trading for. Most of the Maltaani officers he'd known were more interested in returning home than fighting, or they were dead.

His mind made up, Staaber stood and motioned for the two guards to follow as he headed for the basement door.

The stairs creaked as Staaber descended into the basement, escorted by his men. Beck and Mitsui sat together against the wall, while Hahn knelt next to Leighton and dribbled water into his mouth.

"I'll ransom you to the humans," Staaber announced without introduction, and Beck made a noise in his throat when Hahn translated. "I have no further use for you."

The humans traded glances, but said nothing. Staaber examined each of their faces, but they didn't react. He turned and walked to the steps.

"General Staaber, sir?" The female, the daughter of Weldon Krieg, approached. "Thank you."

The general nodded.

"I have a request."

"What is it?"

"In my culture, we value cleanliness."

"We do as well."

She plucked at her filthy clothes and touched her hair. "I need to wash, General. It's been days since I was clean."

"I'll have buckets of water brought down."

Hahn's face fell. "I can't… I mean… I need privacy." She motioned to her companions. "I can't bathe in front of them. It would be inappropriate. Do you have somewhere upstairs that I can use?"

The request was unexpected, and Staaber didn't respond right away. His first instinct was to deny it because it would create unnecessary complications.

"I promise, I won't be any trouble," she said. "I just need to be clean."

Staaber nodded. "Very well. I will arrange it."

Her face broke into a wide smile. "Oh, thank you General. You are as magnanimous as you are strong."

Staaber turned without another word and climbed out of the basement, trailed by his guards.

* * *

"What are you doing?" Beck asked Hahn after Staaber was gone. "Didn't you hear him? We're leaving."

"When?" Hahn sat down next to Mitsui. "We could be here for a long time before the GRC meets his ransom demands. I don't know about you, Beck, but I don't like dirt and body odor. If there's a chance to get clean, I'm taking it. Even if it means I have to kiss his ass."

"I'm not talking about kissing his ass. I'm talking about remaining quiet and cooperative, that's all."

"How is asking for a bath uncooperative?"

Beck shook his head but didn't respond. Hahn still lived in her entitled corporate princess world, and he knew from long experience she would never change.

"Who knows? Maybe when I'm finished, Staaber will allow you to wash, and you can scrub off some of your funk."

"If he does, will you wash my back?"

"Fuck you, Beck."

Beck laughed, and Mitsui shot him a dirty look.

"Don't be a dick, Beck. This basement is way too small for that."

"I just don't think it's a good idea to be high maintenance," Beck said. "I'd rather he forgot about us, except for food and water."

"Maybe he'll forget to lock the door," Hahn said. "Knowing what's upstairs and how to get out of here would be good, wouldn't it? In case we become too high maintenance, I mean."

"You can't argue with her there, Beck."

"Of the three of us, you should be the one most concerned with escape, anyway," Hahn said to Beck. "The GRC will trade a lot more for the daughter of Weldon Krieg than they will for the guy whose record with the PCS has been, well, spotty, no?"

Beck's face flushed at Hahn's barb. She always knew what to say to do the most damage, and she had gotten worse since she was no longer his nominal subordinate. He retorted with the first thing that came to his mind.

"Shut the fuck up."

Beck struggled to his feet, walked to the far side of the basement, and slid down the wall. It was a stupid, immature move, and he realized too late that he was within range of the stench wafting from the honey bucket Staaber had given them to use as a toilet. He sulked for a minute before the stink overwhelmed his pride, and he toiled to stand up and move back across the basement. Hahn and Mitsui grinned as he took his previous seat.

"It's bad enough I have to listen to your shit," he said to Hahn. "I don't want to smell it, too."

The basement door banged open, and one of the Maltaani guards entered the basement. He pointed to Hahn and motioned for her to follow him back upstairs.

"I guess I'm going to get that bath, boys," she said in a lighthearted tone. "Behave yourselves while I'm gone, will you?"

"Go take your bath, princess," Beck growled. "At least it'll be quiet down here while you're gone."

After Hahn was gone, Beck turned to Mitsui. "What are your thoughts about all this?"

"Well, pardner, I reckon this'll work out just fine," the mercenary said. "Mr. Krieg ain't gonna leave his daughter here, and she won't leave unless we all go, no matter what she said about you. It might take a little longer to get back home than we planned, but hell, I'd rather get there late with no charges than rush home and go to prison."

Beck nodded. "That makes sense." He tipped his head toward Leighton, who hadn't moved since Staaber had locked them in the basement. "What about him?"

"What about him? I agree with the little lady. That sumbitch can walk out of here on his own, or he can lie there and die. It ain't my job to rescue government agents. Besides, with this bum leg, it's hard for me to walk on my own, much less help carry him. If I was a horse, I'd shoot myself."

"So, you're okay if Staaber kills another human?"

Mitsui shrugged. "No, I'm not okay with it, but some people need killing more than others. The GRC ain't about to pay a plug nickel for a Justice agent, and the UNT doesn't negotiate with terrorists. If he wasn't brain dead, he'd have a chance. Like that? He's as good as dead."

"You've been hanging around Hahn too long," Beck said.

Mitsui scoffed. "Not enough, I reckon. Beck, I'm a mercenary. I've contracted with some of the meanest, nastiest bastards in the galaxy, and most of them wore suits to work, like the agent over there. I'm not one of these 'Human good, Maltaani bad' types, either. Staaber can be brutal, but what do you expect? He's a Maltaani. At least he's honest about it. I'd take him over half the humans I've worked for."

"You know, I don't think that guard locked the door—" To Beck's astonishment, Leighton groaned and stood up. He shook out his arms and legs and started for the steps.

"You fucking traitors can go to hell," the agent said as he took the stairs two at a time.

Beck heard the door at the top of the stairs slam open, followed by shouts in human and Maltaani as running feet thundered across the floor above. Another loud slam, more shouts in Maltaani, and what sounded like gunfire. The house fell silent, and then Hahn screamed.

* * *

Fortis watched in shock as the human leapt off the back porch and raced across the yard. The sentry dozing in the chair on the porch jerked awake and fumbled for his rifle. Two more Maltaani ran outside behind the fleeing man and raised their rifles, and the trio shot the human before he could reach the tree line.

"What the hell was that?" Bender asked.

Through the open door, Fortis heard a woman scream.

"They're killing the hostages," Ystremski said. "We gotta go."

"Fuck." Fortis raised his pulse rifle. "All stations, this is Team Three. Stand fast, we're moving in. Let's go!"

* * * * *

Chapter Thirty-Three

Staaber jumped to his feet at the sound of gunfire in the back of the house.

"General, a human has escaped!"

Enraged, he stormed to the bathroom door and kicked it open. Hahn screamed, and he jerked her out of the tub by her hair and dragged her into the hall. One of his troops ran up to him.

"We're under attack!"

Staaber heard rifle fire and the unmistakable sound of pulse rifle bolts striking the house.

"Get out there and fight, you fool!"

Maltaani troops rushed toward the back of the house as Staaber pulled Hahn down the hall to the basement stairs. He shoved her through the door, slammed it shut, and locked it.

The volume of fire at the back of the house increased to a roar as more of his troops joined the battle. A blue-white energy bolt whizzed past him and hit the wall next to the front door. Staaber went to the kitchen, picked up a discarded rifle, and headed for the basement.

* * *

Beck stared in surprise as a naked Hahn tumbled down the basement steps and landed in a heap at the bottom. After a pregnant pause, Mitsui elbowed him.

"Help her, Beck."

Hahn groaned and sat up as Beck wrapped her in one of their filthy blankets and helped her to her feet. When they got to Mitsui, she collapsed in the mercenary's arms.

"What happened, little lady?"

"I don't know," Hahn said. "I was in the bathtub when Staaber kicked the door open and dragged me back down here. It sounds like we're under attack."

They heard more gunfire from the kitchen above.

Hahn looked around the room. "Where's the agent?"

"He jumped up and ran out of here. That's when the shooting started."

"What?"

"He must have been playing possum, because as soon as you were gone, he cursed us out and took off running."

"All that firing can't be for him," she said.

"Then who is it?" Beck asked.

"I hear pulse rifles," Mitsui said. "It's Space Marines."

* * *

"Covering fire!" Ystremski shouted as Fortis broke cover and started for the porch. He and Bender hosed down the porch with plasma bolts, but the return fire from the upstairs and downstairs windows was heavy, and it forced them to take cover.

Fortis dove behind a tree after a Maltaani bullet plucked at his shoulder. He stuck his pulse rifle around the tree and fired without aiming, hoping to relieve the pressure on Ystremski and Bender.

"*Hold your fire*," Woody said over the circuit. Fortis chanced a look around the tree and saw the sergeant creeping up along the porch. He threw two grenades, one through the nearest window, and one onto the porch.

"*Frag out!*"

Twin explosions rocked the house, and the volume of fire from the downstairs windows slackened. Fortis rolled over and fired another long burst of plasma bolts into the smoky porch. He saw Woody round the corner as though he intended to mount the porch stairs.

"Wait!"

Woody made it up the steps before a fusillade of Maltaani bullets drove him backwards off the porch and into the yard. He grunted when he hit, and then he was still.

Fortis, Ystremski, and Bender poured fire on the back of the house. The walls glowed as the unexpended energy from their rounds built up, and chunks of wood flew in every direction.

"Covering fire!" Fortis shouted as he lit up the back of the house. "Move!"

The two Space Marines advanced across the yard, firing as they went. There was an occasional *crack* as the defenders returned fire, but neither hesitated as they closed on the porch. Ystremski kept his rifle trained on the door as Bender knelt to check on Woody.

"He's gone, mate," the Aussie said.

"*Fortis up*," Ystremski said, and Fortis jumped up and ran to join his teammates.

"All stations, this is Team Three. We're going in."

Bender was the first in line as they crouched at the door, followed by Ystremski and Fortis. Acrid black smoke from the frags hung in the air, and shredded Maltaani bodies covered the porch.

"Go!"

Bender went in low, Ystremski went in high, and Fortis searched the corners, but they didn't see any live Maltaani in the kitchen. They heard running footsteps somewhere in the front of the house and movement in the room above them. Bender stepped around the corner to move toward the front of the house, and two Maltaani dogs attacked him.

* * *

"You betrayed me!" Staaber shouted at the trio of humans who cowered together in the basement's corner. "I told you my plans, and you still betrayed me."

"General, please," the female pleaded. "We had nothing to do with what that man did. He was our captor, and he had that head wound. He was unconscious."

"Now you've brought the Space Marines to attack us." Staaber pointed the rifle at them, and the barrel tracked Beck as he tried to scramble away.

The sound of the shot was like a clap of thunder in the confines of the basement, and it stunned them all. The bullet hit Beck just below his nose and destroyed the top half of his head. Blood and brains sprayed the wall behind him as his hands flailed for his missing face, and his body fell to the dirt.

Hahn shrieked and buried her face in Mitsui's chest as Staaber pointed the rifle at them. Mitsui stared at the Maltaani, and his lips curled back in defiance.

"Go on, you bug-eyed freak. Do it!"

Click.

* * *

The dogs each grabbed a different arm and dragged Bender down to the floor. They snarled and shook their heads as they tried to tear the massive human apart, but their fangs couldn't penetrate his armor. He picked one up and slammed it on the floor, but the massive jaws wouldn't relent. Fortis and Ystremski tried to get a shot at the murderous brutes, but they couldn't for fear of hitting Bender.

"Fuck this!"

Ystremski drew his kukri and attacked the nearest beast. Fortis followed his lead, and they hacked at the dogs until Bender scrambled free. When it was over, the dead animals lay in bloody shreds.

"Goddamn! Goddamn!" Bender repeated as he rubbed his arms where the dogs had grabbed him.

"Are you okay?"

"Yeah, I'm right," the Aussie said. "Manhandled by a dog. What's next?"

Through an open door in the hall, they heard a woman scream.

"The hostages!"

Ystremski charged through the door and down the stairs, with Fortis hard on his heels. Fortis saw a Maltaani with a rifle pointed at two humans huddled together in the corner. The Maltaani whirled and swung the rifle like a club. It hit Ystremski across the hands. Ystremski shouted in pain, and his pulse rifle clattered across the floor. The force of the blow shattered the rifle stock, and the Maltaani threw it away and drew a sword from a scabbard he wore around his waist.

Staaber!

Ystremski dodged the first swing of the sword, while Fortis moved around and tried to get a clear shot at Staaber. Bender stumbled on his way down the stairs and slammed into Fortis, and they landed in a heap on top of a bucket full of human waste.

Staaber swung his sword again, and the blade struck Ystremski a glancing blow on his visor. The gunny stumbled backward and struggled to draw his kukri. Fortis and Bender slipped and slid as they scrambled to their feet, covered in filth. Before they could get their footing, Staaber was on Ystremski. Fortis watched in horror as Staaber drove his sword low into the gunny's stomach, through the gap between his recon armor top and bottoms. Ystremski let out a guttural cry and pawed at the Maltaani's hands as he fell backwards and pulled Staaber down with him.

"No!"

Fortis found his footing and crossed the basement in three long strides. He swung his pulse rifle with both hands and delivered a vicious blow to the side of Staaber's head. The general slumped sideways, but kept his grip on his sword, and Ystremski screamed as the blade slipped out of his abdomen. Fortis aimed his pulse rifle at Staaber, but Ystremski rolled over and threw his body on top of the general.

"Mine," he spat.

The gunny put his kukri on Staaber's chest, and with his last remaining reserves of strength, drove the blade up under the unconscious Maltaani's chin and into his brain. The kukri wasn't well-suited for stabbing, but the gunny buried the weapon up to the handle before he passed out.

"Man down in the basement!" Fortis shouted over the circuit. "Team Two, move in and get a medic down here now!"

He pulled Ystremski off Staaber and cradled him in his arms. Ystremski struggled to remove his helmet, and when Fortis pulled it off, he saw a heavy bruise already forming across the side of the gunny's head.

"Hang on, Petr," he pleaded as he pressed his hand over the bloody hole in Ystremski's gut. "Please hang on."

"You... smell... like... shit..."

Ystremski's head lolled to the side, and for a second, Fortis thought he'd died. When he pressed his fingers against the gunny's neck, he felt a pulse, and he almost cried with relief.

Bender checked on the two civilians, who'd watched the fighting in stunned silence.

"Are you okay?"

The civilians, a man and a woman, nodded. He looked over at the third man, who was missing most of the back of his head.

"Two alive here, Captain," he said to Fortis.

Fortis nodded. "Get them ready to move. As soon as Doc patches up the gunny, we're leaving."

"I need my clothes," the woman said. "They're upstairs."

"Bender, go."

The Aussie and the blanket-wrapped woman scrambled up the stairs.

Seconds later, the Team Two medic arrived with his trauma kit ready to go. He swore when he saw Ystremski's wound.

"It went all the way through," he said to Fortis.

"I know! Fix him up so we can get out of here."

"I can't—"

"Do it!"

The medic sprinkled antibiotic powder over the wounds and stuffed them with an expanding bandage material that swelled to fill the holes and stopped the bleeding. He wrapped Ystremski's midriff in gauze, and then covered the whole thing with medical tape. The wounded man didn't move throughout the whole procedure.

"Captain, I did the best I could, but he needs a trauma ward, ASAP. I don't think the sword hit any vital organs, but I'm pretty sure it pierced his intestines. He's got internal bleeding, and he's gonna have a world-class case of sepsis."

"Will he make it?"

The medic shrugged. "I don't know. Fifty-fifty if we get him to the hospital in Daarben within the next couple of hours. After that, his chances go down, quick."

"Fuck!" Fortis knew there was little hope of getting Ystremski to the hospital in two hours. On a clear day, the flight was almost ninety minutes. At night, in the rain?

No way.

"Space Marines, coming down!" Warrant Heggie shouted down the steps and then came down. He surveyed the carnage in the basement. "This place stinks."

"What's going on upstairs, Warrant?" Fortis asked.

"The house is clear. Team One shot a bunch running out the front, but more got away out the back. And the second floor is on fire."

An idea came to Fortis.

"Bender, what's your status?"

"Ready to go, mate." The Aussie and the woman, now dressed, had returned to the basement.

The medic pointed at the man leaning against the wall, who had thick bandages wrapped around his leg. "We're gonna need a litter for this one. He can't walk."

"Bender, get the dog heads and grab Woody. Heggie, you and Doc grab that guy, and I'll carry Ystremski."

"What about Beck?" the woman asked.

"That's Beck?"

"What's left of him."

"If he can walk, he can come with us," Fortis said.

Bender laughed. "Where are we going, mate?"

"*Solicitude.*"

* * *

The Space Marines trotted in a tight knot down the center of the street that led into Ulvaan. The rain had returned, and in a rare bit of good fortune, gusting winds from the south propelled them along. Fortis had Ystremski slung over his shoulder in a firefighter's carry, and he prayed he wasn't causing additional damage to the wounded man's midsection. He'd buckled Staaber's sword around his waist, and it banged his legs with every step.

Bender carried Woody's body over his shoulder and clutched a bloody sheet wrapped around the Maltaani dog heads in his empty hand. Two members of Team Two carried Mitsui in a makeshift litter, and Hahn ran right next to them. The rest of the team deployed around them, alert for danger from any direction.

While they ran, Abdullah called MAC-M and informed them of the raid. General Boudreaux demanded to speak to Fortis.

"*What the fuck's going on, Captain?*"

"They started shooting the hostages, so we had to move in. Two hostages are dead, and Sergeant Woods is KIA. Gunny Ystremski is WIA."

"*Where the fuck are you?*"

"We're on the road to the spaceport in Ulvaan to catch a ride to the hospital ship."

"*What?*"

"Doc says Ystremski is going to die if he doesn't get immediate treatment. The weather is shit right now, so we can't fly him to Daarben. There might be a GRC shuttle in Ulvaan we can catch to *Solicitude*, so that's where we're headed."

"*What about Staaber?*"

"Mission accomplished, but some of his guys escaped."

The circuit was silent for a long second.

"*I'm sorry about your men, Captain. Good work, and good luck.*"

"DINLI," Fortis said.

"*DINLI*," Boudreaux echoed.

* * *

When the group reached the spaceport, they ran right past the startled guards and onto the tarmac. When they got to the GRC shuttle, Abdullah pounded on it until the crew opened the boarding ramp.

"Who are you, and what do you think you're doing?" the crew chief demanded. The pilot and copilot stood behind him and blocked their path up the ramp.

"I'm Captain Abner Fortis of the ISMC, and you're going to give us a ride to *Solicitude*."

"We're doing no such thing," the pilot replied. "The weather is awful, and we're waiting for very important passengers. You'll have to find another ride."

The Space Marines ignored the crew's protestations and pushed their way into the passenger cabin. Fortis eased Ystremski into a seat and checked to ensure his friend was still breathing.

The pilot grabbed him by the shoulder and spun him around.

"Leave. Now!"

Fortis drew his kukri and brandished it in the pilot's face.

"Get your ass in the cockpit and get this thing in the air, or I'm going to cut your face off and let him fly it." Fortis gestured at the copilot. "Do you want to fly?"

"Stop!"

Hahn pushed her way between the two men.

"My name is Dalia Hahn, and my father is Weldon Krieg. Do you know who that is?"

The pilot nodded as the blood drained from his face. "We've been waiting for you, Ms. Hahn."

"Then stop arguing and let's go. We can go to *Vast Expanse* after a quick stop at the hospital ship." She pointed to Ystremski. "That Space Marine was wounded saving our lives, and he needs immediate medical care he can only get aboard *Solicitude*. If he dies, I'm going to hold you responsible."

"As will I," Fortis said.

"Okay, get belted in." The pilots ran for the cockpit.

Fortis sank into the seat next to Ystremski, and Hahn sat beside him.

"Thanks," Fortis said.

"I'm the one who should thank you. You really saved our lives."

The shuttle engines wound up, and after a shaky takeoff, the craft made a steep climb into orbit.

* * * * *

Epilogue

Gunny Ystremski cried out at the excruciating pain of Staaber's sword as the Maltaani shoved it deep in his belly. When he tried to pull it out, it wasn't there. He opened his eyes and saw he was in a medical ward, and the sword thrust was just an agonizing memory. There was pain in his abdomen, but it was a dull throb.

The door slid open, and a nurse with a concerned look on her face rushed in.

"Oh, you're awake," she said as she checked his bandages. "How do you feel?"

"Water," Ystremski croaked. His throat was parched, and he swiped at the nasal cannula that blew a continuous supply of dry air into his nostrils.

"You have to leave that in," said the nurse, whose nametag read Stiner, as she pushed his hands away.

"Thirsty."

"I'm sorry, but I can't give you anything to drink," Stiner told him. "I'm sure Doctor Sirico will explain more when she learns you're awake, but I can't give you anything orally right now." She gestured to an IV hanging next to him. "Don't worry, you're getting plenty of fluids."

Moments later, a woman in green surgical scrubs entered the room.

"They said you were awake, Gunny." She smiled and took his hand. "I'm Doctor Sirico. How do you feel?"

"I'm thirsty."

Sirico nodded. "I'm sure you are, but I can't give you anything to drink. You've got quite a wound in your stomach, and the infection is giving us a hard time, too. We can't put anything in there until we get it under control."

Ystremski squeezed his eyes shut for a moment. "Where am I?"

"This is the trauma ward aboard *Solicitude*," Doctor Sirico said. "Your friend, Captain Fortis, brought you here five days ago."

"Five days?"

"Five days. You were in pretty bad shape when you got here, and we had to put you in coma."

Ystremski realized he couldn't see out of his left eye, and when he touched his face, he discovered a wad of bandages.

"It's nothing to worry about," the doctor said as she guided his hand away from his head. "Your left orbital bone was fractured, and you had massive swelling on that side of your head. We removed two bone fragments, but I expect you'll make a full recovery. After a touch of plastic surgery, you'll be as good as new."

"Sword," Ystremski said when he remembered Staaber's stroke across his visor.

"No, no sword," Sirico said. "Captain Fortis left this for you, though."

The doctor picked up a cloth bundle from the bedside table and placed it in Ystremski's hands.

"He made me promise to give it to you when you woke up."

Ystremski unwrapped the bundle and discovered his kukri. Around the handle, someone had replaced the olive drab cordage with dirty crimson.

"He also made me promise to show you this." Sirico placed a portable holo generator on the table. "Would you like to watch it now?"

Ystremski nodded. A miniature three-dimensional Abner Fortis appeared over the table.

"Hey, dickhead. If you're watching this, then you're still alive." Ystremski tried not to chuckle. "I hope you like your gift. I had to use my crimson cord because nobody had any handy, but what the hell, you deserve it more than I do.

"In case you're wondering, we accomplished both of our mission objectives. We lost Woody, and you're laid up, but I suppose somebody in the chain of command will say it was a small price to pay. Maybe it is, if you're not the one paying. Fuck it. DINLI, right?

"I hope you don't mind, but I sent a holo to Tanya to let her know you're on your way home. Do her a favor and don't let her see your face. You were ugly before, but now… sheesh.

"By now, me and Bender are back on the surface, probably dodging raindrops at Zulu-Five. Hug your family for me and heal up. We could use you downrange."

The holo ended.

"Home?" he asked.

"That's where we're headed," Doctor Sirico said. "You picked a good time to get wounded. The defense minister lifted the war zone declaration the day after you got here, and *Solicitude* sailed for home. We'll be in Terra Earth orbit tomorrow."

Ystremski clutched the kukri to his chest as a single tear escaped and leaked down his cheek.

"DINLI."

#####

About the Author

Paul A. Piatt was born and raised in western Pennsylvania. After his first attempt at college, he joined the Navy to see the world. He started writing as a hobby when he retired in 2005 and published his first novel in 2018. His published works include the Abner Fortis, International Space Marine mil-sf series, the Walter Bailey Misadventures urban fantasy trilogy, and other full-length thrillers in both science fiction and horror. All of his novels and published short stories can be found on Amazon. You can find him on Facebook, MeWe, and on the internet at www(dot)papiattauthor(dot)com, or you can contact him directly at paulpiattauthor(at)gmail(dot)com.

* * * * *

The following is an
Excerpt from Book One of The Last Marines:

Gods of War

William S. Frisbee, Jr.

Available from Theogony Books

eBook and Paperback

Excerpt from "Gods of War:"

"Yes, sir," Mathison said. Sometimes it was worth arguing, sometimes it wasn't. Stevenson wasn't a butter bar. He was a veteran from a line infantry platoon that had made it through Critical Skills Operator School and earned his Raider pin. He was also on the short list for captain. Major Beckett might pin the railroad tracks on Stevenson's collar before they left for space.

"Well, enough chatting," Stevenson said, the smile in his voice grating on Mathison's nerves. "Gotta go check our boys."

"Yes, sir," Mathison said, and later he would check on the men while the lieutenant rested. "Please keep your head down, sir. Don't leave me in charge of this cluster fuck. I would be tempted to tell that company commander to go fuck a duck."

"No, you won't. You will do your job and take care of our Marines, but I'll keep my head down," Stevenson said. "Asian socialists aren't good enough to kill me. It's going to have to be some green alien bastard that kills me."

"Yes, sir," Mathison said as the lieutenant tapped on Jennings' shoulder and pointed up. The lance corporal understood and cupped his hands together to boost the lieutenant out of the hole. He launched the lieutenant out of the hole and went back to digging as Mathison went back to looking at the spy eyes scrutinizing the distant jungle.

A shot rang out. On Mathison's heads-up display, the icon for Lieutenant Stevenson flashed and went red, indicating death.

"You are now acting platoon commander," Freya reported.

* * * * *

Get "Gods of War" now at: Coming Soon/.

Find out more about William S. Frisbee, Jr. at: https://chriskennedypublishing.com.

* * * * *

The following is an
Excerpt from Book One of the Echoes of Pangaea:

Bestiarii

James Tarr

Available from Theogony Books

eBook and Paperback

Excerpt from "Bestiarii:"

"Mayday Mayday Mayday, this is Sierra Bravo Six, we've lost power and are going down," Delian calmly said as Tina screamed from the back. He and Hanson began frantically hitting buttons and flipping switches. "Radio's dead, I've got nothing." He had to yell it so Hansen could hear him over the wind.

Mike's eyes went wide. He felt his stomach come up into his throat as the helicopter dropped and began rotating. "Shite," Seamus cursed and smacked the button to drop the visor on his helmet.

"Keep transmitting," Hansen told his co-pilot. "Damn, I've got no electronics, can we do a manual re-start?" He stayed on the stick and the collective, trying to control the autorotation.

Delian had been hitting every button and toggle switch possible. "No, I don't think this is a short, it looks like everything's fried. Mayday Mayday Mayday, this is Sierra Bravo Six, we are going down." He told the younger pilot, "You know what to do. Keep it level, autorotate down, try to control the rate of descent. Time your glide. You see a place to land?"

The helicopter was spinning to the right as it fell, which traditionally was the reason the pilot was the right stick. Hansen looked out the window as he fought the controls. "We're in the mountains, nothing's flat. I've got trees everywhere. Hold on back there!" he yelled over his shoulder.

The helicopter began spinning faster and faster and Mike found himself being pulled sideways in his seat. The soldier on the door gun lost his footing and floated up in the air, then was halfway out the open door, one hand still on the mini-gun, restrained only by his tether as the G-forces made Mike's face feel hot. He vomited, and the bitter fluid was whipped away from his face. The world outside the open doorway past Todd was a spinning blue/green/brown blur. Tina was screaming wildly. The wind was whistling around the cabin.

"We've got smoke coming from the engine," Delian said, peering upward. "What the hell happened?"

"Brace for impact!" Seamus yelled at the cabin, and wedged his boots against the seat opposite.

"Coming up on the mark, keep it level," Delian said calmly. "Get ready for the burn!" he yelled over his shoulder at the passengers. He switched back to the radio, even though he thought it was a waste of time. "Mayday Mayday Mayday, this is Sierra Bravo Six—"

"If they work," Mike heard the pilot respond, then suddenly there was a roar, and he was pressed down in his seat, getting heavier and heavier. The helicopter was still spinning, and out the open doorway and windshield there was nothing but a blur of greens and browns. Mike got heavier and heavier, and Tina stopped screaming. Then the roar stopped, and they began falling again, pulling up against their seatbelts. Tina opened her mouth to scream once more, but before she could draw a breath the helicopter hit with a huge crunch and the sound of tearing metal.

* * * * *

Get "Bestiarii" now at:
https://www.amazon.com/dp/B0B44YM335/.

Find out more about James Tarr at:
https://chriskennedypublishing.com.

* * * * *

The following is an
Excerpt from Book One of Chimera Company:

The Fall of Rho-Torkis

Tim C. Taylor

Available from Theogony Books

eBook, Audio, and Paperback

Excerpt from "The Fall of Rho-Torkis:"

"Relax, Sybutu."

Osu didn't fall for the man steepling his fingers behind his desk. When a lieutenant colonel told you to relax, you knew your life had just taken a seriously wrong turn.

"So what if we're ruffling a few feathers?" said Malix. "We have a job to do, and you're going to make it happen. You will take five men with you and travel unobserved to a location in the capital where you will deliver a coded phrase to this contact."

He pushed across a photograph showing a human male dressed in smuggler chic. Even from the static image, the man oozed charm, but he revealed something else too: purple eyes. The man was a mutant.

"His name is Captain Tavistock Fitzwilliam, and he's a free trader of flexible legitimacy. Let's call him a smuggler for simplicity's sake. You deliver the message and then return here without incident, after which no one will speak of this again."

Osu kept his demeanor blank, but the questions were raging inside him. His officers in the 27th gave the appearance of having waved through the colonel's bizarre orders, but the squadron sergeant major would not let this drop easily. He'd be lodged in an ambush point close to the colonel's office where he'd be waiting to pounce on Osu and interrogate him. Vyborg would suspect him of conspiracy in this affront to proper conduct. His sappers as undercover spies? Osu would rather face a crusading army of newts than the sergeant major on the warpath.

"Make sure one of the men you pick is Hines Zy Pel."

Osu's mask must have slipped because Malix added, "If there is a problem, I expect you to speak."

"Is Zy Pel a Special Missions operative, sir?" There. He'd said it.

"You'll have to ask Colonel Lantosh. Even after they bumped up my rank, I still don't have clearance to see Zy Pel's full personnel record. Make of that what you will."

"But you must have put feelers out…"

Malix gave him a cold stare.

You're trying to decide whether to hang me from a whipping post or answer my question. Well, it was your decision to have me lead an undercover team, Colonel. Let's see whether you trust your own judgment.

The colonel seemed to decide on the latter option and softened half a degree. "There was a Hines Zy Pel who died in the Defense of Station 11. Or so the official records tell us. I have reason to think that our Hines Zy Pel is the same man."

"But… Station 11 was twelve years ago. According to the personnel record I've seen, my Zy Pel is in his mid-20s."

Malix put his hands up in surrender. "I know, I know. The other Hines Zy Pel was 42 when he was KIA."

"He's 54? Can't be the same man. Impossible."

"For you and I, Sybutu, that is true. But away from the core worlds, I've encountered mysteries that defy explanation. Don't discount the possibility. Keep an eye on him. For the moment, he is a vital asset, especially given the nature of what I have tasked you with. However, if you ever suspect him of an agenda that undermines his duty to the Legion, then I am ordering you to kill him before he realizes you suspect him."

Kill Zy Pel in cold blood? That wouldn't come easily.

"Acknowledge," the colonel demanded.

"Yes, sir. If Zy Pel appears to be turning, I will kill him."

"Do you remember Colonel Lantosh's words when she was arrested on Irisur?"

Talk about a sucker punch to the gut! Osu remembered everything about the incident when the Militia arrested the CO for standing up to the corruption endemic on that world.

It was Legion philosophy to respond to defeat or reversal with immediate counterattack. Lantosh and Malix's response had been the most un-Legion like possible.

"Yes, sir. She told us not to act. To let the skraggs take her without resistance. Without the Legion retaliating."

"No," snapped Malix. "She did *not*. She ordered us to let her go without retaliating *until the right moment*. This *is* the right moment, Sybutu. This message you will carry. You're doing this for the colonel."

Malix's words set loose a turmoil of emotions in Osu's breast that he didn't fully understand. He wept tears of rage, something he hadn't known was possible.

The colonel stood. "This is the moment when the Legion holds the line. Can I rely upon you, Sergeant?"

Osu saluted. "To the ends of the galaxy, sir. No matter what."

* * * * *

Get "The Fall of Rho-Torkis" now at:
https://www.amazon.com/dp/B08VRL8H27

Find out more about Tim C. Taylor at:
https://chriskennedypublishing.com

* * * * *

Made in United States
Troutdale, OR
10/09/2024

23607437R00196